BOOK ONE

THE MARIONETTES

KATIE WISMER

THE MARIONETTES

For more information visit: www.katiewismer.com

Cover design by Seventhstar Art
Proofreading by Beth Attwood

Paperback ISBN: 978-1-7346115-5-7

Hardcover ISBN: 978-1-7346115-7-1

First Edition: August 2021

10 9 8 7 6 5 4 3 2 1

ALSO BY KATIE WISMER

Find your next read here: https://www.katiewismer.com/books

YORK TRAINING ACADEMY
SCHEDULE

Breakfast 5:00 p.m.
Class Block 1 5:30 p.m.
Class Block 2 7:00 p.m.
Lunch 9:00 p.m.
Class Block 3 10:30 p.m.
Class Block 4 12:00 a.m.
Dinner 3:00 a.m.

THE ESTATES

New York City, United States
Carrington Estate

Prince Rupert, Canada
Auclair Estate

São Joaquim, Brazil
Queirós Estate

Stockholm, Sweden
Olofsson Estate

Rjukan, Norway
Botner Estate

Dikson, Russia
Vasiliev Estate

Utqiagvik, United States
Locklear Estate

Chongqing, China
Wénběn Estate

Tórshavn, Faroe Islands
Jógvan Estate

Hat Yai, Thailand
Suksai Estate

PLAYLIST

Listen on Spotify
shorturl.at/ajuU3

forget me too – Machine Gun Kelly, Halsey
Wish You Were Sober – Conan Gray
supercuts – Jeremy Zucker
Maniac – Conan Gray
CITY OF ANGELS – 24kGoldn, YUNGBLUD
Electric Love – BORNS
lost cause – KennyHoopla, grandson
Love Spells – POORSTACY
Choke – Royal & the Serpent
Rules – LAYNE
Never Fucking Fall in Love Again – X Lovers
The Search – NF
Bitter – FLETCHER, KITO
3am – Halsey
I'm Not Mad – Halsey
Fake – Lauv, Conan Gray
Without Me – Halsey
Problem Party – Lukr
You should be sad – Halsey
VICES – Mothica
Crush Culture – Conan Gray
Daft Pretty Boys – Bad Suns
Hallucinogenics – Matt Maeson
Painkiller – Ruel

A Change of Heart – The 1975
Losing Grip – Avril Lavigne
So It Goes… – Taylor Swift
Psycho Killer – The Wrecks
that's just how it goes – ROLE MODEL
Frustrated – Lauren Sanderson
idwgtyp – lovelytheband
Apricots – MAY-A
Maneater – Nelly Furtado
ICIMY – Phoebe Ryan
Roses – The Chainsmokers, ROZES
i drive me mad – renforshort
I Did Something Bad – Taylor Swift
…Ready For It? – Taylor Swift
body bag – Machine Gun Kelly, YUNGBLUD
Blood // Water – grandson
you should see me in a crown – Billie Eilish
hangover cure – Machine Gun Kelly
Don't Blame Me – Taylor Swift
title track – Machine Gun Kelly
My Best Habit – The Maine
18 – Anarbor
People I Don't Like – UPSAHL
State of Grave – Acoustic Version – Taylor Swift
Portugal – WALK THE MOON

This book contains material that may be triggering for some readers. Reader discretion is advised. For a complete list of trigger warnings, please visit katiewismer.com/trigger-warnings

CHAPTER ONE

THE LUNAR WITCHES left a dead bird in the field again. At least, it *looks* dead. Blood seeps from its small, black body into the snow, painting a halo of gore around it. Fading moonlight slides through the tree branches, but the surrounding darkness is thick enough to smudge out the details of the clearing. The eerily silent clearing. Whoever did this hadn't been quiet about it—they probably scared away all the wildlife within a mile radius.

An idea curls my lips into a smile as I glance up the hill toward the academy. Whatever spell they did probably won't work without a sacrifice. No one should be up this late, and with the moon clinging to the last few moments of night, I have enough time.

It's the perfect test.

The ring on my middle finger glints as I flip the knife out of the side. It's small—crafted to fit the exact length between my knuckles—but it will get the job done. I shove my sleeve up and carve a line along the back of my arm, but I barely feel the bite of the blade against the cold.

Darkmores don't have the luxury of being squeamish anyway.

I inch forward and let my blood drip onto the bird, willing that familiar heat to flood my veins. "Come on," I mutter under my breath.

The breeze picks up, rustling the tree branches and scattering the dead leaves around me. The cut on my arm heals itself. Heat lingers on my skin as the pink scar fades, but the rest of my body still feels cold.

And the bird doesn't move.

Gritting my teeth, I whip the blade back out and dig deeper. Deep enough to make me wince. As my blood falls onto the bird's wings, matting its feathers and melting the snow clinging to its form, I imagine the blood soaking through to its tiny veins, flooding its heart, and forcing it to pump again.

A wave of dizziness crashes into me, and I lean against the nearest tree, panting.

But then my skin begins to warm.

I keep my eyes trained on the animal as blood drips down my fingers. The bird's head twitches, and then all at once, it leaps up and bursts into flight, the desperate sound of its wings filling the clearing.

Blood continues to run down my arm, and it shows no sign of stopping.

Fucking hell.

I yank my scarf off my neck and wind it around the cut. At least the fabric is a dark enough shade of red that it shouldn't show.

Color blooms in the sky above me—the first trace of morning. I glance down at my arm again. Still not healing. There's no way I'll be able to manage a teleportation spell now.

Which leaves me with only one choice.

By the time I make it back to campus, snow has soaked through my sneakers. White probably wasn't the best idea—splotches of blood litter the tops and laces now. It's quiet this time of morning, and the paths are deserted as I head for the dorms on the east side.

My breath puffs up in a cloud in front of me as the sun crests the clock tower and lights the gargoyles from behind. I don't think I've realized just how many are up there before—one on the corner of every building on this side of campus.

I've been catching myself getting more sentimental, noticing details I hadn't before, letting my gaze linger a little too long. It probably has something to do with my time here being more than halfway through. When you've spent your entire life working toward something, it's difficult to picture what comes after.

Or maybe it's initiation coming up that has everything feeling different lately.

I quicken my pace and keep my head down as I follow along the outside corridor. I eye the windows beside me, and a warped version of my face stares back from the stained glass—my dark eyes and hair the only recognizable traits. Thankfully, no one else seems to be inside. I don't have time to get caught out after curfew.

I slip into the dormitory as quietly as possible and head straight for my room at the end of the hall. I'm halfway there when the door across from mine creaks open. A small, dark-haired girl steps out in a hot pink towel—elemental witch, I think. I can never remember with the first years.

She freezes when she sees me and fumbles with her shower caddy. "Valerie?" she whispers. "What are you doing up?"

"I could ask you the same thing," I say without looking at her and slide my key into the lock.

"I haven't really adjusted to the schedule yet," she admits, her flip-flops squeaking as she shifts her weight.

I glance at her over my shoulder, a single eyebrow raised. It's not uncommon for freshmen to struggle adjusting to the academy's sleep schedule, especially if they don't come from a prominent witch family with a history in the Marionettes. Spending the first eighteen years of their lives on a human timetable must be hard to kick, but to *still* be operating on a daylight schedule—and this late in the semester—how is she surviving? Before I can say anything though, her eyes drop to my arm.

"I—I think you're bleeding." It takes a second for the pieces to click, but I see it in her eyes when they do. She swallows hard and sidesteps toward the bathroom. "Uh, see you," she mutters, then hurries down the rest of the hall, her shower shoes smacking against her feet with each step.

The moment I'm in my room, I close the door behind me and collapse against it, my hands and knees shaking. I am, indeed, still bleeding. Badly enough the blood is fully soaked through the scarf.

It should've stopped by now.

A picture of me and Connor flashes on my phone as a reminder notification pops up—last train leaves in five minutes. I made it my background months ago—a selfie Connor had taken while I was napping on his chest—but it makes me smile every time I see it. A text from him also waits for me on the screen.

Hope you're sleeping well. Call me when you get a chance? There's something I want to talk to you about.

I frown at the oddly formal message, but then my eyes drift back to the time—nearly 8 a.m. I need to hurry. I shouldn't have stayed out this late, but I'd been feeling good when I woke today—better than I had in a while. I'd really thought I'd be able to swing a teleportation spell and not have to rely on this train.

Should've left the damn bird there. Doing a spell like that out in the open was stupid and reckless anyway. But even without messing with the lunar witches, based on how draining a spell that small was, it wouldn't have mattered.

Test: failed. Magic definitely still faulty.

I stride over to the window and shove the heavy curtains aside. The room fills with light, and I get to packing. After throwing enough random pieces of clothing for the weekend into a bag and securing an actual bandage around my arm, I slip off my bloody sneakers and replace them with black lace-up boots. I'm still in my uniform from Friday's classes—red blazer, plaid skirt, black tights—but I don't have time to change. So I throw my bag over my shoulder, slip into the hall, and hurry into the morning sun.

―――――――

THE TRAIN STATION isn't far—it's just down the hill on this side of campus. My eyes droop with each step, both from being up several hours later than usual, but also from the magic's toll. Every inch of my skin feels hot as my body fights to heal the wound in my arm. Something I would've been able to do without breaking a sweat a few weeks ago.

But a lot can change in a few weeks.

The path from campus winds down the hill, framed on either side by snow-covered trees. The sun glitters off the slick earth as I pass the final York Training Academy sign and cross out of the grounds.

A train whistle shrills in the distance.

"Fuck."

My boots slide across ice as I surge down the rest of the hill, hitting the bottom at a run. The platform is empty—the other passengers already boarded. My bag slaps against my side as I sprint, my limbs sluggish and heavier than usual from the spell.

Just fifty more yards.

Steam billows up from the train as the doors start to slide shut. I can't miss this train. I *can't*.

Forty yards.

Elemental magic has never been my strong suit, but it's windy enough out that maybe I can manage. I rip the dressing from my arm and dig my fingers into the wound until blood wells to the surface. My entire arm sings with heat, and I thrust it toward the train, pointing at the nearest door. I will a barrier of wind to form. It stops the door halfway as the rest of them slide closed.

Sweat drips down my forehead as I throw myself inside and the door slams behind me, nearly catching my hair. I collapse onto the stairs, breathless and bloody, as the train rumbles beneath me and starts to move.

My vision swims as I squint up at the surrounding car. It's mostly empty, thankfully, with a middle-aged woman asleep in the back row and a man reading a newspaper on the opposite end. My legs shake as I gather my things and push myself back to my feet. My body is on fire now, protesting that last spurt of magic. I shove the sweaty strands of hair out of my face and slump onto the nearest bench.

The speaker crackles overhead as the conductor announces we'll be in New York City in about two hours. I lean my forehead against the cool glass of the window, finally letting my eyes close, and pass out before he even finishes the sentence.

CHAPTER TWO

HUMANS FILE in and out of the train a few hours later as we cut through the city. They do double takes when they see me curled against the window, then choose the seats as far away as possible. I roll my eyes. Humans can be so skittish. What do they think I'm going to do to them in broad daylight in the middle of a crowded train? *Trust me, I wouldn't be riding this thing if I had any other choice.*

At first I can't figure out how they all immediately know I'm not like them, but then I remember I'm still in my uniform, York Academy's crest on full display—an intricate vine that weaves together the symbols for the five types of witches. Being covered in blood probably doesn't help either. Might as well be wearing a T-shirt that says *Witch. Don't fuck with me.*

At least they can't tell what kind. That would cause a whole new set of issues.

By the time the train reaches the Carrington estate, I'm the only one left on board. It's a short walk from the platform to the front gates, but my body protests every step.

The estate is well-distanced from the rest of the city, so there's nothing around for miles besides the sprawling grounds.

I follow along the fence until I reach the front of the property, passing the gardens and separate living quarters for some of the human servants as I go. The sun relentlessly beats down on me as I jab my thumb against the intercom and lean back for the camera to see my face. I have to clutch the gate with one hand to keep from falling over as the muscles in my legs threaten to buckle.

The towering estate looms in the background, but instead of feeling any kind of warmth at the thought of returning home, my chest fills with something much heavier.

Dread.

The gate buzzes and lurches open, and I start the winding trek toward the door, attempting to strip off my blazer as I walk. Even then, the white button-down underneath traps in the heat building against my skin. The guards stationed along the front lawn nod at me as I pass. I squint against the sunlight and drag my bag behind me, my feet shuffling more than walking.

"Miss Darkmore!" chirps a red-haired servant I've never seen before as I step into the foyer. In contrast to the old-fashioned, rustic look of the academy, everything here is shiny and polished. Marble pillars frame the entryway and reach up toward the vaulted ceilings, where a series of ostentatious chandeliers hangs in a neat row.

I offer her a weak smile and wipe the sweat from my

forehead with the back of my hand. If she's alarmed by my appearance, she doesn't show it.

"How nice to see you. Shall I take your bag up to your room?"

I nod and thank her, half-inclined to follow her upstairs and collapse into my bed, but then someone else appears around the corner. The redhead blanches when she notices the newcomer, does a quick curtsy, then hastens up the staircase and out of sight.

"What could have possibly taken you so long?"

The air in the hall shifts at my mother's entrance, and a sour taste rises in the back of my mouth as she prowls forward. It's past noon—I'd been hoping she wouldn't be awake. Her dark hair is intricately braided and layered into a crown on the top of her head. Sharp, silver spikes dangle from chains attached to each pin, collecting above her shoulders, somehow barely swaying no matter how much she moves. Leave it to my mother to deem her fashion choices dire enough to require magical assistance. Her black dress billows out around her with each step.

The queen must be back if she's dressing up this much. As she draws closer, her lips purse, and her eyes flit over me. "You look horrible."

"Thanks, Mom."

"What's this?" She picks up a lock of my hair between two fingers, pointing out the smear of blood along the tips.

I shake out of her grasp, hating the jolt that goes through me at the contact. It's brief—just a hot flash that travels from my scalp to my toes, leaving no inch of my skin untouched. It's adrenaline. At least, that's what I've always told myself. Because it also feels a lot like fear. "Nothing. It was a long trip. I need to go lie down."

"We have—"

"The ritual tonight, I know. I'll be there."

She looks me up and down one more time, then she's already heading back the way she'd come.

"Nice to see you too," I mutter and turn for the stairs.

The halls are quiet, the only sounds coming from human servants bustling about. Over a hundred vampires and witches live at the estate, but it'll be hours before they're up, not until sundown. A tall woman carrying cleaning supplies gives me a closed-lip smile as she slips past me and down the stairs. The dirty clothes in her hands are stained with blood, and when I glance at her retreating form over my shoulder, I realize there's a splatter down the back of her white uniform too.

Another new face. I'm not sure if they're getting reassigned to different sections of the estate or what, but every time I come here, it seems like they have an entirely different roster of servants. Just when I start to learn names, the humans in the areas I frequent are replaced.

Well, except for Connor. Thankfully, he's never been reassigned.

I head straight for the third floor, which houses current Marionettes and their families, but something makes me pause on the last step. I haven't been home in months, not since before the semester started, and a few more minutes won't hurt.

There's a small section of human quarters on the fourth floor—just for the families who have worked at the estate for generations. Practically in the attic, the rooms are drafty and small, but better than the options in the separate buildings out back. My body goes into autopilot as I head for the last door on the right. Odds are he's not awake if he's still been working the late shift. But just to see him, even for only a second…

I gently turn the knob and poke my head inside in case he is asleep—

My heart drops into my stomach so violently I stagger back a step.

Connor is, indeed, in bed. Handcuffed to it, to be exact. He's splayed out on his back, wrists secured above his head, his curly blond hair spread out on the pillow. A woman with dark skin and darker hair kneels over him, her hands on his chest as she writhes on top of him, moaning with each thrust of her hips. Sweat drips down her spine, and the bed creaks beneath her movements, but all I can hear is the sound of their bodies coming together over and over again.

I'm about to turn away when the woman throws her head back and growls. With a movement almost too fast for my eyes to detect, she sinks her fangs into Connor's neck and drinks. He lets out a small, choked sound, his eyes closed. The woman claps a hand over his mouth as she licks at the blood now trickling down his shoulder and onto the white sheets.

"Oh my God."

The woman whips around, blood dripping from her chin as she hisses. Connor's eyes fly open and lock on my frozen form in the doorway. His mouth starts to move, but I turn and hurry down the hall before I can hear whatever he has to say.

My heart is pounding so loudly in my ears, I don't even

hear the vampire until she's right behind me. She smacks her shoulder against mine as she passes, Connor's blood lingering on her lips. I brace myself for some kind of confrontation, but she keeps going and disappears down the stairs without looking back.

"Valerie, wait!"

I keep walking, my legs suddenly not so tired anymore. My body is thrumming with energy, the heat on my skin scorching and twisting into something stronger. Something darker. I could burn this entire fucking building down right now, defective powers be damned.

I have to get out of here.

"Valerie." A hand circles my wrist and pulls me to a stop.

Connor stands in the hallway in nothing but a pair of boxers, blood dripping down his neck. His eyes are glassy, still hazed over from the venom.

I yank my hand away. "Glad to see you've been coping well while I've been gone."

"It's not like that," he insists.

I laugh and point at his door. "It's *not like that*? Really? Are you kidding me? What, are you some kind of venom junkie now?"

The color drains from his face. "God, no. Valerie, no. It's not. Please, let me explain. It's…" His throat bobs as he swallows, and when he speaks again, his voice is barely a whisper. "It's *work*, Valerie."

My mouth snaps shut, my next words dying in my throat. I look from the door to his face again. "I—what do you mean? They're *paying* you?"

"You know I need the extra money," he continues, his

13

words coming out in a rush. "And it didn't start out like this. It was just letting them bite me at first. But then…and I…I can't say no to them." He raises his eyes to meet mine again, and the emotion there is enough to cut through the haze. "But that's all it is. It's just work, Val, I swear."

I cross my arms over my chest and take a step away from him.

"Val—"

It takes me a few tries before I manage to speak again, and when I do, my voice comes out dangerously quiet. "How many has it been, then?"

His face falls, and he tries to reach for me, but I take another step back.

"How many, Connor?" I demand, my voice rising. "How many people have you been with now? Do you even know?"

His expression is desperate, pleading. He shakes his head. "It's not the same—"

"You want to ask me the same question? Because that's easy, Connor. *You*. I've been with *you*. For six years, it's just been you. And being the only person you'd been with too—that meant something to me. I guess that was stupid, huh? How long were you going to let me go on believing that?"

"Valerie." His voice cracks.

I hold up a hand to stop him, not sure if I can take hearing any more. I clench my jaw, refusing to let any tears come out. "I'm going home," I say, turning away. "It's been a *really* long day."

"I was going to tell you," he insists, but I'm already halfway down the stairs, the sight of two streams of blood trailing down his chest seared into my head.

MY ROOM HASN'T BEEN TOUCHED in the months I've been gone. The same pile of clothes and old sheets of music wait on the bed from the last time I packed, but I push them aside and crawl under the covers. Although sleep takes me almost immediately, I seem to wake just as fast, covered in a cold sweat and my sheets shoved to the bottom of my bed. Glancing at the clock, I realize hours, not minutes, have passed. A knock at the door jolts me the rest of the way awake, and I sit up.

"Come in," I call.

A human servant pokes his head in, eyes lowered to the floor. "You're wanted in the throne room, Miss Darkmore."

"Thank you. I'll be right down."

He nods and silently closes the door again. I stare at it long after he's gone.

The throne room. This can't be good.

I don't have time to shower, but showing up in my current state isn't an option. I peel off my sweaty uniform and duck into my closet for a suitable dress, momentarily overwhelmed by the sheer number of options I have here compared to back at school. The witches' quarters are nothing compared to the vampires' accommodations, but it's better than the academy dorms.

I twist my hair into a bun and pull out something black and old—something I don't care about getting ruined. And at least the long sleeves will cover the gash in my arm. I frown at the wound for a second. The surrounding skin is still very much red and inflamed. I've been healing slowly lately, but this is the worst it's ever been.

A second human is waiting outside the door for me, this one a full foot shorter than I am with blond hair chopped above her shoulders. She says nothing as she leads me toward the throne room, her footsteps nearly silent on the floor.

The estate is darker now—the sun must have set while I was asleep—and all the finer details glitter beneath the light fixtures, just like they were designed to do. I follow the human through the cavernous main floor, and she pauses outside the throne room's golden doors, bowing her head as I pass and step through.

Moonlight rains down from the glass ceiling, acting as the perfect spotlight for Queen Carrington's throne at the back of the room, the purple stained glass offering the only color. Three guards are stationed on either side of her, and my mother stands beside the throne, chin high in the air. She looks at me over her nose as I enter, the set of her jaw even more displeased than usual. I nearly stop in my tracks at the sight of the final person on the dais.

He's much taller than the last time I saw him—or anyone saw him, as far as I know—but that must have been at least ten years ago. His all-black suit blends in with his surroundings, and the golden crown on his head is crooked, tipped onto the left side of his head. He stares off at the ceiling, not even acknowledging my entrance as I join the other witches on the right side of the room. Not all of the Marionettes are here—less than a dozen—so whatever this is about, it must not be that important.

But I'm the only uninitiated witch here, so why did they summon me?

Unlike her son, the queen notices as I fall into place,

and her red lips turn up in a whisper of a smile. She nods at one of her guards, and the back door flies open. Silence blankets the room as two guards drag in an unconscious woman and drop her.

I cringe as her knees hit the floor. She stirs and catches herself before she falls onto her face, the chains around her wrists, neck, and ankles rattling. As she takes in where she is, she draws in a sharp breath. She's directly in the center of the glass circle in the middle of the room, where pools of blood from victims past ripple beneath the surface like waves crashing on a beach.

The queen rises from her throne and steps forward, the sound of her high heels echoing around the room. Her red dress glides across the floor behind her. She stops inches shy of the woman and bends down so they're at eye level. I can't see the woman's face from this angle, but her entire body is trembling now.

"Do you know why you're here?" the queen asks.

The woman shakes her head, a small, animal-like noise coming from her throat.

"Open your mouth," says the queen.

The woman starts to cry in earnest now, but she doesn't move away. The queen tilts her head to the side, and the moonlight catches the cascade of golden hair braided over her shoulder. She reaches out and seizes the woman's chin, her red nails digging in, and lifts her head a few inches. She nods to herself, then her golden eyes flash over to us. I stiffen, but her gaze slides right over me and lands on my mother lingering by the throne.

"Rosemarie?" says the queen. "Be a dear?"

My mother meets her in the center of the room and

leans down to see as the queen points into the woman's mouth. With a nod from my mother, the queen saunters back over to her throne, throwing the skirts of her dress to the side as she crosses one leg over the other.

My eyes drift inches to her right and find Prince Reginald's gaze focused on me. Every line of his face is hard, his eyes nearly black. For a moment, it's all I can do to stare back at him.

I jump as the doors creak open behind me. A man hurries inside in black pants and a matching sleeveless shirt, showing off the thin red tattoo around his bicep. I don't know his name, but he's apparently a Marionette.

"Abdiel?" the queen demands. "You are interrupting."

"My apologies, my queen." He lowers to a single knee and bows his head. The curls of his dark hair fall, obscuring his face.

She makes him wait for a good long while before finally saying, "Rise."

The man quickly stands and clasps his hands behind his back. "There was a breach at the southern border," he explains. "Werewolves. Three of them. They've been detained."

My head whips to the side, really taking in the man now. No one else around me reacts, so I force my expression to remain impassive.

The queen hisses, her fists tightening around the arms of her throne. Slowly, she runs her tongue along the tips of her fangs. "Execute them. Then bring me their heads and figure out which pack master I'll be sending them to, since they seem to have forgotten our laws."

"Yes, Your Highness." The man bows again before hurrying back out the door.

The moment he's gone, the queen looks at my mother. "Continue."

The woman's body shakes with her sobs. My mother's expression is blank as she raises a hand.

"Wait," says the queen. "I'm feeling...*old-fashioned* today."

That, finally, makes my mother smile, and a sour taste rises to the back of my mouth. Taking a step back from the woman on the floor, my mother carves a thin line on her palm with the razors on the sides of her nails. A single drop of blood falls onto the glass circle, and it melts to the other side and joins the waves below.

The woman looks around the room, her expression pleading. She meets my eyes, but I force myself not to show any emotion like the others around me. For all I know, the queen summoned me here as some kind of pre-initiation test and they're all gauging my reactions.

She's skinny, the woman. Probably another human servant taking more food than their ration allows. Her skin is so pale it's nearly translucent, only further highlighting how tightly it's stretched over her cheekbones. I swallow hard as her gaze lingers on me, and a single tear runs down her face.

A guard steps up with a silver platter, holding it out to my mother, and the woman's head snaps forward again—of her own accord or by my mother, I'm not sure. My mother picks up the pair of pliers and dangles them so the woman can see. This time when my mother leans down, the woman pulls her head away.

"No," she begs.

My mother snaps her fingers, and the woman stills. I force my face to remain neutral, but direct my focus slightly over their heads as my mother tilts the woman's head back and opens her mouth wide. A muffled scream fills the room as she yanks out the first tooth and lets it clatter onto the floor beside her. The splatter of blood sinks into the glass. My gaze drifts to the prince, and I realize he, too, is only pretending to watch. His attention is fixed somewhere near the entrance behind us.

The second tooth doesn't come out as easily, and it takes three muffled screams before my mother drops the bloody pliers onto the ground and scoops up the teeth.

The queen rises and tilts her head forward, giving my mother access to her crown. She settles the new teeth near the middle and secures them into place with a drop of blood. The queen straightens, her red lips stretched into a wide smile now as she takes in the woman, who is lying curled into a ball on her side.

"See?" coos the queen. "That wasn't so bad." The smile drops from her face. "Steal from me again, and it'll be your throat bleeding into the floor."

Two guards materialize behind the woman, lift her by her arms, and drag her from the room, leaving a small trail of blood in her wake.

"The rest of you are dismissed," the queen adds as she lounges back into her throne. Her gaze sweeps over our group until finally landing on me. "But not you, Valerie Darkmore."

CHAPTER THREE

THE LOOK my mother shoots me at the sound of my name threatens to turn me to stone. She tries to linger behind, and there's fire in her eyes when the queen dismisses her along with the others. Once they're gone, and it's just me, the queen, the prince, and her guards, I cautiously approach the dais.

"No need to look so concerned, Valerie," says the queen. "You're not in trouble. I just thought it was time the two of us had a chat."

I say nothing and wait for her to continue. The light catches the spikes of gold and rows of teeth in her crown as she leans forward. It looks like she's running out of room. There's no mistaking the two front and center—the only vampire fangs among the human teeth, the ones that once belonged to her husband.

"The Darkmore witches have served in the Marionettes at the Carrington estate for generations. So, of course, whenever a promising, up-and-coming blood witch such as yourself comes of age, I take interest. Especially when your mother has served me so well these past few decades. Truly, I don't think I've ever had a better right hand. And yet." Slowly, she rises from her throne and comes closer until we're a few feet apart. "Skill and hard work can only take you so far. Some people just have more raw, natural power. And don't think we haven't noticed yours." Her eyes burn with each word. "I trust the academy has been preparing you well for the Marionettes initiation?"

I bite my tongue and nod.

"Good." She straightens again, all of the intensity of her expression gone. "And of course, you remember my son?" She gestures to the prince behind her, who merely rolls his head in my direction.

"Of course," I say.

"Good, well, I know how stressful the initiation can be for some of our young witches, and on top of your junior year at the academy, at that. But I wanted to remind you the Darkmores will always have a place here."

The tone of her voice doesn't quite match her words, coming off more like a threat than a comfort. She returns to her throne, the conversation apparently over. Prince Reginald's attention has returned to the back of the room, so not knowing what else to do, I mutter a quick thank-you and cringe as the echoes of my footsteps follow me all the way to the door.

The moment I step into the hallway and the door closes behind me, a hand snatches my elbow and yanks me off course.

"What was that about?" my mother hisses.

I whimper despite myself, and she jerks her hand back

as if burned. Her eyes dart from my face to my arm, then before I can stop her, she seizes my wrist and pulls up my sleeve. The angry wound stares back at her, the skin red and swollen. After casting a quick look over her shoulder, she takes my other arm and leads me toward the stairs.

"Come with me." She doesn't say anything else until we're in her quarters with the door closed behind us. "So you're not healing anymore?" she asks, turning away and striking a match against the fireplace.

A row of a dozen orange candles lines the mantel, and she lights them one by one. A few supplies for the ritual are already laid out beside them.

"It's…recent," I say.

"Is that all? Just the healing?"

I sigh and sink into the velvet armchair by the window, debating the wisdom of telling her at all. But I've already been to the library twice in the past few weeks, trying to find leads on what's happening to my magic. Other than spells that allow you to purposefully transfer some of your powers to another witch, I haven't found much.

"My magic has been a little blocked," I admit. "And when I can manage to draw it out, it's…draining."

Finally, she turns. The flames from the candles cast shadows along the side of her face and highlight the left-over splatter of blood on her throat.

"Now is not the time for weakness, Valerie. Not with your initiation starting this week." Silence settles between us as she sets her hands on her hips and considers me. "It's probably just nerves," she decides, then waves a hand for me to join her by the fire. She stabs her nails into the back of her hand and lets the drop of blood fall on my injured arm. My skin prickles, and the wound heals almost instantly. "I'm sure you'll be back to normal in no time. You just need to relax." She grips my chin with two fingers and frowns at the dark bags beneath my eyes. "And get more sleep."

"Thanks," I mutter, twisting my arm as the heat fades from my skin—

A slap lands hard across my face. My head snaps to the side and my hand flies to my cheek. When I take a step back, she follows me, leaning so close her nose nearly brushes mine.

"Do you know how embarrassing it is to have my own daughter show up last for a trial?" she asks. The calm, quiet rage lurking beneath her words makes every hair on my body stand on end. "When you're late, that reflects on me. And this close to the initiation? Calliope never would have done this. Are you trying to give them a reason to cut you—?"

She breaks off at a knock on the door, but when I glance toward it, she shoots me a warning glare. "Don't."

My cheek burns—half anticipation, half remembrance—but I force myself to stand up straighter. I told myself a long time ago I'd stop cowering under her, bowing to her the way she expects. She notices, because her scowl twists with amusement.

The door opens, but she doesn't turn. Connor steps inside, a small bouquet of red roses in his hands, but he stills as he takes in our stance.

"Mrs. Darkmore—"

"*Not* now, Connor," she says through her teeth.

He steps between us anyway, guiding me behind him with one hand.

Mom lets out a long, low breath, and peels her eyes from me to him. "You can save the chivalry. She'll heal." She looks him up and down. "You won't."

"That's enough," he says lowly.

"You're right," she says. "I have had enough of this."

"Mom—"

"Mind your business, Valerie," she snaps, then draws closer to Connor. To his credit, he doesn't flinch, even when she's right in his face. "You have two minutes to get out of here. If you're still here when I come back, I'll remove you myself."

With that, she turns and disappears down the hall. Neither of us moves at first, and I realize my fingers are fisted tightly in the back of his shirt. I release him and step back, my breath coming out shakily.

"You shouldn't have done that," I say.

He turns, his expression furious. His eyes soften as they fall on my cheek, and he tilts my chin to the side.

"I'm fine," I say, pulling away and eyeing the flowers now crumpled in his fist. "You can't honestly think those will fix—"

"Oh." He looks down as if surprised to find them in his hand. "I actually got these before…" He clears his throat. "I wanted to bring them by for Calla."

As hard as I try to hold on to my resolve, something cracks in my chest as I watch him turn and lay the flowers by the fireplace.

"Calla loved red roses," I murmur. I wave my hand in

the general direction of my mother. "I really can't talk right now."

"I know." He tucks his hands in the pockets of his pants. "I just wanted to bring those by and make sure you were okay. I know today is hard, and I'm really sorry that I made it worse." He meets my eyes again, a million unspoken words flashing behind them. "I know you have things to do, so we can talk about this later."

I nod, and when I don't say anything else, he goes for the door.

"Connor?" I call.

He turns, the faintest flicker of hope lighting in his eyes.

My chest tightens, everything I'd been wanting to say before I'd opened his door still stuck there.

And even though I can see the hurt in his eyes, the remorse, I can also still see the puncture wounds on his neck, and seeing them hurts as much as it did the moment I opened that door.

In the end, all I can manage is, "Thank you."

My mother returns the moment he's gone, and I push past her before the satisfied smirk on her face compels me to say something I'll regret later.

"I'll get the rest of the supplies," I mumble.

The sitting room feeds into a wide hall where flickering torches line the walls with magic-based flames. As I come to the bloodred curtain at the end, a wave of incense hits me. Dark wooden shelves cover every inch of the den's far wall, each containing different-sized glass bottles full of herbs, spices, and...*other* ingredients. It doesn't take long to find what I need, since this particular combination is a regular occurrence.

"Oh." The curtain rustles behind me. "Why is it so dark in here?"

I turn, juggling the vials in my arms as Adrienne snaps her fingers and the torches along the perimeter of the room roar to life—an act she makes look so simple, but I have a sinking feeling if I tried to do the same right now, I wouldn't be able to. She eyes my armful and turns to the wall beside her, plucking three crystals off the middle shelf.

"You forgot these."

"I was getting there," I mutter.

"I didn't realize you were home," she adds, tucking her hair behind her ear. It's hard to believe she's the youngest of us when her face looks the most mature, all angles and sharp edges. It's only further exaggerated now that she cut her hair, the black strands skimming her chin.

"Of course I came home."

She reaches over and takes the jar threatening to fall from my pile and tucks it under her arm. "Mom said you had a private audience with the queen earlier. What was that about?"

I roll my eyes. "Just keeping tabs on the only blood witches she has left, I suspect. Especially now that it's down to the three of us—" Adrienne's entire body stiffens, and I clamp my mouth shut. "We should probably get back." I head for the curtain, but pause beside her. "I know it doesn't seem like it sometimes," I say, "but you're not the only one who misses her."

Adrienne doesn't respond. Her eyes drift to my cheek for a moment, but then she turns away.

Mom hardly looks at me as I step back into the room. She takes the ingredients from my hands and starts mixing them in a bowl on the fireplace. She's laid out a circle of ash on the floor, tracing the line of moonlight as it sneaks through the far window.

I take my usual spot on the left of the circle and wait. Several minutes pass before Adrienne reappears from the back. She wordlessly places the crystals around the circle and finds her place across from me.

When Mom's done, she brings the bowl to me first. The mixture is cool and rough against my skin as I scoop out a handful, rub it between my palms, then drag it down both of my cheeks, wincing at the tenderness still lingering there. The sulfuric scent is momentarily overwhelming. Mom smears her thumb over a cut in her arm, then paints her blood in a straight line down my forehead and chest before moving on to Adrienne.

We each let a drop of our blood fall onto the candles beside us. The flames surge up, flickering violently in the still room. Mom gestures for us to join hands, and Adrienne pauses before accepting mine.

"To the Darkmore blood."

"To the Darkmore blood," Adrienne and I repeat.

"Living and past."

"Living and past."

She switches over to Latin, her words seamless and fluent as she closes her eyes and squeezes our hands. The flames surge up higher, high enough that I can feel their heat.

And it's this moment I always anticipate and dread in equal measure. The barest whisper of a second, the briefest flash in the room. But if souls are defined by the way that person made others feel, I'm certain Calliope's soul fills

28

every inch of the room around us, thick enough that I can breathe her essence in like air. It's like she's standing right beside me, her skin on my skin, her voice in my ear. Mom's eyes flit back and forth beneath her eyelids, and then just as quickly, Calla is gone.

The candles all flicker out, and small plumes of smoke spiral in the air between us. We release hands, and I quickly brush at my cheek, catching the tear that managed to escape.

"Happy birthday, Calla," murmurs Adrienne.

Despite the toll of using magic and my lack of sleep, when my head finally hits the pillow, I'm wide awake. By the second hour of tossing back and forth, I shove off the covers. The halls are empty this time of day—the rest of the estate won't be up for hours, even the early risers—so I take my time heading to the south side of the main floor. My brain churns through everything there hasn't been space for until now—Connor in bed with that woman, what losing my powers this close to initiation could mean, Adrienne's hostile expression when she saw me.

My footsteps echo in the cavernous space as I make my way toward the indoor pool. The room is as white and glossy as the rest of the estate, though windows with special UV-blocking technology cover the far wall. There's a black tint to them that makes it look much darker outside than I know it is. A few human servants bustle back and forth along the grounds, mowing lawns and trimming bushes.

The overhead lights glitter across the water as I perch

myself on the edge and dip my feet in. I wince at the reflection that stares back at me. My cheeks are still stained black from the spell earlier, so I lean forward, scoop my hands into the water, and scrub them against my face.

"Is your shower broken or something?"

The door clangs shut as a narrow figure strides into the room. My face breaks into a grin as I catch sight of her face.

"Avery Varaday," I say. "I thought maybe you retired."

She snorts and drops onto the concrete beside me. "Valerie Darkmore." She's in a similar state as I am—silk red pajamas, blond hair tied up with a scarf, makeup-free. "You're just two years behind me, babe. I'm gonna remember that."

"You couldn't sleep either?" I guess.

She sighs, shakes her head, and kicks her feet back and forth in the water, apparently not caring as the bottoms of her pants get wet. "Getting…nostalgic, I guess. It's my last day here. Twenty-three years, man. Twenty-three years."

My head whips up.

"I requested a transfer," she clarifies and pulls a pack of cigarettes out of her pocket. She holds the box out to me, but I shake my head. "You quit or something?" She lights up and inhales deeply.

I shrug and watch the water ripple as I sway my legs back and forth. Truthfully, if my body can't handle healing a simple cut right now, I probably shouldn't give it any more tasks. "Do you know where they're moving you to?" I ask instead.

She tilts her head back and breathes out the smoke, her entire body relaxing around the exhale. I have to look away.

THE MARIONETTES

My fingers are already starting to itch, so I shove them under my thighs.

"The Botner estate in Norway. So it could've been worse, I guess. They lost a Marionette earlier this year, so they were already looking for someone." She glances at me out of the corner of her eye. "Your initiation must be coming up now, isn't it?" I nod, and she sucks on her cigarette again. "You nervous?"

"Should I be?"

She shrugs. "It can be intense, but you'll be fine, being the golden Darkmore child and all."

I snort. "Maybe I do need one of those."

"Don't let them psych you out. It's not as bad as they try to make it out to be. How's the little one holding up?"

"Adrienne? She still hates me."

Avery shakes her head. "You Darkmores, always at each other's throats these days."

We fall into silence at the words left unspoken—*ever since Calla.* When Calliope was around, things had been different. The much needed buffer in the middle of our sharp personalities. The one voice of reason. Without her, everything feels off balance.

I shake my head, trying to clear it. Thinking of her never brings anything good. "Do you know who your new pair will be at Botner?"

"The queen's youngest son, Harry. We've met once or twice. He seems normal enough. And with me leaving Nathan here, I'm assuming they'll pair him with someone from your class now."

"Are you...sad? Leaving Nathan behind?"

Avery sucks on her cigarette again, inhaling long and

deep. She blows out a slow cloud of smoke as she considers her answer. "The academy will tell you a lot of witches grow close to their partners and they have a mutually beneficial and respectful relationship." She takes another drag off her cigarette, then stubs it out on the concrete between us.

"And you disagree?" I hedge.

She leans on her palms, craning her head back to look at the glass ceiling. "I think it's the luck of the draw, especially when you're dealing with the royals. Not all of us are that lucky."

I furrow my brow, really looking at her for the first time since she walked in. She looks a little different than she had at school, sure, but that easily could've been a product of time. Her face has thinned out, her bone structure more prominent. But there are also deep bags under her eyes, her once dewy, tanned skin now pale and lifeless.

I haven't been around Nathan much—one of the duke's sons. And with all of their family's homes in the different regions, they're rarely here at the estate. In fact, I don't think I've seen Avery and Nathan in the same room since they were officially paired. I'd never thought twice about it. Never considered it could've been bad enough to make her want to transfer.

"Aves," I say quietly.

She clears her throat and kicks her legs hard enough to make the water splash.

Then she's standing and pulling her shirt over her head.

"Avery—"

She tosses the rest of her clothes into a pile, then dives headfirst into the pool. I lean away from the splash, blocking my eyes with one hand. Avery stays under the water for a full minute before surfacing. She sucks in a deep breath, then smooths her hair down and shoots a wicked grin in my direction as she treads water.

"Care to join me? For old times' sake?"

I hug my knees to my chest. "I'm good."

"Suit yourself." She flips onto her back and runs her hands across the water.

"You know they have security cameras in here," I call.

"Nothing they haven't seen before."

She dives back under and comes up again in the deep end.

"Can I ask you something?" I say.

"What's up?"

"It's about Connor. Have you noticed anything…" I trail off, not really sure what I want to ask.

Apparently, I don't have to, because that alone is enough to make Avery's expression shift. She presses her lips together and lowers herself so the water runs over her chin.

"What is it?"

She shakes her head. "I don't know, Val. He's been around forever, so maybe that's the only reason it's noticeable. At first I thought it was the way they were with all the humans who are used to them—I mean, we all know how annoying the worshipping kinds are. But the way the vamps act around him—it's different now."

I lean forward. "Different how?"

She swims a little farther away.

"Different how, Avery?"

She pushes herself back under the water. When she

reappears, she's at the wall beside me, and she lowers her voice so it's barely louder than a whisper. "They're like sharks with blood in the water."

Before I can respond, she thrusts herself out of the pool and grabs a towel from a nearby lounge chair. "*Well,* if you're not going skinny dipping, I guess I'll be on my way." With a heavy sigh, she leans down to scoop her clothes into her hands. She hesitates, then gives my shoulder a squeeze. "See you around—who knows? Maybe they'll send you to Botner's too." She winks, since we both know the probability of that, then disappears from the pool room as quickly as she'd come.

I turn back to the water, kicking my legs back and forth and watching as the overhead lights dance across the waves. Avery's words cycle through my mind, and I imagine Connor in the center of the pool, the surrounding water tinted red.

They're like sharks with blood in the water.

I shake my head, forcing the image away. I can't afford to get distracted like this, not with initiation so close.

I wonder what Calla had been thinking about before her initiation. If she was worried. If she was scared. If she had even the slightest premonition of what was to come.

Maybe it would've been better if she hadn't.

CHAPTER FOUR

I WAKE SURROUNDED by smoke and sit up in my bed, disoriented. It takes me a minute to realize I'm back in my dorm room and not at the estate. The entire trip had been a whirlwind, and although I'd been unwilling to miss Calla's birthday, staying longer hadn't been an option. Not with what this week means.

I roll myself off the twin-size bed, my eyes burning as smoke continues to pour into the room, seemingly out of nowhere. I throw open the curtains and yank at the window —locked. My chest heaves with coughs, and I drop to all fours to get below the smoke and crawl toward the door. I wrap my hand in my sleeve and gingerly reach up, but the handle is cold to the touch, not hot like I'd been expecting.

The door, however, is locked. I still can't figure out where the smoke is coming from. There doesn't appear to be any kind of fire, but that doesn't make breathing easier. The hallway is quiet, no signs of struggle from the other residents. No shouts or pounding footsteps as people flee.

I cough and dig my nails into my palms until they break skin, forcing blood to the surface. But even as the magic's warmth rushes through my veins, I can't get the door open. Something beyond a simple lock is stopping it. Something stronger than I am.

Or maybe I'm just too weak to manipulate inorganic matter right now. The alchemists on the floor probably got out in a heartbeat.

I shift on the floor and wince, glancing down to see what's digging into my knees. I brush away the tiny particles clinging to my skin. It looks like...red salt? Leaning down, I press the side of my face against the ground and squint under the door—sure enough, there's a line of it, probably all the way down the hallway. No teleporting out of here then. No magic that crosses the threshold at all.

But at least that explains what's happening. I just have to wait it out—*that* I should have enough power for. I force my nails back into the wounds before they can heal, urging more blood out. Instead of trying to unlock the door, I use the building magic like an invisible barrier, the blood creating a protective coating over my lungs, throat, eyes, skin—anywhere the smoke can get in.

When my eyes stop burning and I can breathe in a deep, clean breath, I look around, still trying to find the origin of the smoke, but it's coming from everywhere and nowhere at once. My lungs itch from what I already inhaled, but at least I'm not breathing any more in.

A small patch of smoke parts like a curtain, revealing the blank wall across from me.

Your Marionettes initiation has begun.

The voice of Headmistress Coderre echoes in the room as each word materializes in the air in glowing red letters.

One hundred of you have spent the last three years preparing and training for the honor to be considered for the Marionettes. During these trials, we will put your knowledge and abilities to the test to determine if you are deserving of standing beside the great witches who keep us safe. You can be eliminated at any time. You can be tested at any time. And for the next two weeks, there will be no second chances.

You will continue with your regular class schedule. Your trials will appear to you when we see fit, and at the end of the first week, we will announce those of you who will be continuing on to the second and final week of trials. Shortly, you'll receive a note under your door with the time for your pairing appointments. The vampire you are paired with is who you will answer to for the next two weeks. From this moment on, you are officially undergoing your initiation, which means you are bound by the following rules:

Discuss your tasks with no one. Receive help from no one. Offer aid to no one. Breaking these rules or failing to complete tasks will be cause for immediate elimination. Poor performance in written and practical tests provided by your teachers will also be grounds for elimination.

Today is day one. Whether you succeed or fail will be up to you.

With her last word, the letters disappear, the smoke along with them.

Then I'm left sitting alone on the floor, my heart racing in my chest.

So it begins.

THE ACADEMY IS SHROUDED in fog today, the moon barely visible behind the clouds. Torches flicker around the path that cuts through campus, mingling with the array of artificial light sources that keep York Academy brightly lit throughout the night schedule.

Smoke still clings to my hair despite the two showers I took. All of the third years on the floor had looked a little shell-shocked coming out of our rooms, but no one spoke. If figuring out a way to breathe through the smoke was some kind of first task, it looks like no one got eliminated.

Or maybe everyone saw something different. I have no idea if the message manifested the same way, and I didn't ask. If I'm going to be on edge every second of the day for the next two weeks waiting to see whatever trials they throw at me, I can't afford to waste my energy worrying about anyone else.

Which is probably why I haven't touched the six missed calls and three voice mails from Connor waiting for me on my phone.

I stare at my boots as Kirby and I head to our first class of the day—Advanced Poisons. Now that the adrenaline has worn off, my mind is back to its incessant drowsy state, like a fog has settled over my brain. No matter how much sleep I get these days, it's never enough.

"I can't believe initiation starts today. When do you think the first task will be?" Kirby asks beside me. "It feels weird to go along with classes as usual, doesn't it?" When I don't respond, she nudges me with her elbow. "Hey, are you okay? You've been awfully quiet."

I blink, forcing myself to focus on her face. Her cheeks are flushed from the cold, now nearly as pink as the tips of her hair. She has it tied up in two pigtails on the top of her head today, the blond curls whipping against her cheeks with each step, as round and rosy as when we were kids. She frowns when I still don't respond.

"Did something happen when you went home this weekend?"

I nearly scoff at the question. What *didn't* happen? It had been my most eventful trip back in a while. But the thought of getting into it seems like it would take far more energy than I have to spare right now. In the end, I shake my head and say, "No, no. Just…tired, I guess."

"Yeah, I haven't been sleeping that well either. I was so nervous I couldn't even eat breakfast—"

Something brushes against the backs of my legs, and I let out a small yelp. A black cat prances in front of us, the bell around its red collar ringing, its tail held proudly in the air.

"Damn it, Monroe," I say, kicking snow at her. "Stop being a stalker, would you? You're not that sneaky."

The cat hisses, but slowly shifts back into a human form. Monroe rises up, uniform severely rumpled now, and winks at us.

"Sorry, ladies." She falls into step on my other side, winding her long, black hair back into a ponytail as she walks, then pulls out the red streaks at the front to frame her face.

The classroom is mostly empty when we slip inside and find our usual table in the back of the room. Monroe swats aside the plants hanging from the window and throws her bag onto the table.

"That's a lot of poison," Kirby mutters as she eyes the line of glass vials in front of us.

The three of us exchange a look.

"Not it," I say.

"Not it!" says Kirby.

Monroe scowls. "Fuck me."

Other students hurry into the room and fill the desks around us as Kirby leans down and inspects the different ingredients on our table.

"What time are your pairing appointments?" she asks. "Mine isn't until practically dawn, so I'll be waiting around all night."

"Same," says Monroe.

"Mine's at nine."

Monroe's head whips up. "Does that mean you're skipping our study session?"

"Nah, I'll still come. Probably just have to leave a bit early."

A hand appears on the table and knocks with two knuckles—Daniel. He's leaned so far back in the seat in front of me he looks like he's about to fall over. He flashes his perfectly straight smile. "Hey, Darkmore. Heard you went home for the weekend."

I glance at Kirby and Monroe on either side of me, but they both shrug.

"How does everyone know everyone else's business around here?" I mutter.

Daniel's smile doesn't falter. "Small school. How was our beloved queen? Did she ask about me?"

I roll my eyes. "Yes, Daniel. In fact, the entire estate is

now wallowing in your absence. They've even erected statues in your honor."

"As they should."

Beth lets out a snort beside him, then immediately flushes red from the roots of her hair all the way down her neck.

Daniel brings his hand to his chest and looks at her, aghast. "I can take it from Darkmore, but *you*? That hurts, Bethy."

She runs her tongue over the gap between her front teeth and shrugs innocently. "Someone's gotta knock you down a peg."

Mrs. Lavigne strides to the front of the room, her entrance casting a heavy blanket of silence over the class. Daniel winks and turns back around as she flicks her wrist and the blinds fall over all of the windows. A single candle sits on each table, and they alight at once, along with the torches on the chandelier in the center of the ceiling.

"Just one assignment for you today," says Mrs. Lavigne as a single sheet of paper floats from her desk to each of the tables.

I quickly scan our copy, my eyes darting from the instructions on the page to the materials on our desk. We're supposed to create a lethal but slow poison and its matching antidote, but there's no specific directions. A small bottle of a clear liquid sits at the center of the other ingredients, where we're meant to add a single drop of the poison we create. If the liquid turns red, the poison is approved for testing…which is to be done on one of our group members.

Kirby slides a few of the bottles to me and Monroe, her eyes narrowing as she considers the remaining ingredients.

She's always been the best of us at poisons, so I sit back and let her do her thing.

Monroe meets my eyes, scowling. "You guys better not kill me."

I blow her a kiss and start mixing the antidote ingredients together in a bowl as Kirby hands them to me. Monroe reaches over to add something to Kirby's poison mixture, but Kirby rips the bottle out of her hand before she has the chance and smells it. She's shaking her head before the bottle is even all the way to her nose.

"This would just suppress your powers."

Monroe compares that bottle to another one with a near-identical green herb in front of her. "How can you tell the difference? They look exactly the same."

"Here." Kirby holds the vial out to her. "Smell it. Much earthier, right? This one's sweeter."

Monroe frowns. "They smell exactly the same."

Kirby pulls the vial back and stoppers it. "Which is why *you're* taking it, not making it." She peers at me sideways as she grinds another ingredient into the bowl. "How was Mommy Dearest? You wanna talk about it?"

I roll my eyes. "I think I'd rather take the poison."

"Done!" shrills Elle at the table to our left.

Wes lifts the poison in a toast to the rest of the room and casually brings the glass to his lips. He swishes it around in his mouth, swallows, and lets out a long *ahhh.* Chloe, the other little blonde girl beside him, hands over the antidote, and he throws it back like a shot.

The rest of the groups return their focus to their stations, but I keep watching from the corner of my eye. To anyone who doesn't know Wes, he'd probably look calm.

He works the piercing at his lip with his tongue and pushes the mop of dark hair out of his eyes, but his hand has a small tremor. He bounces his thin leg up and down against his chair, making the chain hanging from his pants rattle. He must feel me looking at him, because he glances over at me and winks. Another beat passes, and blood rushes to his face, turning his skin bright red. He brings a hand to his throat.

Then he crumples to the floor.

Chairs scrape back as his group members jump up from the table and surround him.

"Wes," Chloe whispers, holding her hands out like she wants to touch him but is too afraid to as his limbs start spasming.

Mrs. Lavigne sighs and watches impassively from the front. "What did you do wrong?" she asks calmly.

"I—I don't know!" shrills Elle.

"Think back," continues Mrs. Lavigne. "Where could it have gone wrong?"

Wes gasps desperately for air, the skin of his neck turning a deep red.

"Help him!" cries Chloe.

"Think. Back," Mrs. Lavigne repeats.

"I don't know!" screams Chloe.

Wes arches against the floor, his neck turning purple now.

"Your teammate is dying," says Mrs. Lavigne, her voice still entirely calm. "You have everything you need on that table to save him. So what are you going to do?"

When neither girl moves, Chloe openly crying now, Mrs. Lavigne approaches them, slips out a small vial from the pocket of her skirt, and leans over Wes on the floor. The moment she pours the liquid into his mouth, he stops spasming, and she tucks the vial back into her pocket.

"The two of you are dismissed," she says. "Pack your things. And don't bother coming back." She scowls at the rest of the groups turned in their seats to watch. "And the rest of you, get back to work."

The two girls hurry from the room as Mrs. Lavigne helps Wes off the floor and back to his seat. I guess there will be some eliminations on day one after all. I wait to see if she'll send Wes on his way too, but after murmuring something to him in a low voice, she paces back to her desk at the front of the room. Not being able to think under pressure must have been the last straw, not messing up the antidote.

"You two better not fuck this up," Monroe mutters under her breath.

Kirby grins. "Comforting to know she wouldn't have let you die though, right?"

"No, Kirby," says Monroe. "I don't find that comforting at all."

YORK ACADEMY HAS few options for lunch—the handful of shops on Main Street within walking distance, and the dining hall in the center of campus. Food is included with admission here, and it's not half bad. But most importantly, it's the best place to eavesdrop on academy drama.

The hall is already bustling with activity by the time Kirby, Monroe, and I get our trays from the food line. We find an empty wooden booth near the stained glass in the back, surrounded by blissfully ignorant first years gossiping about what they think will happen this week. I can't even be angry at the students betting on our fates—two years ago, that was us.

"I heard last year," whispers the boy behind me, "they pushed an elemental off the clock tower to see if she could summon enough wind to catch her fall."

I roll my eyes to the wooden beams overhead. Definitely not true, though to be honest, I wouldn't put it past them.

I push the mashed potatoes back and forth on my plate, my appetite nonexistent, as it has been for days now. Maybe I'll shove down a protein bar later instead. My second class of the day—Treaties and Foreign Affairs—had passed even more slowly than usual. It's one of the few classes I don't have with Monroe or Kirby, which makes it that much worse.

"Honestly, I don't think I've ever been more jealous of your magic, Val."

I blink back to the table to find Kirby and Monroe looking at me.

"What?" I ask.

Kirby huffs. "I was *saying*, we were practicing cleaning up bodies in Protective and Legal Studies this morning— and I was reading about how different the procedures are for blood witches. I had to cremate a guy—and getting fire to that temperature is *hard*—and Monroe had to get buddy-buddy with the alchemists for their chemicals."

I shrug. It all basically does the same thing. My blood magic leaves my strengths in manipulating organic matter— like bodies. The advantage is I can draw from the magic in my blood—or someone else's. Kirby has to rely on having the particular element around. Air, obviously, isn't an issue. Water and fire are easy enough, too, as long as she carries around a water bottle and a lighter. She started wearing a tiny glass necklace filled with dirt for earth a few years ago. Though we can all draw on the elements, hers is to a much stronger degree.

"I offered to just eat the body." Monroe tosses her hair over her shoulders and sighs dramatically. "They didn't go for it."

I snort out a laugh. I probably shouldn't find the image of Cat-Monroe eating someone as funny as I do.

"Hey, isn't that Weici?" says Kirby.

I glance over my shoulder as two people amble through the aisles between the tables. The girl is about half the height of the man beside her. Her straight, black hair hangs down to her hips, and a thin red line is tattooed around her upper bicep.

"Didn't she graduate already?" Monroe asks.

"Last year," says Kirby. "That's Dante, her partner."

Dante looks at our table, his eyes the same dark brown as his skin. It's the stillness that gives him away as a vampire. The rest of his body doesn't move, just his eyes, as he takes in his surroundings.

The girl—Weici, apparently—laughs at whatever someone says at the table in front of her, and Dante turns back around, smiling too.

"What are they doing here?" asks Monroe.

As the words leave her mouth, Weici hops up on the nearest empty table, her movements fluid like a dancer's. That alone is enough to get most of the room's attention, but then she claps her hands over her head a few times for good measure.

"Excuse me!" she calls out, her voice pretty and light. As more heads turn in her direction, she smiles wide and holds her hands together in front of her chest. "Sorry. Hi. I don't mean to interrupt your lunch, but Headmistress Coderre requested that me and my partner, Dante, come and visit today."

Dante steps up on the table beside her and waves.

"All of you third years should be receiving your temporary pairs tonight, and I know how nerve-racking that can be. Dante and I have been paired for—"

"A little over two years," he finishes.

"Right!" She throws an arm around him—seeming to aim for his shoulders, but with their height distance, it ends up somewhere near his waist. "We're here to answer any questions you may have—"

"So we'll be walking around," says Dante.

"But feel free to come find us if you want to chat!"

My head ping-pongs between them as they finish each other's sentences.

Dante grins, letting his fangs show. "I don't bite. Promise."

As the two get down from the table and the room's buzz of conversation builds to the level it was at before, Dante murmurs something and Weici throws her head back with her laugh.

"I hope I get paired with someone that cute," mutters Kirby.

Monroe rolls her eyes.

"What! If I have to get that close to a vampire, it might as well be someone easy to look at."

Monroe scrunches up her face. "I heard the blood bond can make you feel…weirdly connected to your pair. Like a sibling."

"Not for everyone!" Kirby insists. "They don't look like siblings." She nods toward Dante and Weici. They've moved on to another table, and Weici has her head leaned against Dante's shoulder as they talk. There's an inherent physical ease between the two of them, something beyond just friendship. It's like their bond magnetizes the space between them—not quite visible to the naked eye, but you can still *feel* it, even from across the room.

"How weird is that to think about?" I add. "What if you feel, like, super close to your partner, but if you got reassigned and broke the bond, suddenly you didn't feel anything for them anymore, and it was all just…" I trail off, not sure what word I'm looking for. Superficial? Contrived?

A lie?

Monroe frowns. "I'd never really thought of it that way."

"What if you get weird, fake romantic feelings for them?" adds Kirby.

"Ooo." I snap my fingers. "Or what if you can hear their thoughts and they're secretly talking shit about you in their head?"

Kirby nods and points at me. "I don't want to know what anyone is thinking about me! Ugh, what if I can't even be a bitch in my head in peace anymore?"

Monroe covers her face with her hands. "Now you guys are getting me all freaked out."

I hold up my palms. "Sorry. Sorry. Thinking out loud. I'm sure it'll be fine. Stuff like that is uncommon."

"It better be," mutters Monroe. "What if I get an old, shriveled-up man and I end up falling in love with him?" She wags a finger between us. "You two better stop me."

Kirby salutes her. "Officially on *don't let Monroe fall in love* duty."

The two of them exchange a sideways glance, and I push away my untouched tray.

"I've gotta head back to the dorms to change, but I'll meet you guys in half an hour?" I offer.

Monroe's eyes cut to mine. "You better not ditch us."

I grab her soda before she can stop me, tip the remaining contents of the can down my throat, and grin. "Wouldn't dream of it."

———

"IS THIS PAYBACK FOR THE POISON?" Kirby pants. The treadmill screeches below her as she shuffles along, dragging her feet against the belt. "Because I swear I didn't know it was going to taste that bad."

I stifle a laugh as the image of Monroe gagging in class rises up in my mind. It had been so loud the people at the table in front of us backed out of the line of fire in case she hurled.

"What are you laughing at?" Monroe demands. She jabs the increase speed button on Kirby's treadmill, then leans over to turn up the resistance on my bike. "Neither of you are going to pass the physicals at this rate."

I focus on the two guys lifting weights in front of me—

the only other people in the gym—as I force my legs faster. My entire body feels like it's moving through wet cement. Sweat drips down the bridge of my nose, and I lean back, letting my legs slow to a stop as I fish around the bottom of the machine for my water bottle.

"Okay, Kirby, your turn," says Monroe.

"I can't...talk and...run...at the...same time," she gasps.

Monroe ignores her and flips the page in her notebook. "How many of the estates currently have a branch of the Marionettes?"

"Eight," Kirby pants.

"Seven," I correct.

Monroe points at me, then narrows her eyes when she sees I've stopped. Sighing, I brace my forearms on the bike and start pumping my legs again.

"Correct. Brazil discontinued their program last year. Okay, Valerie, which regions currently have peace treaties with ours?"

I hesitate, my mind working. "Rjukan, for sure, and Utqisgvik, Stockholm, Prince Rupert, Hat Yai..." I trail off.

"Tórshavn," Kirby pipes up.

"Correct." Monroe clucks her tongue. "See? It's really not that hard, guys."

Kirby mimics her behind her back, and Monroe whips around just in time to catch the last of the words. She raises a single eyebrow, reaches over, and increases the speed on Kirby's treadmill a little more. Kirby curses and grabs the handlebars with both hands, her legs flying behind her.

"Valerie." Monroe turns back to me. "Name one viable exception from the weekly blood donations."

Connor's face rises up in my mind. Apparently that exemption hadn't been much of a priority for him if he decided to offer up his blood for fun. I lock my jaw, forcing the image away. Whenever I picture him now, I can't seem to manage it without those puncture marks on his neck.

"Val?" Monroe prompts.

I clear my throat. "Any human who's already currently working for the vampires for another job."

"Correct. Kirby, what was the sixth witch classification before they went extinct?"

Kirby jabs the off button on her treadmill and sets her feet on the sides of the conveyor belt, breathing hard.

A knot forms in my stomach at the question, but I try not to let it show on my face. A bit of heat creeps up the back of my neck just the same. I close my eyes, waiting for my heart rate to slow, and beads of sweat drip down the sides of my jaw.

"You have two more miles to go," says Monroe.

Kirby braces her hands on her knees and hangs her head between her shoulders. "Just give me a minute. My lunch is going to come back up."

"You still didn't answer the question. Stop stalling. The sixth classification of witches was…"

"Necromancers," I breathe.

Monroe points at me. "Right again!"

"Can we be done with the quizzing?" says Kirby. "This basics test is a formality anyway. No one ever fails this one."

Monroe raises her eyebrows. "Kirby, you got like half of these questions wrong."

Kirby waves her hand and restarts the treadmill, this

time barely shuffling along at a jog. "I'll study more. The test isn't for another few days."

"How about a really simple one?" says Monroe. "What is the acceptable turning process for a new vampire?"

Kirby sighs. "You have to get permission ahead of time —apply through the estate of your region. If approved, one of the Marionettes will cast the turning spell on the vamp's blood before they feed it to their human, kill them, then feed them more blood upon their awakening."

"And then…?"

Kirby makes some vague gesture with her hands. "And then the new vamp has to be monitored to make sure the turning didn't go wrong. If they show signs of being unmanageable, they're put down."

"Finally she gets one right!"

Kirby rolls her eyes. "How come you aren't answering any of the questions, huh? I don't see you running either."

I smirk and pull a leg up onto the bike's handlebars to stretch.

"I'm done," Kirby announces. "I feel like my brain is about to explode." She grabs the handrails and jumps off the track, the treadmill still speeding by below her. It starts beeping when it no longer senses her weight.

"Kirby, you have to—" starts Monroe.

"I know, I know." She jabs the off button and grabs the towel off the side to wipe her face. "I need to get my pace up. But throwing up on this machine isn't going to do it."

"Fine. We can be done. *For now.*" Monroe tosses an identical towel to me, and I run it along the back of my neck. "In other news, I heard something interesting from Wes today."

I raise a brow, still chugging my water.

"*He* said the prince came back with the queen, and he's at the estate now, maybe for good."

"What?" gasps Kirby. "Since when?"

Monroe narrows her eyes at me. "You don't look surprised."

I shrug. "I might have run into him when I was home."

Kirby throws her towel, and it hits me square in the chest. "And you didn't *tell us*? Does he look as good in person as he does in the pictures?"

"You know, Kirbs, *Vampire Weekly* doesn't count as an actual news source," says Monroe. "*I'm* more interested in why he's back."

I shrug again and fold myself over the bike, trying to stretch out the aches around my spine. "I don't know any more than you do."

"Well, is he back for good?" asks Kirby.

"How would I know that?"

She lets out an impatient huff. "Well, if you don't know anything, I'm going to find someone who does." And with that, she struts off toward the group at the front of the gym.

Monroe and I exchange a sideways glance.

"Isn't your pairing appointment soon?" she asks.

"Half an hour."

I dig my teeth into the inside of my cheek, thinking back to that conversation I had with Avery by the pool. I've never really been anxious about who I'd get paired with... until now. What if it turns out to be someone awful and I'm...*stuck* with them? At least this practice round will only be for the next two weeks.

"Okay, not to be all up in your business, but you've been acting weird ever since you got back. Is everything okay?"

"Just...nervous, I guess. About initiation and everything. You know, to be thinking about something for the past twenty-one years, and now it's here? And it could end at any time. And then what? Start a shop down in the city turning tricks for the humans? Get a healing job in a hospital?" I shake my head. "I can't even imagine that kind of life enough to picture it."

I half expect some derivative of *You don't have to worry about that. Of course you'll get in—you're a Darkmore!* like everyone else loves to say. But she just shakes her head. "We're all nervous." She reaches over and squeezes my arm. "But I know for a fact you don't have anything to worry about."

I start to roll my eyes, but she tightens her hold on me. "And *not* because you're a Darkmore. You work hard, Val. You *deserve* this spot, okay?"

I grimace, my face burning a little under the praise, and she nudges my shoulder repeatedly until I smile.

"Okay, okay," I laugh. "So do you. Anyway, I should get going. Don't want to be late."

She nods, but I can feel her watching me as I gather my things and head for the door. I don't know why I brought it up. I hadn't been planning to say the words until they were out of my mouth.

The air smells like rain as I step outside, and I head straight for Headmistress Coderre's office on the other side of campus. The cold immediately melts through my skin, and I hunch my shoulders up to my ears.

It's probably just the stress about my powers not acting

right that has me thinking this way—subconsciously trying to prepare myself for what would happen if I somehow don't get in.

Which is dumb. Honestly, even if I bomb every task this week, I have a feeling the queen still wouldn't let me go. But if I'm going to beat out someone else for this spot, I want to *earn* it.

The headmistress's secretary glances up from her computer as I step into the room, her cat eye glasses taking up the majority of her face. Her fingers stop typing. "Ah, Valerie Darkmore."

I nod, and she gestures toward the door at the back of the waiting room. "You can go in. She's expecting you."

I hesitate before crossing to the door and turning the knob. The moment I open it, I freeze in the doorway.

Coderre is standing behind her desk, head bent as she talks in hushed tones with the man beside her.

Not just any man—the prince.

CHAPTER FIVE

"VALERIE DARKMORE," she says, exasperation slowing her voice. "We received an...unusual request for your pairing." She gestures for me to step inside. A chill raises the hairs on my arms as I cross the threshold, her office somehow drastically colder than the waiting room was. The dark bookshelves lining the walls paired with the heavy curtains over the windows make it feel like a cave.

Unusual is a bit of an understatement. Why the hell would the queen send her son to mentor a student for two weeks when she has thousands of lower-ranked vampires at her disposal? Doesn't he have anything more important to do? Unless this is more about keeping an eye on me.

I watch warily as Prince Reginald nods and steps out from behind the desk in black slacks and a white buttondown, his dark hair free from his usual crown. His expression is unreadable, but his eyes flit over my face like he's... looking for something. I bristle a bit under his stare as my gaze swings from him to Headmistress Coderre.

"You can't be serious," I say.

Her mouth tightens, and something about the look in her eyes tells me she's not happy about this either. "The queen insisted."

"Well, come on then." The prince nods toward the door. The deep, hypnotic quality of his voice sends a jolt through my nerves, and I realize this is probably the first time I've heard it in over a decade. "We're on a tight schedule, and we've got a long way to go."

"I—oh."

He strides from the room without another word. Coderre raises her eyebrows as if to say, *Well, what are you waiting for?* I hurry after him, but it's not until we're outside and several yards from the building that I manage to catch up.

"Where are we going?"

He strides along the path, long legs covering distance so quickly I have to jog to match his pace. "The estate," he says.

"I—what? I can't go back to the estate *today*. It'll take hours."

"Which is why we're leaving now."

"I have other classes—"

"No, you don't," he says, voice oddly cheery. "I got you out of them."

"I—" I look around as if someone nearby can help, but the paths are empty. "The train station is that way." I point behind us.

He snorts, but doesn't slow down or look at me. "You're funny."

"Look, all due respect, Prince Reginald, but—"

"Please, call me Reid." He stops abruptly and turns toward the road, where a sleek black car is idling. I stare at the car, then him, my brain still trying to catch up. He opens the back door and waits for me to climb in. When I don't, he sighs, his expression serious. "Get in the car, Darkmore. Unless you'd like to decline your first task."

Finally coming out of my shock, I step forward and slide into the seat.

He gives me a humorless smile as he closes the door behind me. "Wise choice."

It's the longest car ride of my life. Thankfully, the prince's driver has a healthy respect for exceeding the speed limit by at least ten miles per hour, but the fact remains: it's a long drive.

The prince and I share the back seat, but almost immediately into the drive, he tilts his head back, closes his eyes, then doesn't move again. I can't tell if he's actually asleep—it's hard to tell with vampires sometimes. My body, however, refuses to relax. I don't know if I've ever been this close to him—certainly never *alone*. I glance at him out of the corner of my eye, but he seems to be apathetic to my presence.

My sweaty gym clothes cling to my skin as I shift my weight. God, he can probably smell me. I'd thought the appointment would be a quick in-and-out at Coderre's office. If I'd known I'd be spending the rest of the evening with him, I would have at least showered.

As we pull away from the academy, the light outside the

car shifts from the bright, artificial lights that fill the campus to the hollow glow of the moon. Sometimes I get so used to the day-like lighting at school that I forget how *dark* night can be, especially as we drive through the rural areas of upstate. Miles go by without seeing another car.

Despite the absolute exhaustion gripping my body like a second skin, I can't sleep. Not in this car, not when I have no idea what the prince is about to make me do or why the queen wanted me paired with him, and not with the never-ending rampage of images in my mind—Connor's blood on the pillow, Avery's expression when I'd said his name, the look on my mother's face when she'd seen the cut in my arm.

So instead, I pull my notebook out of my bag and rifle through my notes. Might as well do Monroe proud and squeeze in some studying.

The prince stirs beside me, making a low sound in the back of his throat. He reaches up and unbuttons the collar of his shirt, then twists his head toward the window. The moonlight illuminates his face, making the deep bags under his eyes look even more pronounced.

I flip the page and sigh, my brain refusing to retain any of the information I'm reading.

"Could you keep it down over there?" he mutters.

I scowl in his direction, but he's smiling.

"All due respect, again, *Your Highness*, but I have to study for these exams. You're making me miss class right before our finals—I'm going to have to deal with the consequences of that."

A single eye opens, and there is far too much amusement in the set of his mouth. "Who would've thought?" he muses. "A Goody Two-Shoes Darkmore."

I make an unintelligible sound and flip the page again.

"Well," he says, clearing his throat. "Might as well get used to it. We're stuck together for the next two weeks."

I close the notebook. "Where exactly are you taking me?"

"The Carrington estate," he says without missing a beat.

"Yeah, you already said that. *Why?*"

"Part of your training is being able to think on your feet and handle surprises. Who am I to deprive you of that?"

"Fine." I turn away and press the side of my face against the window. "Don't tell me."

We lapse back into silence for the rest of the drive, and I'm just starting to doze off when the car stops. I blink my eyes open, expecting to see the front of the estate, but instead, we're parking outside the entrance at the back of the property. The one almost exclusively used by the human servants.

I squint over at the prince. "What are we—?"

He throws his door open and hops out. "Come along." He takes off toward the entrance without waiting for me, and I have to hurry out of the car and jog to catch up.

The back entrance is nearly hidden by low-hanging tree branches, and it's especially difficult to see in the dark. Prince Reginald heads straight through as if he's done this countless times before. He grabs a handful of the branches and pushes them aside, but instead of ducking in and leaving me behind again, to my surprise, he holds them up and glances at me over his shoulder, waiting.

"After you."

It's too dark to see anything, though I suppose he has an advantage with his vampire vision. I slow and reach my arms out in front of me, then a hand presses against my lower back and guides me forward.

"Sorry," he mutters. "I forgot how dark it would be for you. It's right here." He swings aside a heavy metal door, and I blink against the sudden brightness. Instead of opening to the kitchen as I'd been expecting, the door leads to a metal staircase.

He goes down first, rolling his shirtsleeves up to his elbows as he walks. I follow closely behind, the smell in the air shifting as we go farther down to something metallic and humid. There's a second metal door at the bottom of the stairs, and everything clicks into place.

Oh, God.

Reginald shoulders the door open, and it lets out an earsplitting screech. He holds it and waits for me to pass. My heart pounds in my chest as I take a few steps inside.

The first thing I notice is the stench. It hits me like a wall the moment I step through the door, easily doubling what I'd smelled in the stairs. The dim overhead lights reflect off the damp concrete floor, which is marred with bloodstains and dirt. Metal cells line the walls, and plastic tarps cut off the second half of the room from view.

Bodies upon bodies are crammed into the cells, their skin covered in dirt and sweat. They don't react as Reginald and I step inside, but the people in the cell closest to me— three women and two men—shrink away when the metal door clangs shut behind us.

Reginald steps up beside me as he finishes rolling up his

sleeve. The line of his jaw is sharp enough to cut glass, and his throat bobs as he swallows. But when he turns to look at me, his expression is carefully blank.

"Ready to get started?"

I glance around the room again, a cold sweat collecting on the back of my neck as I think through the possible reasons he would take me to a blood farm.

But the possibility I keep getting stuck on is: *What if he wants me to use magic on them?*

And: *What is he going to do when he realizes I can't?*

"This way." He starts down the line between the cages and comes to one near the end. There's three people inside —two boys, both no older than teenagers, and a middle-aged woman. He gestures to the woman with two fingers, and she shakily climbs to her feet. The other two stare at him with something like reverence in their eyes.

For fuck's sake, even in a cage, they look at him like he's a god.

The woman is in a white tank top, so stained with dirt it's nearly brown, and a loose pair of drawstring pants. Her dark hair is slicked back in a greasy ponytail, but instead of showing any fear or concern upon seeing the prince, her expression is as blank as his is.

The ring of iron keys jangles as he unlocks the door and motions her toward the back of the room.

I follow along at the rear as he pulls the curtain aside, revealing half a dozen sectioned-off areas with thick metal walls. The three of us enter the closest one, and the door makes a loud click as it locks behind us.

There's a chair in the center of the room, right on top of the drain in the floor. Metal drawers line the walls, and I don't even want to venture a guess as to what's inside. The woman sinks into the chair and folds her hands in her lap, a resigned look on her face.

I glance at Reginald, waiting to see what happens next, but he's staring at me as if he's waiting for the same thing.

The cold sweat reappears on the back of my neck. I've heard rumors of the vampires using the Marionettes' magic against their enemies or for getting information, but I've never been able to get a straight answer from any of the witches on what really goes on. If he's expecting some kind of magical torture from me…

"We're looking for the vampire James Westcott," he says, and his voice echoes around us. "And we have reason to believe you can help us."

"I don't know anything." A muscle in her jaw jumps, and there's a fire in her eyes as she looks at me that wasn't there before. "I didn't know anything before you brought the witch in, and her being here doesn't change that."

She nearly spits the word *witch*.

Interesting.

Reginald tucks his hands in his pockets and rocks back on his heels. "We'll see about that." He turns, fishes the keys from his pocket, and opens the door again. When I try to follow, he holds up a hand to stop me. "Your job is to get us the information we need."

I stare at him, wide-eyed. "How am I supposed to do that?"

He shrugs, saying nothing more on the matter, and closes the door between us.

CHAPTER SIX

SOMETHING SHIFTS in the woman when Reginald leaves. She straightens her spine, her eyes narrowing as I pull a metal folding chair from the corner and drag it toward her. But the way her hands tremble before tightening them around the bottom of her seat gives her away.

It's almost as if she isn't afraid of him...but she *is* afraid of me.

How many other Marionettes has she seen come down here? How many times has she heard through the walls whatever they've done?

"I'm not telling you anything," she says.

"Oh, I know." I drop the chair in front of her and sit, trying to keep my posture casual, as if that will somehow convey I'm not the threat she thinks I am. "What's your name?"

She doesn't say anything.

"I'm Valerie."

Still, nothing.

I sigh and run my hands up and down my thighs. How am I supposed to get anything out of her when I don't understand what I'm looking for? How am I supposed to know what questions to ask? Maybe the nice face had been for show and it was Reginald's plan all along to set me up for failure.

I chew on my nail and glance at the door. I can already hear the rumors like buzzing insects in the back of my mind.

A Darkmore got eliminated on the first task?

Unheard of.

A disgrace to all blood witches.

How humiliating.

I can't even imagine what my mother would say. Probably nothing at all. She'd just never speak to me again.

"Madison," says the woman. "My name is Madison."

I must look really pathetic if *she's* taking pity on *me* right now.

The tension in her shoulders eases, just a little, and I notice for the first time how *skinny* she looks. Her shoulder blades protrude like the tips of bird wings. They're supposed to be feeding everyone in here rations, so either she was skinny to begin with, or she's been here a while and the portions haven't been generous.

I pull my backpack into my lap and search around in the front pocket. Madison eyes me as I remove a protein bar and hold it out. She doesn't reach for it, but her eyes fix on my hand and dilate.

I wave it in her direction again. "It's not poison, I promise. It's just my lunch. Take it, please."

Her hand shakes, but she reaches up and takes it, a

diamond ring glinting on her finger under the light. I narrow my eyes and watch quietly as she rips it open and shoves half of it in her mouth. I offer her my water bottle, but she shakes her head.

"Do they have your family here too?" I ask.

Her gaze shoots to my face, and she stops chewing. "They have nothing to do with this."

"How long have you been here?"

Her forehead creases, and her eyes unfocus a bit. "I... don't know," she admits.

"Do you think they're doing okay without you?"

As quickly as they had come down, her walls slap back into place. I curse myself for not weighing my words more carefully. She pushes herself back as far as she can in her chair and clenches her jaw.

I lean my elbows on my knees and lower my voice. "Look, I don't know why you don't want to tell them what they want to know. I don't even know what they want to know in the first place. But *I* can't leave here without you telling me something, so how about we work something out?"

"By threatening my family?" she asks tightly.

"By offering to *help*."

"I don't believe you." Her eyes flicker around the room, repeatedly finding the door behind me.

Is she worried he's listening?

I shrug and dig around in my bag again. "You don't have to." I push a notebook and pen into her lap. "Write something on there that they want to know, and then on a different piece, write what *you* want me to do to help. And then we can be done here."

She frowns, but she picks up the pen. "Why would I trust that you'd actually do it?"

"Well, I don't see anyone else around here offering. So I'm the only chance you've got."

———————

"Here." I shove the paper into Reginald's hands and cross my arms over my chest, the other paper tucked away in my backpack. The prince quirks an eyebrow at the messy hand-writing, but instead of asking questions as I'd expected, he tucks the paper into his pocket, escorts Madison back to her cell, and leads me out of the cellar.

The other humans look up when we pass. Instead of the fear or hatred I expect to see there, there's just…curiosity.

When we're back outside, I take a deep breath and close my eyes. The air is much cooler out here, and it helps clear my head as I work through my options of what to do next.

Madison's right—she has no way of knowing if I do what she wrote on this paper. But she kept up her end of the deal, and now there are several people depending on me to keep up mine.

The prince's footsteps crunch in the earth behind me, but he says nothing. There's something more unnerving about his silence than anyone else's—the way he always seems to be watching, observing, filing away everything he sees, all the while giving nothing away himself.

A pair of headlights cuts through the darkness—his driver is still idling beside the curb. To take him where, I have no idea.

KATIE WISMER

"Why did you need me to ask her? Why didn't you just glamour her?"

He inclines his head. "Good question. I tried."

"You…tried?"

He turns, and the headlights from the car catch the sharp angles of his face. "There's some kind of magical block in her mind. Maybe I could've had a witch remove it, but there was no telling how much damage that would cause. She knew something." He holds up the paper in his hands. "But it couldn't be taken from her unwillingly."

A small smirk pulls at the corners of my mouth. "And you thought I could be more persuasive than you?"

He tucks the paper into his pocket and pops his eyebrows. "Seems I was right."

He walks toward the car again, and when he notices I'm not following, he lets out an exasperated sigh. "Get in the car, Darkmore. Let me take you back."

"Why would you drive all the way back to the academy just to come back here?"

"Because I'm not coming back here. I have some business upstate."

I shift my weight and tighten my fists around the straps of my backpack. I can't leave with him. Not yet. I don't know the next time I'll be back at the estate. And by then, it could be too late. This has to happen tonight.

"No thanks," I say. "I—I need to go see my family first. I'll grab the train home."

He studies me for a moment, and there's nothing in his expression to tell me whether he believes me. Finally, he shrugs and climbs into the car, closing the door between us without another word.

I turn like I'm heading for the estate's front entrance. Once his car pulls off and disappears around the corner, I allow my steps to slow to a stop and strain my ears, listening.

A light breeze picks up and rustles through the trees, but I'm alone.

I plunge back into the darkness, passing the blood farm's door. The other entrance must be close by. A hint of light emerges up ahead. My steps quicken, and I'm too focused on the light to notice the thick roots crisscrossing below me.

"Shit." I stumble and steady myself against a trunk. The light falls on my face, and I squint against it. Straight ahead, there's a single bulb illuminated above a screen door.

The door isn't locked, and it's all too easy to slip into the kitchen. It's mostly empty this time of night, aside from a few workers cleaning up or preparing food for dinner.

A tall woman in the corner nods at me as I duck into the walk-in pantry and start shoving anything I can find into my bag, preferably nonperishables.

If any of the servants question my presence or what I'm doing, they don't say anything. Questioning Marionettes or other witches in the estate isn't looked upon kindly. The divide among the humans and the rest of us has always made me uncomfortable, but tonight, I'm grateful.

It takes three tries to yank the zipper over all the food, but then I slip the straps over my shoulders and head toward the door.

The rest of the kitchen continues on unperturbed, but I freeze in my tracks as Connor walks into the room carrying a tub of dirty dishes. He nods, smiling, as a few of the other workers greet him. He notices me a moment later and stops. The dishes clank together, and he opens his mouth like he wants to say something.

But then my gaze drifts to his throat. Two bite marks are still plainly visible, and there's bruising around the puncture sites. The image reappears in my mind as fresh as it was the first time—another woman on top of him, his blood dripping from his shoulder to the sheets.

I turn and push out the exit.

If he calls after me, I don't hear it over the roaring blood in my ears.

I don't have time for this right now. I need to get into the city, and in a way no one will question or follow me. Which means I can't take one of the estate's cars, and none of the public transport comes out this far other than the train, and those are few and far between.

I venture back into the thick of the trees and out of sight, shooting a quick glance over my shoulder to make sure I'm alone.

"This is such a bad idea," I mumble to myself as I flip the blade out of my ring.

I don't even know if I *can* do this. Teleportation is a taxing spell, even on a good day. It's not like manipulating a single part of body chemistry—it's manipulating my entire *being.* At least I'm not trying to teleport someone else. That would be even worse. And teleporting into the city should take far less power than trying to get all the way back to the academy.

Hopefully it takes whatever amount I've got left.

I pull the paper out of my bag to look at the address again, then prick my index finger so I can smear my blood over the words. The wind picks up, and I shiver as I make the second cut.

I sway on my feet, and my vision swims, but the heat keeps building in my blood, almost hot enough to burn, and I imagine myself shrinking down smaller and smaller, folding in on myself and condensing until I'm microscopic. Then the trees around me disappear.

When I blink my eyes open again, I'm on my knees on the pavement of a quiet street. The streetlight overhead buzzes—the only one still lit on this side of the block. I take in the house in front of me—single story, red front door, windows boarded up—and double-check the address.

It's the right place.

I clutch my bag tighter as I make my way up the fissured concrete driveway and hesitate in front of the door. What if Madison gave me the wrong address on purpose, and this is some kind of setup?

The door cracks open before I have the chance to knock. A single brown eye looks out at me.

"Who are you?" a deep voice asks.

"I—uh—" I slide the pack from my shoulders. "I'm here to help."

The man starts to close the door.

"Madison sent me!" I call. "I brought food. You have two kids, don't you?"

The door stops.

"Madison," he says, his voice rough. "She's still alive?"

"Yes. I just spoke with her."

The door cracks enough for him to peer out again, this time with his eyes squinted, assessing me.

"You don't have to trust me," I say. "But will you at least let me give you the food?"

His gaze travels over my head, then flickers up and down the street. After another moment of hesitation, he pulls the door the rest of the way open and juts his chin. "Come on. Hurry."

I slip inside the dark house, the only light coming from the kitchen at the back. The man closes the door behind me, and my throat tightens. Usually I wouldn't give being alone with a human a second thought. If he tried something, I could handle myself. But with my powers acting so strangely and me already being exhausted from teleporting here, I'm not sure what I would do.

He heads for the kitchen, apparently expecting me to follow. I search for signs of the kids—toys are strewn across the floor, and there's a second, smaller table beside the large round one in the kitchen—but the house is quiet.

"They're downstairs," the man says gruffly as he yanks open the refrigerator. As the light falls on him, I see how rough of a state he's in. His clothes are tattered, like he hasn't changed in days. His hair is cropped close to his head, but there's a trace of a beard along the lines of his jaw. Despite the harsh lines carved into his face, he doesn't seem as old as I'd first thought. He might not even be thirty.

There's a staircase behind me—the basement must be where the bedrooms are, since there's no place for them on this floor. It occurs to me it's the middle of the night for humans, not the middle of the day.

"Sorry to show up so late," I say.

The man reappears with two beers, pops the caps off, and slides one across the table to me. He nods for me to take a seat.

"You're on the vamp schedule," he says. It isn't a question.

I nod anyway as I sink into the chair and unzip my backpack. "I grabbed as much as I could fit." I start unloading my finds, and the man watches me silently, sipping his beer. Once I've finished taking the last of the food from my bag, we stare at each other.

He tilts his head and licks his lips. "She in a blood farm?" This time, it is a question. And I can see in his eyes how much he's hoping I'll tell him otherwise.

I swallow hard and drop my gaze to the table.

He lets out a slow breath and reaches forward to take one of the cans—beans—and rolls it in his hand. "Why'd you come here?"

"She and I made a deal. I'm just holding up my side."

He sets the beans back. "She's anemic," he says, eyes still trained on the can. "Couldn't keep up with the weekly donations and work full-time. It was taking too much out of her. She'd spend days in bed recovering, then at the end of the week, have to donate again, and it would start all over." He takes a slow drink of his beer. "She won't last long in there."

"She looked okay," I say quietly. "Like they hadn't really been taking from her."

He stares at me like he's not sure if he should believe me.

After several moments of silence, I grab my bag and stand. "I don't know when I'll be back in the city. But I'll try to come by again with more." I turn to go, but pause, something gnawing at the back of my brain. "You're sure she was taken for skipping donations?"

He nods, but he doesn't quite meet my eyes.

I furrow my brow. "Does the name James Westcott mean anything to you?"

His entire expression darkens, whatever trust we'd managed to build in the last few minutes shutting down. "You should go."

"You know that's the real reason they're keeping your wife there, don't you? They think she knows something about him."

"You should *go*," he repeats, his voice firm, but not unkind. This time when he meets my eyes, his expression is stricken. Scared.

I pace back toward the door, trying to show I'm not a threat. "I'm not trying to cause any trouble. I'm just saying —if you work with them, you might be able to get her out—"

The man pushes up from the table. "You don't know anything." Then he turns and disappears down the stairs, apparently unconcerned about leaving me in his house. That or he's off to get a gun.

I let myself out, the door creaking behind me as I close it. A dog barks somewhere down the street. Hugging my arms to myself, I glance up at the moon glowing overhead, then squint, trying to see the street signs. I don't have it in me to teleport back. I know that much. But there has to be a train station or something nearby to get back to the academy.

Maybe I should've asked the guy in there before burning that bridge.

A car pulls around the corner, illuminating the street with its headlights, and every muscle in my body tenses. It glides down the street, its engine humming, until it comes to a stop in front of the house. The glossy sheen of the door flashes beneath the streetlight as someone steps out.

Not someone.

Prince Reginald.

I gape as he strides toward me, frowning, his eyes sweeping our surroundings.

"What are you doing here?" I demand.

How did he find me? How could he possibly have followed me here?

His eyes flicker from my backpack to my face, then away just as quickly. "Get in the car."

"I—"

"Valerie." The sound of my name coming from his mouth makes me freeze. I think it's the first time he hasn't called me *Darkmore*. "Get in the car." It comes out less demanding this time, and there's something about the way he keeps shooting wary glances down the street that makes me follow him.

We sit in silence as the driver pulls away from the curb, but when I catch a glimpse of him, there's a shadow of a smile on his lips.

"Very bold," he says. "Were you not afraid I'd report you for stealing food?"

I hadn't planned on getting caught. "Well, are you going to?"

He shrugs, his mouth twisted up in amusement now. "No."

I shift my weight and watch the neighborhood disappear into the darkness behind us. "How did you find me?"

"Madison may have been blocked from glamours about James Westcott, but that doesn't make her resistant to all glamours."

Something twists in the pit of my stomach. Making someone do something against their will has never sat right with me, especially if you have the power to make them think it was their idea or forget it altogether. It just feels so…invasive.

"Do you do that often?" I ask, my voice coming out stiff. "Glamour humans."

"No," he says simply. "Only when I think my partner might be doing something stupid and putting herself in danger."

I glance at him, but he's not looking at me anymore. He's turned toward his window.

"What will happen to her? Now that she's given you what you want."

The amusement disappears from his voice. "That's not up to me."

"That doesn't answer the question."

"No," he sighs. "It doesn't."

We lapse into silence as the car turns back toward the academy.

"Why are you doing this?" I ask.

That, finally, makes him look up. "Doing what?"

I wave my hand between the two of us. "Getting paired with me. Wasting two hours driving me home. They have plenty of others who could've done the job. Why make the prince waste his time training some student?"

The curl of his lips returns. "Surely you think higher of yourself than that, Darkmore."

"So that's it? It's just because of my name?"

He inclines his head, acknowledging this. "Since I currently find myself without a partner, my mother decided this would be the best way to test if you and I could work together. Had there been another, older blood witch available, I'm sure she would have paired us instead. But alas…"

He doesn't finish the sentence. He doesn't need to. *I'm the only one left.* And with Adrienne not even eighteen yet, it will be years before she's eligible to pair.

I chew on my lip and watch him as we pull onto the main roads of the city. Lights flash across his face. "What happened to your last partner?"

"Oh, he tried to kill me."

At first I think he's joking, but his expression is serious.

I'm not sure what emboldens me to say it, but the next words tumble out of my mouth of their own accord. "Did you deserve it?"

He smirks, and laughter dances in his eyes as he meets mine. "Probably."

"Is that why you've been gone all this time?"

His expression darkens, and he turns away, the conversation apparently over.

"There are all kinds of rumors about where you've been," I say, trying to lighten the mood again.

"Oh, I'm sure there are."

I sigh and glance out the window. Although the human side of town is quiet and asleep, the heart of downtown is buzzing with life, the sidewalks crowded with passersby, the store windows bright.

"I suppose if I ask you what's so important about James Westcott, you wouldn't tell me that either."

"You catch on quick," he says. "Maybe we will be a good pair after all."

CHAPTER SEVEN

THE PRINCE'S car gets me back to the academy at a reasonable time, but I still don't get much sleep. Dusk rolls around far too soon, and I head out early to the academy's library before my first class, barely able to keep my eyes open.

The library is empty when I step inside, the rows of shelves looking much different than they usually do cast in the light streaming through the windows. The dark-haired woman behind the information desk glances up at me, but she says nothing and goes back to whatever book she's reading. She tried to help the last few times I've been in here, but after I shut her down and insisted on finding everything myself, it seems she's given up.

Nothing personal. I just don't need to advertise what I'm doing.

I cross to the grand staircase in the center of the room. A peek through the shelves confirms the human workers aren't even here yet. I head straight to the third floor, not sure what I'm looking for, considering my last few visits produced exactly zero leads. Just anything that could hint to what's happening to me.

I may have lucked out with the first task, but there's no way I'll make it through this entire initiation with barely any magic. There must be some documentation about this —a reasonable explanation. A *reversible* explanation.

And, ideally, some information on James Westcott would get my curiosity to leave me alone so I can focus on the rest of my tasks.

I start in the reference section and search for any books related to blood witches or the Darkmores that I haven't tried—only two are obviously labeled, so I grab them. This might not be a blood witch thing at all, but it's a place to start.

I work my way back on each of the blood witch family trees from this region—the Darkmores, the Hawthornes, the Abrams, and the Blackwoods. I'm not expecting it to be explicitly documented, but maybe I can find something in *someone's* history that hints at a loss of magic. Any promising leads end up in my notebook to look into later.

There isn't a lot of time, so I skim then move over to the computers against the wall once I have a few names. I double-check over my shoulder for any librarians, but the rest of the floor is empty. I don't want any search history to be tied back to my login info, so I have to be smart about this. Instead, I look for holes. Gaps in information. Empty spaces. Anywhere secrets could hide.

The first few names I try turn up with nothing. I'm about to give up when a girl from the Hawthorne family who died about a hundred years ago catches my eye. She was in the running for the Marionettes, but all mentions of her disappear a year after she didn't make the cut. This isn't entirely unusual—witches have several paths they can take in society, the Marionettes being the roles with the most prestige. Witches who choose a different path—to work on their own or for the humans—often fall off the map, whether it be because of the unexceptional nature of their lives or their families disowned them. The latter being more likely if they came from a bloodline that's remained in the Marionettes across centuries.

The Darkmores, for example. There hasn't been a single one who's chosen a path other than the Marionettes as far as our family tree stretches back.

I frown when I happen upon the girl's obituary. There's no cause of death—just a date. There's not much information about her life aside from her family name. It doesn't even mention what she did in lieu of the Marionettes.

Whoever chose the photo must have had it out for her too. I can still tell she was pretty, but aren't obituary pictures supposed to show the deceased at the peak of their life? This one looks like it was taken in the peak of an illness—a near impossibility for witches, especially blood witches with how fast we heal.

The picture is cropped below her collarbone, showing off the thin, lifeless waves of blond hair spilling over her shoulders. Her eyes look sunken into her face, her lips cracked. She's not smiling, just staring blankly into the camera.

There's something in her eyes that makes it seem like she's staring back at me. Something that makes me stop and print out the page.

I click out, lean back in my chair, and circle her name on my list.

Samantha Hawthorne.

It's a dent on the surface of all of my current problems, but at least it's something. I chew on my pinky nail, my mind drifting back to last night. I probably wouldn't have thought twice about the name James Westcott if the prince hadn't been so secretive about it. And a magical block in Madison's mind? So there must be at least one witch involved too.

A book clatters to the ground in the stacks behind me, and I jump. A human boy ducks to retrieve it, then resumes pushing his cart along, restocking the shelves. He glances my way, his brown eyes locking on mine, but he looks away just as quickly and disappears into another row.

I cock my head. I can't exactly ask the librarian for help, and something tells me I don't want this showing up in my search history either. If the prince is so tight-lipped about James Westcott, maybe others would be too. Or at the very least, if the prince is trying to keep this a secret and it gets back to him that I've been asking around, I doubt that would go over well.

Books shuffle a few rows down as the boy returns more to their shelves.

I squint in his direction over my shoulder, considering. What harm would there be in asking the human for help? He probably knows these books better than anyone, and I could always make him forget afterward.

A murder of crows launches into flight outside the window, cawing and scattering up toward the sky. I lurch back as the sound of their beating wings fills the library, then hurriedly pack my notes into my bag and follow the boy into the stacks.

"Excuse me?"

He jumps as I round the corner, and the book in his hands tumbles to the ground. He mutters a soft "sorry" as he bends to pick it up.

"I was hoping you could help me find a book," I say.

The boy shifts his weight, his eyes still flickering around the room. His anxiety is so high I can practically smell it on him.

He jabs his thumb toward the librarian at the front. "She would probably be more help."

"I'm looking for information on a vampire named James Westcott," I say, lowering my voice.

The boy stops fidgeting.

I narrow my eyes, studying him as he slowly puts the book in his hands back on the shelf. A hint of red creeps up the side of his neck.

"What do you know?" he asks, not looking at me.

What do I know? Nothing. Absolutely nothing at all, but I'm not going to tell him that. Because for some reason, he thinks I do. And that...*worries* him. But why would a human care?

And why would a human and Prince Reginald have this in common?

A bead of sweat rolls down the side of his face.

Maybe I don't need a book.

"Please," he whispers. "I don't know anything."

His body is shaking now, and I take a step back, trying to show I'm not a threat. "What's your name?" I ask.

Instead of defusing the situation, the question only makes him more tense.

I sigh. "Look, I really am just looking for a book—"

"There's nothing in this library with the information you're looking for," he says quietly. "And even if there was, if I were you, I'd stop looking. While you still can."

I frown, but he turns and walks swiftly from the library before I can respond—or before I can cast a forgetting spell. *Shit.*

"Ryan!" the woman at the front desk calls as the library door swings shut. She glances back at me, perplexed. I hurry after him, but as I burst out the doors and onto the sidewalk, he's nowhere to be found.

Students stream past in both directions, heading to the first class block. A few shoot me questioning looks as I stand there looking around.

Damn, for a human, he's *fast.*

I glance at my watch and curse—if I don't hurry, I'll be late for class. I search for him in the crowd again, but he could be anywhere by now. Erasing his memory will have to be a problem for another day.

The trip wasn't a complete bust though. While I may not have gotten any concrete information about James Westcott, I do have a potential lead about my magic with Samantha Hawthorne. And somehow, Ryan's reaction feels better than some book. More significant. How many other humans on campus know something?

I turn right, falling into step beside the other students as I head toward the clearing for physical conditioning. With only twenty students in the class, it will definitely be noticeable if I'm late. The last thing I need is a lecture from Zouche right now. She always spits when she yells.

And with it being initiation week, who knows, maybe I'll get worse than a lecture.

A shriek cuts through the air.

We all stop, looking around, trying to find the source. But then up ahead, I see a tall man grab a dark-haired girl from behind. He throws a black bag over her head before I can figure out who it is. My entire body tenses, but he smiles when he sees he has an audience, flashes his fangs, and winks as he throws the girl over his shoulder and takes off into the trees.

He's taking her for a task, I realize.

After another stunned second, everyone along the path starts walking again. I stare at the place the vampire disappeared through the trees for another moment, but then like everyone else, I turn away and continue on.

"WHAT WAS HE LIKE?"

I glance at Monroe out of the corner of my eye as I finish tying my hair into a ponytail. The sun is still setting in the distance, painting the sky above the clearing a light pink. Fifteen of us stand in a line in the field, waiting for the rest of the class. Zouche paces back and forth in front of us, her entire face pinched together.

"You're obsessed." I roll my eyes. "What was *your* partner like?"

"Being late is more than enough reason to be eliminated!"

Zouche's voice cuts through the group's chatter as Daniel and Wes, attached at the hip as usual, run toward us and join the end of the line. They duck their heads as she continues to yell, pointing her finger so closely it almost touches Daniel's nose. The moment she looks away, the two exchange a smirk.

Monroe nudges me with her elbow before leaning forward to touch her toes. "Who cares about mine?" she whispers. "I have one of the old guys who takes on a student every year, so I know he won't be my final pair. Besides, don't change the subject. You got paired with *the prince*. That never happens."

I tuck my fingers into my jacket's sleeves and start jogging in place, trying to urge some warmth back into my body. My legs already feel numb from the cold through my leggings. "He was…normal, I guess."

Even after he'd caught me last night, he'd just driven me home, saying nothing else about it the entire ride back. I'd managed to sleep for the majority of the trip, but even once we arrived at the academy and he dropped me off by the dorms, all he'd said was *Good job today*, then driven off to wherever his *business* was around here.

"Normal?" Monroe demands, shifting herself into a side lunge. "Did he say where he's been for the last, like, ten years?"

"Yes, Roe, he told me his entire life story, then we painted each other's nails and shared a bottle of wine."

"I have done nothing to deserve this sass." She shifts into a lunge on the other side and lowers her voice. "What did he have you do?"

I suppress a shudder as images of that cellar flash back through my mind—the dim lights, the bloodstains on the floor, the stench. The resigned look in Madison's eyes, her husband…

Another human who'd reacted badly when I'd said the name James Westcott. Another human who knew something.

I shake my head. "You know I can't tell you that."

She sighs, straightens, and grabs her ankle for a quad stretch. "You know, you're very *selective* on when you decide to follow the rules."

I narrow my eyes, considering the wisdom of saying anything at all, but my curiosity gets the best of me. "Does the name James Westcott mean anything to you?"

"No. Should it?"

"I don't know," I admit, stretching my arm across my body.

"All right, everyone!" Zouche yells at the front of the line. "Three laps around the academy on the designated trail—four miles. You have thirty minutes to complete it, *max*." Her whistle cuts through the air, and we take off.

Monroe and I have a pretty similar pace, so we fall into step beside each other, our breaths puffing up around us like fog. The first part of the trail is the easiest since it's mostly downhill. A couple boys take off sprinting and get so far ahead I can't see them anymore. They'll burn out after a mile or so though like they always do. I focus on the steady rhythm of my sneakers hitting the dirt to distract myself from the cold, counting each step in my head, but even that can't stop my mind from wandering, wondering who else around here would know something.

And would any of them actually be willing to talk?

I don't know why I care so much. I certainly have plenty

KATIE WISMER

of other things to worry about. But I can't get it out of my head.

A group of girls runs around us as we approach the corner near the gates. The tallest of the three whispers something to her friends, and they peek at me over their shoulders before disappearing around the bend in the trail.

"They're just jealous," Monroe assures me. "You got the best vamp. Pretty sure she got some middle-aged man. Isn't the prince like twenty-six or something? Older, but not so much older that it's not hot anymore. Damn. Maybe *I'm* jealous."

I snort and push my legs harder as the path shifts to more of an incline. "I think it has more to do with his mom wanting to keep an eye on my family than anything else." The thought makes me pause though. I actually *don't* know how old he is, but he was born, not bitten, so at least he's not one of those two-hundred-year-olds in disguise. And he hasn't had one of the witches freeze his aging…that I know of.

My only memories of him before he left the estate are fuzzy with age. All I remember is having to crane my neck back to see his face when I was eight because he was so much taller.

Monroe's ponytail whips around her face. "If she wanted to spy on you, she could've used literally anyone from her estate. It wouldn't have had to be her son."

She's right, of course. Any vampire in her territory would be loyal to her. But that wasn't what I was talking about. I don't correct Monroe as we pass our dorms and start up the steep hill behind the clock tower. It's not that I think Queen Carrington is trying to spy on me. Keep tabs on me, maybe. But it feels like something else. Something I can't quite put into words.

With blood witches in short supply, keeping us close had always felt like collecting trophies more than anything, but lately, it's felt like something more. Blood witches are nice to have around since our magic isn't as limited as other witches. We can still do a bit of everything, but there's no need to rely on drawing power from a moon or an element when you can get it from your own blood—but what does she need all of that power for? A precaution…or a plan?

"Val? You good?"

"Yeah, sorry." I shake my head. "You think Zouche is gonna make us do the circuits after this?"

Monroe groans. "I hope not. My legs are still sore from last time. Oh hey, how's Connor? Did you have a chance to see him when you went home?"

His name hits me like a punch to the stomach. I nearly trip over a dip in the path and stumble to a stop, then brace my hands on my knees to catch my breath.

Monroe stops a few paces away, eyebrows drawn. "We're only on the first lap!"

I glance over my shoulder at the others coming up behind us and quickly catch up to her.

Images from that night fill my head. Sweaty sheets. Bruises on his neck. The blood still on that vampire's lips as she passed.

"I caught Connor in bed with a vampire," I say through gritted teeth.

"*What?*"

"And she was feeding on him."

"You are *shitting* me. What the fuck?" Monroe's voice

echoes around us, and a group of blackbirds in a nearby tree takes off into flight. "I'm so sorry, Val, I'm seriously speechless right now."

"You and me both."

She shakes her head. "I can't believe it. Men are trash, we know this, but *Connor*? What did he say—not that there's any excuse—but did you talk to him?"

I pump my arms hard at my sides as we round the next corner, and Monroe pants beside me as she tries to match my pace.

"He said it was *work*. The vamps are *paying* him for it, and he can't say no—to them or the money."

"Fuck," she breathes.

"Maybe it wouldn't have been as big of a deal if he'd told me about it beforehand, you know?"

"Definitely. Like how else were you supposed to react after finding out like that? Ugh, so you actually caught him *in bed*?"

"Literally in handcuffs, Roe. *Handcuffs*. And he's got bite marks all over him, so it was obvious he's been doing this a lot."

"You want me to castrate him? You know I could be real sneaky about it. In and out. No one would be the wiser. Just a cat and a penis."

I let out a breathless laugh. "I think we can hold off on that for now."

She shrugs. "We'll call it Plan B."

We run in silence for a bit, my body fully warmed from the mixture of exercise and rage now. We complete the first loop of the trail, passing the girls from before, but the first few guys are still nowhere in sight.

"Fuck," Monroe mutters under her breath.

I glance at her sideways. "What?"

She mimics zipping her lips shut. "Nothing. Keeping my opinions to myself."

"That's exactly the opposite of what I'm asking for! What are you thinking?"

"You're not going to *like it*," she singsongs.

"Just spit it out!"

She hesitates, then sighs. "Do you want a voice of reason or someone to bitch with right now?" When I don't respond, she adds, "This sucks, but come on, Val, it's *Connor.* That boy has been in love with you since you still had baby teeth. He'd do anything for you. And I know this has to hurt, but we will *never* know what it's like for him in that house as a human. Especially with his parents gone—he's only got himself to count on. *You're* all he's got. Whatever he needs that money for, if this is how he's doing it, he must need it bad. All I'm saying is, you should talk to him."

I press my lips together, my brain pointedly deciding to discard any of that logic. After a beat, I say, "I guess I just wanted the bitching partner."

"I can do that too!"

Daniel and Wes swim into view up ahead, and I nudge her with my elbow. "We should pass them."

They disappear over the top of the hill, and I push my legs until my muscles burn. The sun is fully set now, the darkness falling over the campus like a blanket. Most of the artificial lights don't reach this far out on the grounds, leaving long stretches of near-darkness as we run. I squint, trying to see the boys' shadows or outlines—they can't be that far ahead—but there's nothing.

A scream cuts through the air. Monroe and I look at each other, then sprint even harder. We pause when we hit the top of the hill, looking around for the source of the yell. Nothing but darkness and trees surrounds us, and there's no sign of the boys.

Monroe shrugs. "Maybe it was just—"

A second yell, this one louder and coming from the trees on the right. Monroe takes off, shifting midstep, her cat form blending in with the darkness.

"Monroe!" I call, hurrying after her. My heart thuds painfully against my ribs, an unfamiliar fear flooding my veins. Without my magic, I don't have many defenses left. The ground beneath me slopes as I head through the trees. The wind whistles, and then I hear it—muffled cries, crunching snow, and the distinct sound of slurping.

My blood goes cold as I see Daniel's body slumped against a tree, held up by a pale hand around his throat. The vampire is bent over, his face tucked against Daniel's neck. Monroe's tail brushes against the backs of my legs, and then she's shifting back into her human form beside me. I look around for Wes, but don't see him—or his body—anywhere.

Monroe turns to me with wide eyes, the silent meaning clear: *Do something.*

Of course she's expecting me to make the move—weeks ago, I was the most powerful in our class. I can hardly remember what that felt like anymore.

Still, I whip out my ring and dig a line into the back of my forearm, deeper than I'd usually go. The vampire straightens the moment the blade breaks skin, inhaling deeply at the smell of my blood. Daniel crumples to the ground as the vampire turns to us, baring his teeth. Blood drips down his jaw, his eyes wild, and black veins stand out against his skin.

I raise my arm, letting my blood drip onto the snow, and I imagine my magic crawling under his skin and filling his blood like liquid cement, then I clench my fist, making the cement solidify. The vampire freezes in place and snarls. His body twitches unnaturally as he tries to fight against me.

"Hurry," I grunt to Monroe.

She drops to her knees and searches the ground for something to use.

"Oh my God," gasps someone behind me.

I can't afford to break my concentration and turn, but based on the sound of footsteps, a few others have joined us.

"Help her," I growl, nodding toward Monroe.

My hand shakes, and the vampire keeps fighting against my hold, now starting to gain ground. He realizes it, too, because his mouth breaks into a grin with each step forward. Deep fissures trail down the imaginary cement I built in his blood, chipping and breaking it apart. He snaps his teeth over and over again like a rabid animal. My vision swims.

"Roe," I warn.

Someone raises their hand beside mine, and a gust of wind surrounds us. The vampire's progress forward halts, now just a few paces away. Light flashes in the corner of my vision, and the air around me warms.

"Duck!"

The witch beside me—Beth—grabs my wrist and pulls

me down a moment before a burst of fire consumes the vampire. A shrill, animal-like wail splits the air as he flails backward and lands on his back. Steam rises around him as he hits the snow, and the moment his body stops moving, the flames flicker out.

"Daniel!" Two of the girls rush toward his body, still slumped against the tree.

"He's alive!"

I let out a breath. *Thank God.* "Does anyone see Wes?" I call.

A few other girls disappear into the trees to search.

I push myself to my knees and crawl toward the vampire. His skin is badly burned, and he doesn't move again. Monroe appears at my side and looks over my shoulder.

"Something was wrong with him," she whispers.

I nod, frowning down at the lingering trails of dried blood coming out of his ears.

"You think maybe he was just turned?" she asks.

It would make sense. Most vampire attacks are chalked up to newbies. Newly turned vampires are always the most vicious, the most bloodthirsty. A lot of the time, their instincts take over, and they don't even realize they've killed until it's over.

But this seemed like something different. More than just bloodlust.

"How did he get on the grounds?" someone murmurs behind me.

Monroe meets my eyes, and her mouth is set off to the side as if she's thinking the same thing I am. The turning process is highly monitored. Everyone who wants to turn goes through a thorough approval process, and even then, they become the responsibility of their maker—a maker who would know the laws against attacking potential Marionettes. If he was recently turned, he shouldn't have been alone. Whoever turned him should've been there to make sure something like this didn't happen—especially on academy grounds. It doesn't make any sense.

I glance back down at the body, and my vision darkens at the edges, the afterburn of the magic lingering on my skin. Blood is still dripping down my fingers, the cut failing to heal.

"Val? Val?"

I feel myself start to fall, and everything goes black before I hit the ground.

———

IT STARTS with a buzzing in my ears. Slowly, the sound around me trickles back in. The field is an explosion of chaos. Voices layer over one another, building and building until I can't make out the individual speakers. My vision is gray and grainy, too blurry to make out the face hovering above me, just the faint outline of their features.

"Valerie."

I blink again, and my vision clears. Monroe looks down at me, eyes wide. I couldn't have been out for more than a few seconds.

I clear my throat and push myself onto my elbows. "I'm fine."

Her expression doesn't change. "What happened?"

"Nothing," I insist, trying to shake off the lingering

dizziness. "I tripped. There was a tree root."

Her eyebrows lower, no longer looking surprised. Instead, a hint of suspicion creeps into her expression, but she doesn't say anything else. She grabs my hand and helps me back to my feet.

I know she saw me faint. But no one else really seems to have noticed. They're all too busy getting Daniel up. He lets out a low moan as a group of four guys hoists him into the air and starts carrying him back toward the academy. Beth and Andie linger by the vampire's body, whispering to each other.

"Did you guys find Wes?" I ask.

Beth presses her lips into a hard line and shakes her head.

"Go get Zouche," says Monroe.

The two girls take off. When it's just me and Monroe left, she looks at me again as if expecting more of an explanation.

I don't know why I haven't told her or Kirby about what's been going on, probably because I still don't understand it myself. Or maybe it's something else. Maybe I don't want to admit what's happening, and I certainly don't want an audience, at least not until I can figure out how to fix it.

So I shake my head again, then nod back the way we'd come. "We should get going. Zouche might still make us finish those laps."

Monroe hesitates before responding. And then, finally, she says, "Knowing her, she'll use this as an excuse to push us even harder. Say this should be *good motivation. Oh, Daniel got mauled by a vampire? Probably because he should've been* running faster."

I snort out a laugh and brush the dirt from my hands. "He looked okay, though?"

She nods and leads us back through the trees. "He'll heal. You good to walk back?"

I nod, but I can feel her watching me. She doesn't ask about the fainting again, and I don't offer.

By the time we make it to the starting point, there are half a dozen other faculty members standing with Zouche, one of them being Headmistress Coderre. She waves her arms impatiently when she notices us coming up the hill.

"Is there anyone else behind you?" she calls.

"We're the last ones," says Monroe.

"Good, good. Go on inside. Class is dismissed for the night."

"Do you want us to show you where he is—?" Monroe starts to ask.

"Go on inside, ladies," cuts in Coderre. "We'll take it from here."

A boulder of a man steps out from behind her—Mr. Garret, one of the other poisons teachers. He tilts his head back and sniffs the air, then juts his chin in the direction we'd come. The group heads off, but Zouche lingers behind.

She looks us up and down, arms crossed over her chest. "Was anyone else injured?"

Monroe peers at me, but then shakes her head.

"Good." She claps her hands on our shoulders and gives us both a slight push back toward the academy. "Get inside."

And with that, she takes off after the group and disappears into the trees.

CHAPTER EIGHT

I SLEEP WELL into the next day, only rolling over long enough to pop in more iron and vitamin B pills before falling back asleep. Typically, my body has no problem replenishing blood loss on its own, but I figure given the state of things, a little extra help couldn't hurt.

When I manage to pull myself out of bed, I'm not nearly as dizzy as I'd thought I'd be. A dull ache still drums against the cut in my forearm as I pull a sweatshirt over my head and spray a quick cloud of perfume around myself instead of jumping in the shower. The rest of the dorm is quiet as I slip outside, everyone probably already out and about enjoying the weekend.

Kirby's and Monroe's doors down the hall are closed as I pass, no light coming from underneath. When I make it to the hospital wing, the room is empty save for a single bed. I glance around for a healer, but there doesn't seem to be anyone behind the curtain in the back—no noise, no light, no movement. My footsteps echo around me as I approach the bed, and Daniel glances up.

He's pale, save for the nearly black bruises along his neck. His lips pull into a weak smile, barely a ghost of his usual grin.

"Darkmore. What the hell are you doing here?"

"Here to finish the job, obviously." I grab a chair and pull it up beside his bed.

He chuckles, then starts coughing.

I frown. "I was going to ask how you're feeling, but I guess that answers that."

He lays his head back against the pillow for a minute, catching his breath. "They don't know why I'm not healing," he says. "They're bringing in some expert." He pauses and takes another deep breath. When he speaks again, his voice is barely above a whisper. "Did you see him? The vampire?"

I nod.

He swallows hard. "Did you see how he wasn't…right?"

I nod again and lean forward. "What did it seem like to you?"

Daniel shakes his head. "Not like anything they've taught us. He seemed…sick. Can vamps get sick?"

"I don't know," I admit. I reach forward and lay my hand on his, but when I open my mouth, nothing else comes out. What can I say? Daniel and I have never been that close, but we both grew up at the Carrington estate since his mom has been in the Marionettes nearly as long as mine has. We've known each other since we could walk. And now, looking at him with his veins standing out against his skin, his lips cracked, his eyes drooping, a sharp pang of panic fills my chest. For him, but also for what this could mean. What kind of vampire bite does *this*?

"What are you doing in here?"

I whip around as Headmistress Coderre struts into the room, followed by a man in black robes I've never seen before. I stand as they reach the foot of the bed, and she raises her eyebrows at me.

"I came to check on Daniel." I sidestep out of the way but pause before turning to the door. "The vampire—have you figured out where he came from? Or what was wrong with him?"

The headmistress's eyes lock on to mine with a striking intensity. "Wrong?"

I wave my hand at Daniel as if to say, *Obviously there was something wrong.* "He seemed...rabid."

Her eyes tighten, but the rest of her expression gives nothing away. "I can assure you, the issue is being looked into, and the campus has been secured. There's nothing to worry about, Miss Darkmore."

I meet Daniel's eyes, but she steps to the side, blocking my view of him.

"I'm afraid visiting hours are over." A muscle ticks near her eye, and I realize what was first coming across as hostility is just...fear.

She's worried.

"I'll see you around, Daniel," I say, then head back into the hall. Even once I'm back to the dorms, I still can't get Coderre's face out of my head. I've never seen her look like that before.

"*There* she is."

I blink back to the hall in front of me to find Monroe and Kirby outside my door.

"We were just looking for you," says Kirby. "How are you feeling?"

"I'm fine." If there's any truth to it, honestly, I can't tell. I don't feel like I'm going to faint again, so at least there's that. But I never do—not until the moment it's happening.

"Do you still want to come tonight?" asks Monroe.

I squeeze my eyes shut for a moment. I'd completely forgotten about the blood moon.

"You have to come," Kirby says. "I'll carry you down on a stretcher if I have to."

"There's definitely no need for a stretcher." I edge around them to the door.

"Where have you been?" asks Monroe. "We thought you'd still be sleeping."

I hesitate with my key still in the lock. "I went to see Daniel."

They follow me inside, and I sink onto the edge of the bed, suddenly exhausted.

Monroe leans against the doorframe, her teeth working her bottom lip. "How was he?"

I shake my head, thinking of his veins standing out, almost black. The nearly translucent quality of his skin. He looked as close to death as he had against that tree. "Sick."

"There have been rumors all over campus," says Kirby, taking my desk chair and spinning it around to sit on it backward. "People saying it was some secret test for initiation."

Monroe rolls her eyes. "That's ridiculous."

"Plus, we all would've been kicked out for helping him if that were the case," I add.

Kirby purses her lips, acknowledging this, then shrugs. "It's either that or someone purposefully set that vamp free on the grounds. How else would he have gotten in here?"

And yet, people clearly aren't *that* worried if they're carrying on with the celebration tonight.

"Anyway. Can we please not talk about this anymore?" says Kirby. "It's all I've heard about all day." She jumps up from the chair and heads for my closet. "How long will it take you to get changed? I can pick out your outfit."

"Kirby," Monroe warns.

"What?" She starts flipping through my hangers, landing on a long-sleeved black top that ties around the waist. "We're not leaving her behind, and we're not missing the bonfire, so either you pick out the shoes, or I will."

"Not the boots," Monroe and I say at the same time.

Kirby scowls, then shoots a loving glance at the pink cowboy boots shoved in the back of my closet. She gifted them to me forever ago, and they haven't seen the dark of night since.

"Fine." She tosses the shirt on top of me, then turns to rifle through my drawers. "You have five minutes to pull yourself together, and then we're heading down."

WE HEAR the party long before we find it. Kirby takes the lead as we cross out of campus and into the main woods of York. We still have a few hours before the moon is at its peak, but the party is already well underway. The roar of the bonfire stretches through the woods, the glow of the flames flickering off the damp underbrush. The dense trees give way to a broad clearing, where the bonfire sits at its center. Drums beat somewhere nearby as more people filter in through the trees.

Kirby takes off in search of drinks, her high heels sinking into the earth with each step. Monroe lingers by my side, the red streaks in her hair glowing by the light of the fire.

I wrap my jacket tighter around myself despite it not being nearly as cold tonight as it has been this past week, especially with the fire. I just can't get warm lately.

"If you want to leave, just say the word," says Monroe.

I shake my head and wave at Wes across the field, relieved to see he's okay. My stomach sinks a little at the empty space beside him where Daniel would usually be.

He's going to be fine. There's nothing to worry about— that's the message the academy is pushing—yet, I still catch myself scanning the area, my shoulders tense.

"You don't think maybe it was a bad idea to go through with this after what happened today?" I say.

Monroe nods her head to the side, acknowledging this. "The academy did a sweep of the area, and they're looking into it. If they're not concerned, then it's probably fine and was some random fluke, right?"

A group of the lunar witches have all huddled together near the fire, setting up their props and getting ready for a ritual. Beth and Amber—girls from our class—stand at the head, surrounded by a bunch of underclassmen I don't know. They start by setting their crystals together in a line, and one of the younger girls pulls out a massive spell book.

"You think they're trying to secure a spot with the Marionettes?" Monroe mutters.

I snort, because really, who *ever* knows with the lunar witches?

Ben, one of the elementals in our class, sneaks up behind them and reaches his hands toward the fire. Its flames leap up and expand, close enough to the lunars that they shriek and retreat back several feet, a few of their crystals getting consumed in the throw.

"Ben!" screams Beth as she grabs a handful of dirt and throws it at him.

"Here you are." Kirby reappears through the crowd, three bottles clutched to her chest. She hands one to each of us and nods back the way she'd come.

Monroe pops off the top of hers and drinks. Her eyebrows shoot up, and she takes another sip. "Who made the juice this year?"

Kirby shrugs as she leads us along the outskirts of the clearing and over to the opposite side of the fire. The crowd is thicker here, and I immediately recognize more people from our year. "Hopefully not the skinwalkers. No offense, Roe, but they totally fucked up the spell last year."

We manage to snag the last remaining seats on a fallen tree trunk near the fire where another group is currently passing around a flask. I take a sip from my bottle, and the sweetness floods my senses. The potion is always the same, one intended to work with the blood moon tonight. "Recharge" everyone's powers, bring good fortune—that kind of thing. It's tradition. But each group always puts their own spin on it, changing the flavor ever so slightly year to year. This year's has a distinct blueberry taste to it, though the alcohol still comes through loud and clear. It burns the back of my throat. I quickly screw the cap back on and set the bottle at my feet.

The girl to my right nudges my knee with her flask.

I glance from it to her face. "What is it?"

The rest of her friends laugh.

"You'll like it," says the beefy guy beside her.

The girl on his other side elbows him hard and whispers something in his ear. The arrogant grin quickly falls from his face, and he looks away.

"It's spiked venom," explains the girl next to me. "Way better than that stuff." She nods at my discarded bottle.

My stomach flips, but I keep my expression neutral and shake my head.

The girl shrugs and passes the flask to the next person.

"Shouldn't you be joining in over there?" asks one of the other guys, nodding toward the groups of witches preparing their rituals and showing off their party tricks.

I raise an eyebrow. "And why would I do that?"

The guy shrugs. "I don't know. Blood witch, blood moon."

"You realize the blood moon doesn't actually have anything to do with blood, right?"

He blinks at me, the haze from the venom already casting a heavy gloss over his eyes.

I rise from the trunk, and Kirby shoots me a concerned look.

"I'm gonna stretch my legs," I tell her. Then before she or Monroe can try to follow me, I disappear into the crowd, working my way farther and farther from the fire. A couple of vampires from town are in attendance tonight as well, swaying along to the drums and sucking at the wrists of their human companions.

I find a spot where I can still see the fire, but there's enough distance between me and the rest of them. Each of the groups has joined together for their different rituals— the skinwalkers throwing bones they've collected into the fire as they chant, the alchemists mixing their potions, the elementals adding different herbs.

I can't help but wonder what traditions have been lost over the years. Not being able to participate in the blood moon rituals has never bothered me, but sometimes I let myself imagine what it would be like to have other blood witches at the academy—in the region at all, really. The Darkmores are the only ones left, as far as we know, and there's no telling what else we've lost along with the other family lines.

Even Monroe—one of only six skinwalkers at the academy—has a group, whether she likes them or not.

My fingers itch—for a cigarette or my violin, I'm not sure. I suppose either would do, just anything to calm me down. But the violin is safely tucked away in my dorm, where it has been for months, untouched. Even though I've tried to cut the cigarettes out the past few weeks, with everything going on with my powers, tonight, that logical part of my brain is much quieter. I slip one out of my bag and prick my finger to light it.

The moment the smoke enters my lungs, relief courses through me. My shoulders relax, and I close my eyes as I let my head fall back against the tree.

"Those things will kill you, you know?"

I startle and turn to see the tall outline of the prince

step out of the darkness and into the flickering glow of the fire. Instead of the perfectly tailored suits he's worn every other time I've seen him, tonight he could almost blend in with the rest of the leather jackets in the crowd. He leans against the tree beside me. As he crosses his arms over his chest, he keeps his gaze on the fire.

I take another drag on my cigarette. "So, what? Are you stalking me now?"

He chuckles lightly. "I told you I had business in town."

"And your business was…a college party?"

He twists his face to the side. "Not exactly."

"Right."

We lapse into silence as a group of elemental witches manipulates the fire, taking away oxygen to shrink the flames, then making them rise to twice their original height. Onlookers cheer, and the energy in the air buzzes louder.

"We do have some unfinished business from the other night," he says.

My shoulders tense. Has he changed his mind about not reporting me?

He still looks as relaxed as ever as he rolls his head to the side to look at me. "The blood exchange," he explains. "Should've been our first order of business."

Somehow, of all things he could've said, this is the worst. I *wish* he'd said he's going to report me. That he'd come here to drag me back to the estate kicking and screaming. I breathe the smoke into my lungs, long and slow, my fingers tightening around the cigarette.

"It's standard," he continues. "Every pair has to do it—"

"I know," I snap.

Blood exchanges are done between witches and their paired vampires upon entering the Marionettes, but they also have all initiates do it during training to get used to the way the blood bonds work and to learn how to work with them. Of course I'd known this was coming. There's no getting around it, no matter how many ways I've imagined to make it otherwise.

Leaves crunch as he paces over and stands in front of me, blocking my view of the fire. He tilts his head to the side, his eyes narrowed like he's trying to read me. I stiffen as he rolls up one of his sleeves. He notices—of course he notices. Damn vampire senses.

"It won't hurt any more than all the times you've had to cut yourself for your magic," he says slowly.

"I know," I snap again, dropping my eyes despite myself. "It's not about that."

"Then…what is it?"

I drop my cigarette to the ground and stomp it out with the heel of my boot. I stare at the glowing red end until it dies. "My sister was a venom addict."

He doesn't say anything, not at first. And, mercifully, he doesn't ask any questions. Though being from the Carrington estate, he's probably already heard all of the rumors. Queen Carrington losing one of the few blood witches she had left was no small news.

"Calliope," he says quietly.

I nod. Somehow hearing her name in his voice hits twice as hard as hearing it in my own head. They hadn't let me or Adrienne see her body. Mom had sat us down, her voice far too calm, not even flinching around the words *overdose* or *gone*. She said she didn't want us seeing her like that. Wanted us to remember her the way she'd been before.

And naturally, she was to be buried at the academy instead. It would be too shameful of a memory at the estate.

"And you think that's going to happen to you?"

It's a rare condition, but it *is* hereditary, is what neither of us needs to say. I sniff and look away, my eyes starting to burn from the smoke. "I don't know. But it was this task when she was going through initiation—it was the first time she'd ever had it. And she never came back from it."

He pauses, his eyes flickering over me. I expect him to make some kind of joke or snarky comment, maybe tell me I'm being ridiculous. But instead, he says, "Do you have a blade?"

I blink. "What?"

His eyebrows lift. "Do you have a blade on you? So you can cut yourself, and I'll drink your blood that way. No venom involved."

"I—yeah." I flip the knife out of my ring.

"Perfect." He waves his hand. "Do it wherever you want. It doesn't have to be big either."

I stare at him for a moment, my body still wound tight, but then I dig the blade into the soft skin on the inside of my wrist, just enough for the smallest trace of blood to well to the surface, and mutter the binding incantation under my breath.

"May I?" He gestures to my arm.

I nod, mute, and hold it out for him.

He takes my hand with one of his, the other bracing farther up my forearm, and brings my wrist to his mouth.

His gaze never leaves mine, even as he leans his head down, dark hair falling across his forehead, and he slowly runs his tongue from one end of the cut to the other.

My breath catches in my throat, and a small tingling of heat spreads over my skin, but I don't look away. The fire roars behind him, the sounds of the celebration all fading to the background as he drinks.

His hands tighten around my wrist as he lets out a sharp breath. A slight sheen settles over his eyes, and I realize he's fighting back his fangs.

I stiffen, but then he releases me, his tongue slowly running across his lips. He swallows hard and winces.

"What?" I pull my arm back and cradle it against my chest. "I don't taste good enough for you?"

He narrows his eyes and brings his fingers to his mouth. "It…tastes like there's something in it. It almost burnt my tongue."

"Something in my blood?"

He shakes his head once like he's trying to clear it. "Are you…are you feeling okay?"

"I—what do you mean?" I hold my arm tighter against myself. My mind jumps to my powers, the exhaustion, the chill that never leaves me alone. "What did it taste like?"

He scratches the back of his neck, then shakes his head again. "It tastes like poison."

CHAPTER NINE

A PAIR of fingers snaps twice in front of my eyes. A small jolt goes through me, and I blink back to the classroom. Kirby clears her throat and nudges the book on the table between us. It's only then that I notice Madame Darlington headed straight toward us, perpetual scowl in tow. She's a scarecrow of a woman, all angles and intimidation—she fits right in with all of the creatures and spirits in our textbook. Her high heels click against the floor until she comes to a stop directly in front of our table.

"Miss Darkmore. Miss La Doux." She glances from us to the book on the table. "Have you chosen a creature for your paper yet?"

I peek back at the pages Kirby set in front of me. A gaunt, ash-gray creature stares back. Blood drips from the tattered remains of its lips. "A...wendigo," I say.

Madame Darlington tilts her head, the sour expression on her face softening. "An interesting choice." She turns abruptly and continues to the table behind us, pulling one of the pencils out of her bun to jot something down as she walks.

I glance at Kirby sideways. "A wendigo?"

She shrugs. "It was the first page I turned to, and you were basically asleep."

I sigh and flip through the pages, cringing more with each illustration. "Creepy cannibal spirit it is then."

"You want to head down to town and hit a coffee shop later this week to knock this out?" she offers.

I rub my eyes with the heels of my hands. "Yeah, sure."

"Hey." She reaches over and touches my elbow. "Are you good? You know, Monroe and I looked everywhere for you when you disappeared from the party. We would've left with you."

"Yeah, I'm sorry. I should've told you, I just…" I shake my head, my mind already trying to come up with some fake excuse. I study Kirby's face for a moment. I don't know when it became such second nature to keep all of these things from her. But if anyone could figure this out, it would probably be her. "Actually," I say, lowering my voice, "something kind of happened at the party last night."

Her forehead wrinkles. "Something?"

A sharp bell fills the air, and I startle.

"You're awfully jumpy today." Kirby braces a hand on my back as everyone else gets up and the room fills with noise.

"All papers are due before your final trials next week!" Madame Darlington calls as students hurry out the door.

I brace my elbows on the table and lean in. "Do you know how to do a blood test?"

If Kirby's surprised by the request, she doesn't show it. She listens along silently as we make our way back to the dorm and I explain what happened. She heads to her room first, and as I wait for her to collect all of the supplies she'll need for the spell, I search my room, not sure where to start. It could've been slipped in anywhere—things I've eaten, pills I've taken, clothes I've worn. I stand in the center of my room, hands spread and too afraid to touch anything.

Where the poison is coming from is only one part of the question. The second part I haven't let myself think about yet: *Who* has been poisoning me?

And the third: *Why?*

The effects have been consistent for weeks, so it must be something I interact with regularly.

A soft knock sounds behind me. I turn, expecting to see Kirby, but Monroe's head appears through the door.

"Kirby told me." She meets my gaze, and I see the understanding there, the pieces clicking into place. I brace myself, waiting for her to yell—maybe slap me—for not telling her sooner, but all she says is, "So, where do we think it's coming from?"

I glance around again, hands on my hips, and sigh. "I have absolutely no idea."

Monroe slowly paces around the room. "It would have to be something someone else would have easy access to— maybe something someone gave you?" She glances at me over her shoulder. "How are you feeling today?"

I shrug. "Okay. I haven't touched anything in here."

"I'm here! I'm here!" Kirby shoulders in, arms full of supplies, and kicks the door shut behind her.

"Have you ever done this before?" mutters Monroe.

"Nope," says Kirby cheerfully as she lays out her finds. She starts by spreading a white tarp on the ground, then digs through the tote bag on her shoulder and produces a dozen or so glass containers. "It better be one of these—I grabbed everything even remotely poisonous that I could find." She hands the containers to Monroe and points to the tarp. "Start putting a tiny sample of each on there. Make sure they're at least a few inches apart. And you." She turns to me. "Lie down and take off the shirt."

I resist the urge to ask if she knows what she's doing— *I'm* the one who asked for help in the first place—and comply. I strip off my sweater, leaving me in a tank top and my drawstring pants, and lie flat on the ground beside the tarp.

"Stay still." She pulls a handful of crystals out of her bag and starts laying them on my skin—amethyst, clear quartz, and bloodstone. She holds up a needle so I can see. "Any preference?"

I lift my left arm, and she carves a line along the back.

"Monroe, can you light those?" She nods at her bag.

Monroe pulls out three black candles and quickly positions them in a triangle.

Kirby carries my blood over and closes her eyes. "*Manufesto, ostendo, exsero.*" The blood falls and collects into a perfect circle on the tarp. "*Manufesto, ostendo, exsero.*"

Monroe reaches out and takes Kirby's hands. "*Manufesto, ostendo, exsero,*" they chant, and the flames in the candles strengthen. "*Manufesto, ostendo, exsero.*"

I tilt my head to the side to watch as the blood starts to move. The crystals feel warm against my skin as the blood trails across the tarp, passing poisons one by one, until finally settling below the final sample in the line.

Kirby opens her eyes, and the flames die down. She releases Monroe's hands and frowns.

"Which one is it?" Monroe demands.

Kirby shifts through the glass containers again and produces one full of green herbs. "It's Vexillium."

"What does that mean?" I ask.

Kirby reaches over and lifts the crystals from my skin, her teeth working at her lower lip. "It means whoever did this didn't want to hurt you, exactly. Vexillium just suppresses your powers."

Suppresses your powers.

A chill washes through my entire body. It hasn't all been in my head. Someone has purposefully been making me sick for weeks, probably watching from the shadows with some twisted satisfaction. But to what end? To keep me from getting into the Marionettes? With initiation ongoing, it's the only thing that makes sense. But there are so many other witches in the running. Who would want to stop *me* specifically from getting in?

"Now we need to figure out where it's coming from," mutters Monroe.

"There has to be a spell to do that, but I don't know how." Kirby winces. "I'll do some research and try to find something. In the meantime, here." Kirby holds out the container toward me. "This is what it smells like. If *anything* you eat smells like that, stay away from it."

I inhale deeply. The scent is so faint, it's nearly nonexistent. Just the smallest earthy tang. It could be anywhere, in anything, and the smell is so slight, I'd have no idea.

I look around my room at all of the possibilities, of all the places it could be coming from. I can't assume anything is safe.

My chest constricts and my breath gets stuck there, refusing to go down to my lungs. The walls feel like they're closing in. It could be in the air in here…somehow. I could be breathing it in with every breath.

I need to get out of here.

I can't stay here anymore. I need to get out of here *now*.

"Val—" Monroe starts.

"Thanks for the help, guys." I push myself to my feet and grab the duffel bag from under my bed.

"Where are you going?" Kirby asks.

"I need to get out of here for a bit," I manage, shoving my toothbrush and a change of clothes into my bag.

"Okay, let's not panic," says Kirby. "We can fix this. We'll find it."

"You can sleep in my room if you want," Monroe offers.

"Thanks, Roe. I appreciate that." I yank my hair up into a ponytail and pause with my hands fisted in my hair, my eyes closed. "I just need to…not be here for a bit, you know?"

Monroe squeezes my shoulder as Kirby sweeps everything back into her bag. "Val, we're going to find whoever did this."

"And then *I'm* going to kick their ass," adds Kirby.

I can tell by the looks on their faces that they have more to say, probably more questions to ask, but I just give them the most reassuring smile I can muster and squeeze each of their hands as I pass.

"I'm just going to get some air, okay? I'll see you guys in class?"

They nod, still looking at me like I'm a wounded animal. But if I stay in this room for another minute, I very well might explode. So I head out the door and down the hall, not really sure where I'm going, but anywhere must be better than here.

———

MY BODY DECIDES FOR ME, going on autopilot when I step out of the building. The train is full today, so I find one of the last seats available toward the back and spend the entire trip working through what I'll say when I get there. Yet as I step up and knock on his door, my mind goes blank.

Connor stands in the doorway, hair tousled and eyes bleary with sleep. He's shirtless and wearing a pair of gray sweatpants. I hate where my mind goes, but the first thing I do when he opens the door is search behind him for another vampire in his bed.

The room is empty.

"Val?" He glances at the hallway behind me, then at my own disheveled appearance. At least I'd slipped on some sneakers, but I'm still in my sweats with no bra and no makeup. "What's going on?"

I swallow the lump in my throat and wrap my arms around myself. "I'm sorry. I didn't know where else to go. Can I come in?"

"Of course." He steps back and opens the door wider to let me pass.

I hadn't been sure what I'd feel when I saw him again—anger? Hurt? But as he closes the door behind me and I turn to face him, I drop my bag and throw my arms around him. He crushes me against his chest, his face burying in the side of my neck. Then, mortifyingly, I start to cry. And I tell him everything—the poison, the dizziness, the way my healing hasn't been working. He pulls back to guide us over to the bed—me sitting on the edge, him kneeling in front of me. When I'm done, I wipe the back of my arm along my nose and pull in a deep breath.

Connor reaches up and brushes the remaining tears from my cheeks with his thumb.

"And I'm sorry I haven't been answering any of your calls." I sniffle.

"No, no, Val, you were right to be mad. I should've come to you about it sooner. I was just…" He looks down at his hands. "I was just embarrassed."

"Why did you do it?" I whisper.

A long beat of silence stretches between us, and he sighs as he leans back on his heels.

"I've gotta get out of here, Val," he whispers. "I thought if I could save up enough money, maybe I could get myself settled and start over somewhere else before you finished school, and then maybe we'd have a real chance, you know?"

I blink, my mind slowly processing his words. "You want to…leave the estate?"

He meets my eyes, and it's a look on his face I've never seen before. Not once in the twenty-one years I've known him. He just looks…done. "The protection from working here hasn't been all it's cracked up to be, has it?"

There's no mistaking the tinge of bitterness in his tone.

"Where would you go?"

"Maybe to the city—maybe farther. I don't know."

My stomach drops. "You want to leave the region altogether? But—"

He grips my hands tightly between us. "I'm starting to think a lot of the information they've been pushing around here might not be the whole story. At least not for humans. Of course they'd want us to stay in their regions—we're their *food*. Maybe it's not as bad outside of the boundaries as they make it out to be. Maybe there's something better, Val."

I stare at him, the thought of him venturing out of the boundaries making another tear fall down my cheek. They put up the borders for a reason—order, yes, but also to keep out the more dangerous species. Who knows what's out there anymore? And for a human? He'd be utterly defenseless.

At least if he stayed in the city, there are rules in place to protect the humans—as long as they follow the laws and keep up with their blood donations. Granted, they're not as enforced. When humans go missing, not many people ask questions.

I'll never be able to fully understand how it feels for him working here, but at least I've always known it would keep him safe.

But maybe that was selfish. Maybe that was just what I liked to believe.

"Connor," I whisper.

He clears his throat and shakes his head. "Anyway. One of the vampires approached me a few weeks ago. It was just to bite me. I don't know why—it's not like there's any shortage of blood around here. But he offered me fifty bucks, so I let him. Then I guess word got around, and suddenly, after you've said yes to so many of them, when you try to say no, they take it really personally... It wasn't even about the money anymore. I was just trying not to..."

I reach out and cup the side of his face, forcing him to look at me. I have no idea what to say, so I slide off the edge of the bed until I'm on my knees in front of him and wrap my arms around his neck instead. He pulls me tightly against him, his hand winding around my hair.

"I'm so sorry that I hurt you," he whispers. "That was never—I never wanted to—Valerie, I never wanted you to find out about any of it." He pulls back and holds me at arm's length as his eyes scan over me. He presses the back of his hand to my forehead, and I push him away.

"I'm fine."

The crease between his eyebrows doesn't let up, but he doesn't push it. "You don't know where the poison's been coming from?"

I shake my head.

"You think it was someone from school?"

"I honestly have no idea."

He presses his lips together for a moment. "And you're sure this isn't another one of those trials they have you do? Like a test?"

"If it is, it's only happening to me, as far as I know. And it started well before initiation."

He frames my face with his hands and pulls me closer

until our noses almost touch. "Don't go back. Stay here until it's out of your system, at least. I'm *worried*, Val."

"You know I can't do that."

His jaw tightens, but he sighs and says, "I know." A small, sad smile stretches across his face. "I've missed you so much."

I lean my forehead against his and close my eyes. "I've missed you too."

Gently, his lips press against mine, testing, searching. I open my mouth to him, sighing as the familiar feel of him washes over me, immediately making my muscles relax. His hands slide to my hips and pull me against him as I wind my hands through his hair.

"Stay," he murmurs against my mouth. "At least for tonight."

I nod, push his chest until he's on his back, and brace my hands on either side of his head.

He smiles up at me and pushes the hair back from my face. "I love you."

I lean down and cover his mouth with mine. "I love you."

One arm sweeps around my waist, the other coming up to protect my head as he flips us over and presses his weight down on top of me.

"Connor," I breathe as he hooks both of my legs up around his waist and trails his lips down my neck. I run my hands along his skin, digging my fingers into the muscles of his back as they tighten.

Our movements turn frantic as he lifts me up to yank my tank top over my head and I pull at the waist of his pants. Our clothes quickly collect into a pile, and then he's inside of me. I gasp out his name as he drives over and over, his arms braced on either side of my head, his head buried against my shoulder.

And for a few moments, I can forget about everything else that's going on and lose myself in the familiar feel of his skin, his breath on the side of my neck, his voice in my ear.

I flip us over again, bracing myself above him with my hands planted on his chest. His fingers dig into my thighs as I move against him. Then he grabs me by the back of my neck and pulls me down flat against his chest, holding me there as he drives up with his hips, hard enough that I let out a breathless moan in his ear.

"Fuck," he grunts as he comes undone, and it's over nearly as quickly as it started. I collapse against his chest, breathing heavily, and listen to his heart pound against his ribs. He brings a hand up to clutch the back of my head as his lips trail small kisses along my forehead.

"Sorry that was so—"

"It's okay." I lean up and kiss him on the cheek, not wanting to talk about it, especially not now. Every time we do, the conversation doesn't really get anywhere, and the experience doesn't change much.

And it's not that I don't enjoy it, in my own way. It's nice being close to him, and I know he feels bad about it. I don't know. Maybe other people would care more. Maybe I'm not that sexual of a person.

Maybe I gave up a few years ago and decided it wasn't that important.

I start to disentangle myself from him, but he tightens his arms around me.

"Can we just…stay here? For a little?"

I let out a breathless laugh but nestle back against him. "On the floor?"

"We've had worse."

A full laugh breaks out this time, and I tighten my arms around him, the exhaustion starting to crash back into me. With each sweep of his fingers up and down my spine, my eyelids grow heavier and heavier, until sleep finally takes me.

I WAKE to a stream of light coming from the window across from me. Covering my eyes with my hand, I roll over, the smell of Connor on the pillows nearly overwhelming.

"Sorry if I woke you."

I blink my eyes open and see him standing by the dresser as he buttons his white work shirt. I glance back toward the window.

"The sun hasn't even set yet," I mumble.

"I know." He leans over and presses a kiss to my forehead before disappearing back toward his closet. "I have the early shift."

I lift my arms over my head and do a full body stretch as he sits on the edge of the bed to tie his shoes. He tilts his head to the side, and I catch sight of the faded bruising along his collarbone, the skin now more yellow than purple. My mind drifts back to that conversation with Avery by the pool.

They're like sharks with blood in the water.

"Connor?"

He pushes the hair out of his eyes and glances at me over his shoulder. "Yeah?"

"You know you can talk to me, right? About anything."

He reaches over and squeezes my leg beneath the blankets. "I know I should've told you about all of this sooner. I just didn't want you to worry."

"Should I? Be worried?"

He rises from the bed, then leans down to brace a hand on each side of me and kisses my forehead again. "I can handle it."

I reach up and squeeze his wrists. "Connor—"

"I promise if there's something to be worried about, I'll come to you, okay?" He brushes the hair out of my eyes, and a small, rueful smile rises to his lips. "I have to get going. You gonna be okay here alone?"

I nod.

"Call me if you learn anything new." He hurries over to his dresser and quickly shoves his wallet, keys, and phone into his pockets.

I sit up and tuck the sheets around my chest. "Just don't...tell anyone, okay? About the Vexillium."

"Of course." He offers me one last wave, then silently slips into the hallway and closes the door behind him.

I fall back onto the bed and stare at the ceiling, my head surprisingly clear. Clearer than it's been in weeks. No dizziness. No cloudy vision. No exhaustion. I might even be able to swing a teleportation spell so I don't have to waste half the night on the train.

A sniff of yesterday's clothes informs me that they will not, in fact, be good enough for today, so I grab my bag and head down to my own room to change.

The entire floor is quiet as I slip into my room, it still being much earlier than most of the estate's occupants rise. I set my phone on my dresser, and a notification flashes on the screen—a text from Reginald.

Meet me at the estate at three. Don't be late.

I stare it for a moment. Considering I saw him two days ago, I wasn't expecting another task so soon. However, this is undeniably good news. 3:00 a.m. is a good eight hours away, giving me plenty of time to shower, relax—maybe go back to sleep. And the fewer times I have to ride that train until my powers are fully back, the better.

And maybe I'll be able to catch Connor again at the end of his shift. I know he wants to brush this under the rug and pretend like it's all okay, but I can't. If it's noticeable that *Avery* of all people seemed worried, then there must be a lot he isn't telling me.

I'm about to start the shower when someone knocks on the door. I'm halfway there when the person knocks again, louder this time.

"Valerie?" calls my mother. "I know you're in there!"

I throw my head back and let out a long, calming breath. I debate ignoring her, but I know she's not going to leave. My shoulders tense as I swing the door open. She stands in the hall in a floor-length black gown and equally dark lipstick, her fist raised and prepared to knock again.

"Oh." She smiles and drops her hand. "I thought I heard you over here." She struts past me and situates herself on the foot of my bed. Even though our quarters aren't attached like some families' are, we do share a wall, which is honestly just as bad. Somehow she manages to hear *everything*, like being around vampires all her life has somehow rubbed their heightened senses off on her.

There's a reason Connor and I have always hooked up at his place.

"What are doing home? How's initiation going?" she asks. "You must have had your first task by now."

I debate telling her about the poison, but a small voice in the back of my head stops me. It's ridiculous to think my mother of all people could be behind this—she's pushed me to join the Marionettes since I could cast my first spell.

She rises from the bed again and paces toward me, eyes narrowed as she studies my face. "What's wrong?"

"What? Nothing." I look away and busy myself with the skincare products on my desk. "It's going fine. You know I can't tell you anything."

"I can tell when you're lying. Are you still not healing? Is that it?"

When I glance back at her, the hard expression is gone from her face, replaced with what I'd think was concern, if I didn't know any better. She's always carried the title of *mother* as an inconvenience more than anything. She's the last person I would ever go to for a favor.

And yet.

Connor's been around since we were kids—practically part of the family. That must mean something to her, right? And if there's anyone in this estate with the power to make a difference with this, unfortunately, it's her.

"What is it?" she asks again.

"I'm worried about Connor," I admit.

She digs in her eyebrows. "Worried?"

I shrug and pace the length of the room, putting more

distance between us. "I've heard some things…the vampires seem to have taken a particular *interest* in him. I just—it's probably nothing to worry about and I'm just being paranoid, but would you look out for him?"

"Did something happen?"

"No—I—just—"

She flicks her wrist as if exasperated by the conversation. "I'll keep an eye on him."

I sigh, the smallest bit of tension easing from my shoulders. That's about as good as I'm going to get from her. "Thank you." I jab my finger over my shoulder toward the shower. "I really need to get ready though. I have another task with the prince today."

"Oh." She smiles, and something about it looks forced. "Well, I won't keep you then." She hesitates, but then without saying anything else, she slips from the room and closes the door behind her.

CHAPTER TEN

It's probably not my best idea, but I take one of the estate's cars into the city before meeting the prince. It's a minor detour, and I shouldn't have any trouble getting back in time. After giving the driver a street name I remember passing on the way back with Reginald last time, I sit quietly, the only sound coming from a pop song on the radio.

There's a club on the corner—I've never been there, but I've heard some girls from school mention it once or twice. This is where the driver drops me off, and I linger on the curb as I wait for his car to disappear back into traffic.

The lights and buzzing nightlife roar around me. It's momentarily disorienting. Though I've only been at the academy for three years, I've grown used to the quiet, small town. Comfortable, even. At first I'd thought I'd miss the bustle of the city, but there's something charming about York.

There's a line wrapped around the building beside me,

waiting to get into The Blood Lounge. Vampires and humans alike sway in high heels, laughing and edging toward the doors.

The girl closest to me has bite marks all over her throat, and a sheen over her eyes that doesn't look like it's from alcohol. She blinks a few times, then forces a smile as someone behind her says something. She looks a little like Madison, to be honest. I've always wondered why the humans who frequent these kinds of places do what they do, but maybe there's a side of it that I don't understand.

A broad-shouldered vampire leers behind her as he braces his hands on her waist. She tenses under his touch, but then he leans down to murmur something in her ear, and her body relaxes.

I clench my jaw—I know a glamour when I see one— but then the bouncer ushers them on, and the two disappear into the club.

A group of humans rounds the corner, whispering to each other. They shoot shy glances at the remaining vampires in line and bow their heads to them as they pass.

I squint past them toward the club's entrance with half a mind to follow that girl, but they wouldn't let me in there if I tried, not looking like this. Especially not with this bulging purse on my shoulder. It digs into my skin beneath the weight of the food—not as much as last time, but hopefully better than nothing.

I sigh. If I don't get moving, I won't make it back in time to meet the prince.

It's a decent walk to the residential areas, but the fresh air feels nice. The streets all look the same back here, but my feet carry me confidently forward. I'm not sure if it's a magic thing or a me thing, but I've always had a way with directions. At least, if I've been somewhere once, I can always find my way back.

The streetlights blink as I pass, but the nervous fear I'd felt the first night I was here is noticeably absent. Maybe it's finally knowing *why* my magic has been faulty lately, or maybe it's being away from my room and the poison long enough that it's filtering out of my system. If it came down to it and I really needed it, I don't think my magic would fail me tonight.

The street is as dark as last time, the front windows of the house still boarded up. But when I knock on the door, it swings open, revealing the dark entryway.

"Hello?" I call.

No one answers, and I tentatively reach a hand inside to find the switch on the wall. The lights flicker on and reveal…nothing.

A fine layer of dust coats the wooden floor, broken up only by the marks where furniture used to sit. But it's all gone now. The house is utterly empty. I pace into the kitchen to be sure, opening cabinets and closet doors. Everything is gone.

I drop my arm, letting my purse slump against the floor. A can of soup springs free and rolls across the hardwood.

Where could they have gone?

And the question I don't want to think:

Had it been willingly?

I check the door to the basement before I leave, flicking on the light and peering down the stairs. But it, too, has been cleared out.

I leave the food on the kitchen counter—maybe

someone who needs it will come by to scavenge the house—
then slowly start my walk back.

I wonder if Madison knows her family is gone.

The thought makes me flinch. Because maybe she's
gone now too.

———

A FEW HOURS LATER, Prince Reginald picks me up at the
front of the estate in the same black car as before. Streetlights fly past as we make our way toward the city. I scowl
out the window, still thinking about that vampire glam-
ouring a human outside the club, when I notice the prince
is aggressively drumming his fingers against his knee. If I
didn't know any better, I'd think it was a nervous tick.
When I glance up at the side of his face, the line of his jaw
is hard.

Despite the silence in the car—his driver doesn't even
turn on the radio—I pick up on the somber mood; at first
I'd thought it was coming from me, but no, it's clear something else is going on. The tension is so thick in the air I feel
like I'm choking on it.

Does he somehow know about Madison's family?

Would he tell me the truth if I asked?

"Where are we going?" I ask instead.

"We're almost there," he says without looking at me.

The driver passes the busy heart of the city and keeps
going, the surrounding buildings becoming progressively
more run-down the farther we drive, the streets and sidewalks less occupied. We end up at an abandoned parking

garage behind an old factory. I frown at it through the window, trying to figure out why he would bring me here.

Reginald and the driver exchange a look I don't understand as the prince climbs out and heads straight for the garage. I hurry after him, the night coaxing out goosebumps along my arms.

He pauses in the center of the ground level, head cocked to the side like he's waiting for something. Or...*listening* for something.

Of course, my stomach chooses that moment to let out a long, loud growl. I haven't eaten anything in nearly a day, too paranoid of what might be in it.

Reginald slowly turns to look at me.

I wince and mouth, *Sorry*.

The overhead lights buzz and flicker, half of them already burnt out.

Reginald turns abruptly and heads up the ramp toward the second level. I have to jog again to keep up with his long strides. Something about the stiffness in his shoulders keeps me quiet. He sniffs the air and veers toward the back left corner. I inhale deeply through my nose, but whatever his senses are picking up is too faint for me.

A cold sense of unease washes over my skin as we venture farther away from the pockets of light. We're about halfway across the level when I finally smell it. My steps slow as I slap a hand across my mouth, trying not to gag. Reginald continues on, his steps even faster than before. I force myself to follow, the rotting smell getting stronger with each step. The cold unease turns to ice against my skin as I realize why he's brought me here.

I catch up to him as he reaches the bodies—three of

them, by the looks of it, but it's difficult to tell. Arms, legs, and heads are strewn about, though the majority of the body parts are piled together in the corner. The concrete around them is nearly black with dried blood.

"Rich pricks," mutters the prince.

My head snaps toward him, thinking he's talking about the dead humans, but his gaze is focused somewhere through the open window, toward the city.

"They've taught you how to clean up these messes, I'm assuming," he says.

I nod even though he's not looking at me.

"Are you…feeling up to it?" He turns, but the shadows over his face mask his expression.

We haven't talked since the blood exchange in the woods—we didn't even complete it by having me take his blood. I'd been too consumed by the confirmation that there was, in fact, something happening to me, and it wasn't all in my head.

"I'm fine," I say, and for the first time in a while, I think I actually mean it. The weakness in my body is from needing food, not a poison eating away at my powers.

I'm no stranger to blood or death, and yet, the pile of bodies makes me wince. I want to ask—there are *so* many things I want to ask—but before we'd ever learned any spells, the first thing the academy taught us was to not ask questions. Stay out of vampire business as much as possible.

Stupid rules, if you ask me.

"But if you want my help with this, I'm going to need something in return."

Reginald's eyebrows shoot up, a hint of amusement

bleeding into his expression. "Is that so? What makes you think you're in a position to make demands?"

I cross my arms and lift my chin.

He lets out a low laugh and shakes his head. "What is it you want?"

"What happened to Madison?" I ask.

He watches me, a shadow of curiosity passing over his face. "The human? I let her go."

I narrow my eyes, not sure if I believe him. "I went back to check on her family," I say, gauging his reaction. "They were all gone."

His brow furrows. "Gone?"

"The whole house was cleared out."

"Interesting," he murmurs. His eyes flit back to mine, expression still thoughtful. "Any more questions?"

I glance at the pile of bodies and swallow hard. "Why won't you tell me anything about James Westcott?"

I half expect him to ignore me, but the thoughtful expression doesn't leave his face. His eyes sweep me up and down. "Why are you so interested?"

"You can't just drag me into the middle of your business and then expect me not to ask questions."

A single corner of his mouth lifts. "You do realize that's *exactly* what you're supposed to do in the Marionettes, right?"

"And you don't see a problem with that?"

"I see plenty of problems with it." He turns away toward the city again. "The truth is, I've kept my investigations on James Westcott to myself because I don't know if there's anything to find. He may very well be dead like everyone else believes."

"Wait, he's *dead*?"

He shrugs. "Possibly."

"If you've been keeping this to yourself, then why bring me down there and involve me in the first place? Surely there were other tasks we could've done."

"That"—he turns back around and nods toward the pile—"is a very good question. Now, I think I've given you enough answers for one night. Unless you're stalling for another reason."

I stare at him, but it's clear I've already gotten all he's willing to give tonight. And I have a feeling if I push too much, he won't give me any more again.

"I'm not stalling," I mutter. I breathe through my mouth as I take a few steps closer and flip the blade out of my ring. If I'd known what we were doing today, I would've brought something bigger.

Dead. James Westcott is…dead? But then why had that human reacted so badly in the library? Why would Reginald be looking into him in the first place?

I can feel his eyes on me, but I force myself to focus on the task at hand. I start with a cut along my right wrist, then make an identical one on my left. The blood splashes near my feet, the wounds already healing. Damn. They'll need to be deeper. I glance down at the blood on the concrete and freeze, my heart sinking in my chest.

"What is it?" Reginald says behind me.

I squat and slowly run my fingers over the piece of metal beside my shoe, wiping the blood away. The necklace is small, just a chain and a circle of silver. Engraved is an image of antlers backlit by the moon—the skinwalker symbol. I jerk my hand away as if burned.

Reginald appears at my side, trying to see what I saw.

"They're witches," I say quietly.

I glance over the body parts again, looking for any indicators that they were in the Marionettes, but their clothes look tattered, worn. No trace of the thin red line that gets tattooed on your bicep after your initiation. There's nothing.

They might as well be human.

He takes in a slow breath beside me but offers no words of comfort. No promises of justice. He just steps back and gives me space.

After a moment, I make a second cut, higher on my arm this time, and slowly walk around the remains, letting my blood create a circle around them. Once the circle is complete, I press my hands against the cuts, covering my palms, and hold them both to my chest, muttering the incantations under my breath.

Reginald lets out a soft sound beside me, so I know it's started. When I drop my hands to my sides and open my eyes, a wave of dizziness rolls over me, but I grit my teeth against it.

The bodies in front of me quickly cycle through decomposition, time wearing down on them in a matter of seconds. The blood on the ground glows as they become nothing but bones, and then nothing but dust.

A hand presses to my back, and I realize I'm swaying on my feet, my vision marred by tiny splotches of black.

The regret over what I've done is immediate. I didn't know them, but if my life had gone differently, if I hadn't been in the running for the Marionettes, that could've been me. The simple lack of a title making me less important, forgettable.

Disposable.

No justice, no investigation. Just another witch covering it up.

As Reginald leads me back down, I murmur, "They're going to get away with it, aren't they? Whoever did that."

He doesn't respond as we climb into the car.

They're going to get away with breaking the law, and I'm the one who covered it up.

The prince reaches over and squeezes my knee, the lines of his face hard. And I see in his eyes that he doesn't like this any more than I do. Whatever vampire did this must be important—most likely royal.

"Where to?" asks the driver.

"Back to the estate," says Reginald. "You can drop us off at the kitchens." He glances at me sideways, and as if on cue, my stomach growls again.

THE KITCHEN IS empty when we slip inside, and I prop myself on the edge of the counter and swing my legs over the edge as Reginald rummages around in the cabinets. I wonder if Connor is done with his shift yet, or if they'll have him cleaning dishes in here all night again. My eyelids strain to keep open as my body continues to burn off the spell—the biggest one I've done in weeks.

"Here." Reginald pushes a banana into my hand, then pulls out a pan from the cabinet beside me.

"You don't have to cook for me," I mumble, half of the banana already inhaled.

"You think the poison is coming from your food?" he asks as he rolls up his sleeves, sets the pan on the stove, and digs around in the fridge for some eggs. It strikes me as odd that he knows how to cook at all. Vampires can eat regular food, but they don't need it. And they certainly don't have to make it themselves if they grew up in an estate.

"I don't know," I admit.

He quirks an eyebrow at me over his shoulder. "So your plan was to just…what? Never eat again? Brilliant."

I scowl, but my mouth is already watering at the smell of the eggs as they sizzle in the pan. "What would you rather have me do? At least I figured out what kind of poison it is. I just don't know *where* it is."

He shakes the pan and flips the eggs like he's done this a million times before, then sprinkles in some salt and pepper. "What kind is it?"

"Vexillium."

He frowns, dumps the eggs on a plate, and slides it toward me. "Odd choice."

We fall into silence as I quickly devour the food and barely hold back from licking the plate clean. When I glance up, he's already back at the cabinets, pulling out a loaf of bread, this time to make toast. That, too, I demolish immediately. I swallow it in three bites, barely tasting it.

"Why are you helping me?"

He shrugs, takes the empty plate from me, and sets it in the sink. "You're my partner. Isn't that the point of all this?"

"I don't think it works that way. I'm supposed to be the one helping you."

He leans against the counter across from me, arms crossed over his chest. "I don't see why it can't work both ways."

I narrow my eyes, trying to figure out why he's being forthcoming all of a sudden. Either way, it would be a missed opportunity if I didn't take advantage of it. "Do you know who killed those witches?"

He sighs and pinches the bridge of his nose. "We have some…*visitors* from the royal family at the Russian estate. They've never been known for their discretion. My mother is negotiating new peace treaty terms with them—it's thin ice."

I look down at my hands in my lap, digging through my memory from royal history classes. The Russians were the group most recently added to the peace treaty, and the alliance that's the most unstable.

"Doesn't look like they're that interested in *peace*," I mumble.

He gives me a small, rueful smile. For a moment, it's all I can do to stare back at him. I guess I'd never given much thought before to what he'd be like, especially with how long he's been gone. But I never would've guessed he'd be like…*this*.

Whenever I've seen the other royals at the estate— usually in a formal setting in the throne room—they've been perfectly polished and composed, their faces practically made of glass with how little emotion they show. I suppose he is like that, sometimes. When the walls are up and he's avoiding my questions. But right now, as he's looking at me with his expression open and tiredness weighing on his eyes, I can forget that he's a prince.

He just looks like a person.

I cough and drop my gaze, my face suddenly feeling hot.

"My driver can get you home before dawn if you go now," he says.

I nod and hop down from the counter, too exhausted to argue.

"Before you go." He rolls his sleeve a little more and gestures to his forearm. I'd almost forgotten about the blood exchange we never completed. "You can make the cut, if you'd rather. Just to play it safe."

I meet his eyes again as I take his arm, the muscle taut beneath my fingers.

"You'll have to press harder," he murmurs as I pull out my blade.

I put more pressure into the cut than I usually would on myself, but it still doesn't break skin. I grit my teeth and try again, and his hand clenches into a fist as I finally manage to draw blood. I don't look at him as I lean down and run my tongue along the cut.

The moment I swallow, my body contracts. An utter sense of *wrongness* consumes me, and my chest squeezes so violently I can't breathe. I grasp at my throat and meet his eyes.

His mouth moves, but I don't hear the words. The room spins around me, and then I'm falling. Blood roars in my ears, muffling every other sound. The floor is cold against my back, but I barely feel the impact.

Reginald leans over me, eyes wide.

Everything in my body tightens, squeezes, thrashes against itself.

A door bangs open, and a voice rises above the buzzing in my ears.

"What did you do to her?"

Connor. It sounds like Connor.

Reginald yells something back to him, but I can't make out the words. Someone holds my head while another pair of hands presses down against my arms. I gasp, desperately trying to pull oxygen into my lungs.

"Just help me get her up."

The entire room dips and spins, and I squeeze my eyes shut as two pairs of hands heft me up, and then we're moving. Everything blurs by so quickly, I can't make sense of any of my surroundings.

"You can't tell anyone about this," says the prince.

"Why?" asks Connor, his voice hard. "Because whatever you did to her is illegal? She's going to be a Marionette— you're not supposed to touch her—"

"*Because*, if you tell anyone, you're going to get her killed."

I try to raise my head, but a violent wave of black crashes into my vision, and everything else around me disappears.

CHAPTER ELEVEN

When I wake up, my head is on fire. The barest streak of light slants in from a window, and squinting sends a piercing knife of pain straight into my brain. My hands skim along the bed—twice as large as mine is, and I can *feel* how expensive the silk sheets are. Thick, red curtains with golden stitching hang from the bed's four posts.

I groan and squeeze my eyes shut again. Pricking one of my fingers, I smear the blood across my forehead, and the pressure instantly eases. I let out a low, shuddering breath, slowly sit up, and look around. The room has towering vaulted ceilings and more square footage than I've ever seen in a single bedroom before. There's a fireplace on the far wall, surrounded by a chaise longue and oversize chairs. But there's nothing personal about the expensive furniture and meticulously cleaned surfaces. The room could belong to anyone.

Anyone rich, that is.

I roll myself out of the bed, and deliciously soft carpet

meets my bare feet. I sway as I tiptoe to a wardrobe door, but when I peel it open, it reveals a metal ladder that disappears down into darkness. My breath catches in my throat, and I slowly close the door and take a step back.

I'm in a vampire's room.

But if the sun's out, and they're not here…they must be asleep somewhere else.

I desperately search my memory, but the entire last twenty-four hours are missing. I must have come back to the estate, but when? And why? I'd had class with Kirby, and then…

The door cracks open, and I whip around, a scream lodging in my throat.

"Master Reginald, I—" A maid pokes her head in, and a soft blush rises to her cheeks at the sight of me. She quickly presses her lips together, bows her head, mutters something about coming back later, then slips into the hallway.

It's not until she's gone that her words register.

I'm in the *prince's* room?

I look down at myself—the leggings and T-shirt are mine, thankfully. But if *that* isn't what's happening, then why am I here? Why isn't *he* here? All of the vampire rooms have the underground sections, just in case, but their windows can be UV-blocking if they want them to be.

My throat aches, and I run a hand along my throat. God, I'm so *thirsty.* I grab the glass of water from the nightstand and swallow the entire thing, but it doesn't help much. My hand shakes as I set the glass back, and I search the ground, but none of my other belongings are here.

I poke my head out in the hallway, making sure the

coast is clear before slipping out and heading down to my floor. I'm not sure why I'm bothering—I've already been seen by one person. With how fast rumors travel around here, the rest of the estate probably already knows and is speculating all about my relationship with the prince.

My vision focuses and unfocuses on the hall around me, and I sway so violently I have to keep a hand braced on the wall to walk in a straight line. The headache is already creeping back in, but it's nothing compared to the burning in my throat. I've never really been able to get sick before with how fast my body heals itself, but *fuck*, this doesn't feel normal.

The first thing I do when I make it back to my room is fill another glass of water in the sink, swallowing it in a single gulp. It's nearly sunset—if I want to make it back to the academy before classes tonight, I'll have to hurry.

Bag in hand and yesterday's clothes still on my back, I jog down toward the train station, my head pounding with each step. I just need to get on the train, then I can sleep the rest of the way there, and hopefully sleep off whatever is going on with my body right now.

The train lets out a whistle as I climb on board and find a seat toward the back.

THE TRAIN MAKES it back to campus a few hours after dark, and despite not sleeping the entire ride here, I've never felt more awake. I'm the only one to get off at my stop, and I collapse onto one of the benches on the platform—my throat *throbbing* now—before starting the trek up toward campus.

The snow from the other day is mostly melted, leaving behind a disastrous mess of mud along the paths. It's not nearly as dimly lit back here as I remember it being— maybe maintenance finally listened to the complaints and added some more light fixtures. But as I crane my neck back and glance around, all I see are the usual trees and the moon's silhouette behind the clouds.

My phone goes off in my bag, and the ring pieces my ears like little knives, bringing the headache back full force. I rip open the zipper and yank it out. *Connor.*

"What do you want?" I snap.

"Val? Val? Where are you?"

"What do you mean, where am I? I'm at school."

"Val, I'm so sorry—I had to leave for a second for work, I thought you wouldn't wake up yet—"

"What are you talking about?"

He continues on as if I hadn't spoken. "Just stay where you are, okay? Are you in your dorm? We'll come get you."

"*We?*"

The breeze rustles my hair, bringing with it the smell of something so delicious my mouth starts to water. I freeze in my tracks. My stomach growls at the reminder of my neglect these past few days. The trees on my side sway in the breeze, and a flash of movement catches my eye. I squint but only manage to see a shadow before it disappears. A hint of unease creeps up my spine.

"Valerie?"

"I've gotta go," I mutter, then shove the phone back into my pocket.

My legs don't burn as much as they used to as I hike up the steep path—maybe those physical conditioning days are starting to make a difference. I'm halfway back to campus —the tips of the towers swimming into view in the distance —when the scent hits me again, stronger this time. I'm veering off the path and into the trees before I realize it, my feet moving of their own accord, barely making any noise as I creep through the underbrush.

There's a girl a few yards away surrounded by a circle of lit candles. She hasn't noticed me yet, her back facing me. I creep forward, sniffing the air as another gust of wind confirms this is where the smell is coming from. The rest of the forest blurs around us, my vision focusing on the girl as she tilts her head, her hair falling away and revealing the pale skin of her neck.

Heat flashes across my gums, and then I'm on top of her. A shriek fills the air, but the sound is muffled. All I can hear is the girl's pounding heart. I wrench her head to the side and bury my face in her neck. The moment her blood hits the back of my throat, the agonizing ache starts to ease. I moan and dig my teeth deeper into her neck, desperate for more. The girl's screams turn to sobs, then trickle off into little more than a choking sound.

I pull my head back to lick the blood from my lips and inhale a deep breath.

"*Darkmore.*" A hand grabs the back of my shirt and rips me away from the body. I hit the ground on my back and skid away several feet, a growl ripping through me. I flip over onto my hands and knees, ready to pounce again, but the same hand grabs me by the throat and slams me back to the ground.

"Look at me," a deep voice growls.

I bare my teeth, and he tightens his hold on my throat.

Finally, I blink, and my vision slowly returns to normal. Reginald's face hovers above me, his mouth set in a hard line. "Look at me," he repeats.

I gasp, and he loosens his hold.

Whatever he sees in my expression must be satisfactory, because he releases me and turns away. I push myself into a seated position as he walks over to the girl's splayed form on the ground.

"Oh, God," I whisper.

Her blood is splattered everywhere—on the trees, the ground. When I look down at myself, I realize I'm covered in it.

She's not moving.

Reginald crouches over her, lifting her head into his lap. He bites his own wrist, then lets the blood drip into her mouth. After a few moments, she stirs, then starts screaming again. Reginald grabs her by the chin, forcing her to look at him. She relaxes more with each word he says, and when he's done, he helps her back to her feet.

It's Beth, I realize, and my stomach drops so violently I feel like I'm going to throw up. How had I not recognized her before?

"Oh hi, Valerie!" She waves at me, smiling.

I stand there, stunned, and slowly wave back.

"Well, see you in physical conditioning tomorrow!" She gathers her bag off the ground, abandoning her candles, which are now mostly snuffed out and turned over in the dirt, and heads back toward the academy.

Reginald slowly turns to face me, his suit covered in dirt, a line of blood dripping from the corner of his mouth.

I blink rapidly, my heartbeat thrashing in my ears. "I don't—I didn't—"

He sighs, pulls a handkerchief out of his suit pocket, and wipes his mouth. "I know."

CHAPTER TWELVE

I DON'T KNOW if I've ever seen anything stranger than a disheveled Prince Reginald standing in the doorway of my shabby dorm room. He steps in first, and his head immediately cocks to the side. I squeeze in after him, and a flood of different scents I've never noticed before hits me all at once —the sweat from my laundry hamper, the apple on the desk, not quite rotting, but definitely no longer in its prime, and—

I beeline for my desk, searching for the origin of the smell. I bend down, sniffing everything within reach, then freeze at my favorite bottle of perfume. Slowly, I bring it to my nose.

It's faint, even with my senses working in overdrive, but beneath the usual floral and musky scent, there's a distinct hint of something else. Something that doesn't belong.

Something…earthy.

The prince steps up beside me and gently takes the glass

bottle. He turns it over in his hand. "Where did you get this?"

I swallow hard and sink onto the edge of my bed, feeling faint. "I—my mother gave it to me."

Reginald meets my eyes, and we stare at each other for a second. The sounds around me muffle until all I can hear is my pulse in my ears.

"Anyone could have slipped it in there after she gave it to you," he reminds me, then shoves the bottle in his pocket.

I nod, willing myself to believe it. Because if my mother really is the person behind this…it's too much to comprehend. I try to think back to when I first started feeling sick—it wasn't until several weeks into the semester, and my mother gave me that perfume at the start. So it couldn't have been her. It couldn't.

But what if it just took a while for the poison to start affecting me, like it was building up in my system?

"What is happening to me?" I whisper.

He scrubs his face with one hand, then takes a seat beside me on the bed.

I look down at my hands and realize some of Beth's blood is under my fingernails. The entire past few hours are a blur. I barely remember getting on the train, let alone walking back here. Nothing until after Reginald found me.

"I think my blood…woke something up in you. Something that's always been there, but dormant. Feeding someone vampire blood is the last stage of the turning process, and with the magic in your blood, maybe it didn't need the turning incantation. And the way you reacted looked exactly like—"

"You're telling me I'm a vampire now?"

He hesitates, and then, quietly: "Half, I believe."

I stand up and pace across the room, but he continues.

"I'm willing to bet, given your magic tying to your blood, that dormant part of you may have contributed to you being so much more powerful than your peers."

I shake my head and cover my face with my hands. "Beth…"

"I took care of it. She won't remember any of this—no harm done."

I gape at him. "No harm *done*?"

"When turned vampires first transition, they're almost always savage and running on pure instinct until they've had their first feed. It's completely natural."

"Natural?" My voice cracks.

"Which is *why*," he continues, "I *tried* to keep you in my room to help you transition, but then you ran off—"

"So this is *my* fault?" I demand.

"I'm trying to help."

The quietness of his voice freezes my next words in my throat. I cross my arms over my chest and turn to look out the window at the starless sky, my mind trying to process the possibility of what he's saying. "But I didn't… die. Wouldn't that have had to happen first for me to turn?"

"Usually, yes, for turned vampires. In this case, if it was already in your DNA…I don't know."

I try to work through what this will mean for me, to *conceptualize* the idea of this in the first place, but it's like my brain is rejecting the very idea of it, refusing to even consider it. I…can't be.

I shake my head, and my voice comes out little more than a whisper. "What am I supposed to do now?"

"Go about your usual routine. Don't speak of this to anyone else yet—"

"I can't exactly keep this a secret."

"That's exactly what you're going to do. Valerie. I don't think you understand how dangerous—" He sighs and roughly runs a hand through his hair. "Are you familiar with the legends about half-vampires, half-witches?"

Slowly, I shake my head.

"How much do you know about the necromancers?" he asks.

A jolt goes through my body at the word, the same way it always does. I open and close my mouth a few times, momentarily thrown by the change in subject. "Necromancers used to be the sixth classification of witches," I say like I'm reciting from a dictionary. "But what does that have to do with anything?"

He meets my gaze, and the intensity there pins me to the spot. "Did you find anything *strange* about what you learned about them?"

I press my lips together and hold his gaze. The necromancers were wiped out by a mutated strand of a disease— a plague perfectly targeted to take them, and only them, out nearly a century ago. The textbooks call it coincidence, chance. An unfortunate, but inevitable, extinction.

Despite being something that would appear to be a major part of our history, it's rarely discussed in school. It didn't even take a full class period to cover it.

When I don't respond, he adds, "Do you really think a bunch of vampires weren't threatened by witches who could control the dead? You think they didn't know that all it would take was a few necromancers to band together and want to take them down, and they'd be able to do it without breaking a sweat? They probably wouldn't even need to lift a finger if they could get the vampires to start killing each other."

I slowly sink onto the edge of my bed. When I manage to speak again, my voice comes out hollow. "What does that have to do with me?"

"There are legends about this. Stories. Very few have been documented. But the combination of a blood witch and a vampire is said to manifest the same kind of abilities —not as potent as the original necromancers—but an *evolution*, if you will." He searches my face, a small frown crossing his own. "You don't seem…surprised by this."

Slowly, I shake my head. The bird from the clearing takes flight in my mind's eye, dead one minute, airborne the next. That hadn't been the first, of course. I think the first time had been a rabbit at the estate. I'd been nine, maybe ten?

It wasn't until my mother caught me doing it that I realized it wasn't normal. I'd just thought all blood witches could do it. At the time, I'd thought her anger had been about me using magic before my powers were fully formed, something that could be dangerous if not monitored.

It quickly became clear that was not the case.

"Valerie."

"It's nothing new," I say, steeling myself and raising my eyes to meet his. "I've always—" I shake my head again. "It's nothing new."

He doesn't blink for what feels like a long time. Despite

the tension blotting out the air in the room, my chest feels lighter. A weight I've been carrying for more than ten years, a secret I've been forced to keep, is suddenly just…out there.

"I suppose you don't need me to tell you that no one can find out about this."

I look down at my feet. "Why wouldn't you just turn me in?"

He kneels in front of me and tilts my chin up with his knuckle, forcing me to look at him. There's a deep furrow between his eyebrows. "Why would I do that? I don't care about your magic, and whether it was intentional or not, my blood was what turned you. That makes you my responsibility. And I don't take that lightly."

I swallow hard. "Have you ever turned anyone before?"

"No." A smirk pulls at the corner of his mouth. "Too much responsibility."

I let out a small, pathetic laugh. "More than you bargained for when you got paired with me, huh?"

His smile grows. "At least you keep things interesting, Darkmore."

For a moment, I'm caught in his gaze, in the briefest flash when that usual wall behind his eyes is absent.

I'm the first to look away, back toward the perfume in his pocket.

He follows my gaze. "We'll find whoever did this. Do you have any suspicions?"

I try to think through all of the research I've done since my magic started to lag, and an idea scratches at the back of my mind. "Can I…see it for a second?"

His brow furrows, but he hands it over.

I set it on the bed beside me, then dig through my desk until I find the book I'm looking for. Reginald watches silently as I flip through the pages and dig my teeth in my lip. This book is mostly in Latin, and it takes a bit before my mind switches over. If the spell I think I saw is in here, there was a diagram in the center...

"Can you hand me three candles?" I say without looking up.

He grabs some white ones from my desk and adds them beside the perfume on the bed.

"Here!" I open the book wider and grin.

"What is it?" he asks.

"If I'm translating it right, it should be a tracing spell."

I crouch on the floor beside the bed, setting the book in front of me and making a small arc with the candles. I prick my finger to light them, then smear a line of blood between my eyebrows and a second line across the top of the bottle.

Reginald backs up and leans against the opposite wall, arms crossed over his chest as he watches me. The flames grow as I wrap my hands around the bottle, the glass cool against my palms. Closing my eyes, I familiarize myself with the feel of the bottle, the carved lines along its sloping sides, the scent of the candles—like fresh flowers and tobacco. My blood burns, warmer than it ever used to when I did spells, like the magic is bubbling to the surface, ready, eager. I squint a single eye open to read the incantations scrawled at the bottom of the page.

"*Vestigium, indago, pervestigo,*" I whisper. "*Vestigium, indago, pervestigo.*"

The flames surge up in front of me, warming my legs with their heat. Images stain the backs of my eyelids, playing out like a movie in rewind. I watch my hand pick up the bottle time and time again, going backward in time, every time I touched it. As I ran out last minute before class, a second coating before going out with Kirby and Monroe, lifting it as I searched for a hair tie on the desk...

The bottle warms in my hands along with my blood, and the magic rushes through me like a wave, carrying me forward, carrying me—

—directly into a wall.

I physically jerk back, nearly dropping the bottle. The candles extinguish, and my eyes fly open.

"What happened?" Reginald is kneeling in front of me now, a crease in his forehead.

"I—" I look down at the bottle in my hands. The glass still feels warm. "There's some kind of...block. I feel like I ran into a wall."

"That's what the inside of Madison's mind felt like," he murmurs.

"Do you think they're related?"

"I don't know." He frowns and rises back to his feet. "I can take it and see what I can find out, if you want."

I perch myself back on the bed and hand the bottle to him.

He opens his mouth to say something else, but pauses when his gaze lands on something in the corner. The tension in his shoulders eases, and I shift on the bed to see what he's looking at. "You play the violin," he says softly.

My case is still propped up against the wall beside my desk. I took it out a few months ago but never brought myself to open it. It's been sitting there staring at me accus- ingly ever since.

"I—" I stand, suddenly wanting to grab it and shove it back under my bed. "No, not really."

His gaze travels from the case to me, one eyebrow raised.

"My dad gave it to me before he left," I explain. "My mom thought lessons were pointless. I tried to teach myself, but I've never been any good. I don't have much time for it anymore anyway." I have no idea why I say it, and the moment the words are out, I wish I could snatch them back. My face burns under his stare, but something in his eyes softens.

My stomach sinks when I realize he probably knows all about the scandal with my dad. My mother somehow managed to snuff out the rumors to keep them from leaving the estate's walls, but that didn't stop the wildfire on the inside.

I don't remember him. Not really. The face I picture sometimes is probably not even his. He was gone shortly after Adrienne was born—but not before sleeping around with the other Marionettes. Three of them...that we know of.

The only reason I brought the stupid instrument to school was I knew if I left it behind, Mom would probably burn it. Looking at it makes her think of him. And for some reason, even if I never manage to play it again...I can't stand the thought of her having it. And not for some dramatic *it's the only piece I have left of him* reason—even though it is all that I have of him—but it also feels like one of the few pieces of me she hasn't touched.

"That's a shame," he says. "Maybe you'll find the time again someday."

"Maybe," I agree quietly.

We stare at each other for another second, before he finally blinks and nods toward the door. "The academy has visitor accommodations for the day—I'll stay here, and we can talk about this more tomorrow night." He looks me over, his eyes searching my face. "You're not going to kill anyone if I leave, are you? Do you need more blood before I go?"

I shake my head, the burning in my throat just a dull ache now. Whatever I'd managed to get from Beth seems to be enough.

"Okay." He hesitates in the doorframe and looks me up and down one more time, but then he turns and disappears down the hall without another word.

———

MY DAY STARTS bright and early on Friday, a few hours before sundown. I send an apology text to Connor first thing, then stare at my screen for a few minutes, waiting for a response that doesn't come. Maybe he's still asleep. I vaguely remember hanging up on him the night before. The memory is blurry and disjointed, like I'm remembering a movie I saw years ago instead of something that happened last night.

I send him a second text to let him know I'm okay and Reginald found me—apparently he'd had one of the witches at the estate transport him here as soon as the sun went down. It hadn't occurred to me last night to wonder how he'd gotten here so fast. I'm just grateful he found me when he did.

I don't let myself think about what would have happened with Beth if he hadn't.

My mind swims, trying to process everything that happened in the last twenty-four hours, but I shove it aside. I can't afford to think about any of it right now. The written tests start today, the last step for this wave of initiation trials. The combined scores from these tests and the practical trials with our vampire pairs will determine who remains in the running. And if I want any hope of continuing on, they need my full attention.

The tests are held in the dining hall instead of the usual classrooms so everyone can take them together. Coderre stands at the front of the room when I enter, backlit by the stained glass windows behind her. Half of the seats are already filled, so I slide into one of the wooden desks near the back.

My head pounds, the waning sunlight piercing my eyes like needles. My skin had prickled the entire walk over here —not hurting, exactly, but clearly reacting to the sunlight differently than it had before. Yet another thing to worry about. I was fine before I went to sleep, but when I woke up, my throat was on fire again.

I swallow against it, forcing the urges down, but already, I can hear the thudding pulses of everyone around me, elevated and frantic with the stress over these tests. The faster their hearts beat, the more my throat burns, like their anxiety is egging the hunger on.

I squeeze my eyes shut as the wooden doors open behind me. More footsteps sound down the aisle as other students trickle in and find their seats.

"Val," someone hisses.

Monroe slides into the desk in front of me. She stares at me with her eyebrows pulled together. "Where have you been?"

"Please settle down everyone, and no talking. We're about to begin," calls Coderre from the front. Her high heels click against the concrete floor as she begins to distribute the tests.

Monroe frowns, her gaze lingering on me for another beat before she turns around in her chair.

Coderre slides a paper on my desk, and I spin my pencil around my fingers, trying to force my vision to focus. The first exam is on intuitive magic—things that don't require specific incantations or spells. It's one of my favorite subjects, so it should be a breeze.

But as pencils start scratching on papers all around me, a second sound builds in the background. A steady thrum of heartbeats buzzes in my ears. I pinch myself under my desk, forcing myself to fill out the first question, but then the sound of pulsing blood rises to the forefront of my attention again. I squeeze my eyes shut. Heat courses through me, accumulating under my gums.

Logically, my brain knows I need to do well on this test.

With each passing second, the importance of that seems less and less.

The pulse of the girl next to me is racing as she flips through all of the pages of the test, clearly starting to panic. Maybe if I can just make it to one of the breaks between tests, I can follow someone out when they head to the bathroom—

I clench my teeth, and pain flares up my jaw. For a moment, it's enough to center me. I scream the questions in my head as I read them to myself and press the pencil on the page a little harder than necessary, making my fingers cramp as I write. But the pain is good. The pain is enough to distract me.

By the time I make it to the last page of the exam, my hand is aching from holding the pencil so tightly. Just when I feel like I'm starting to get the hunger under control, I feel a sharp tug right behind my navel, like someone's pulling an invisible string.

I sit up straighter, momentarily breathless. Images wash over me like a daydream, but stronger. Heat flashes across my skin, and it's Reginald—I don't know how I know, but I do. I watch out of his eyes as he's walking through the gardens at the estate, only it's in the middle of the day. The sun beats down on his skin, and he tilts his head back to feel it on his face.

I shake my head, the image gone as quickly as it had come. I'm breathing hard now, hard enough for the girl beside me to look over, a strange expression on her face.

I quickly scribble a few lines under the last question and stand up, my chair scraping along the floor behind me. A few heads turn in my direction as I cross the long distance between my seat and the front of the room to hand Coderre my exam. She furrows her brows at me, but I hold my stomach with both hands and mouth *I'm sorry*, hoping it'll be enough to spare me, then turn and hurry from the room.

The corridors are empty, mercifully, and I head straight to the nearest bathroom. I brace my hands on one of the porcelain sinks and splash cold water on my face, my entire body shaking now, a cold sweat breaking out on my skin.

Bloodshot eyes stare back at me in the mirror, and when I open my mouth to inspect the ache spreading across my top teeth, my gums are bright red and inflamed.

There's another tug in my stomach, and I whip around to balance myself against the sink as I'm assaulted with another image—*me*. I'm looking through Reginald's eyes at myself sitting in the back seat of a car, my face slightly turned toward the window. My hair falls down my back in waves, and the moonlight hits my cheekbones. I turn, and suddenly I'm looking into my own eyes. That version of me scowls, and the expression makes her nose scrunch.

I sink down until I'm sitting on the floor as the image shatters and I'm back in the bathroom. It's silent save for the leaky faucet dripping behind me. I wrap my arms around my knees and pull them close to my body, my chest heaving as I try to catch my breath.

What is happening to me?

CHAPTER THIRTEEN

·

I STAY in the bathroom long after I'm supposed to be back for the next test, though I do move into one of the stalls in case someone else walks in. Thankfully, no one has yet. If they did, I don't know if I'd be able to stop myself from pouncing on them. The hunger feels like a living thing inside of me, growing more restless with each passing minute.

Harming witches in the running for the Marionettes is highly illegal for vampires, and I don't think me only being half of one would cut me any breaks, especially since no one is supposed to know that.

The door creaks open, and every muscle in my body tenses. My heart pounds in my ears in anticipation, my mouth watering. A burning sensation builds in my gums as footsteps echo off the floor, coming closer. They stop directly in front of my stall.

My breath comes in short, harsh gasps, and my tongue

runs along the sharp points of my teeth—not quite fangs, but definitely sharper than I remember them being before.

"Open the door, Darkmore."

My muscles relax at the sound of his voice. I rise up off the toilet and unlock the door. Reginald stands on the other side, still looking half asleep, the bags under his eyes darker than usual. A glance out the window confirms the sun must have just set.

He looks me up and down, and judging by his expression, I don't look much better.

"How did you know where I was?" I ask.

"We'll talk about it later. But I think we have some more pressing matters to attend to first, don't you?" He raises his eyebrows, and I swallow hard, my throat burning as I do. He checks the rest of the bathroom, then juts his chin for me to follow. "Not here."

"I think I blew my chances at the Marionettes."

After a scan of the hall, he leads me through the empty corridor in the opposite direction of the dorms.

"They'll let you finish the tests another time," he says.

"You don't know that."

He glances at me over his shoulder, his expression slightly amused. "Yes. I do."

The temperature drops as we step outside. The cold brushes against my arms, but I hardly feel it, like it can't break through that first layer of skin.

"Where are you taking me?" I ask as I follow him toward one of the administration buildings near the clock tower.

He ignores me and circles the building, coming to a set of stairs leading to a cellar door.

"How do you know where the back entrances are to everything?" I mutter, but follow him down the steps.

They open to a dimly lit space that looks like some kind of break room for the administrators. A round table sits in the center, surrounded by a few mismatched chairs, and there's a kitchenette in the corner. Reginald goes straight to the fridge as I hesitate in the doorway, looking around.

"Here you go." He returns with a hospital bag full of blood and pops it open. "It won't be as good cold, but it'll do the trick."

My pride apparently nonexistent at the moment, I take it and suck down the contents as quickly as I can. He doesn't say anything, just waits until I drain every last drop and hand the empty bag back to him. I lick my lips, already wanting another one.

"This isn't normal, is it?" I ask.

He shrugs, paces back over to the fridge, and produces a second bag. "None of this is normal."

I drink the second bag, slower this time, wiping my mouth with the back of my hand and making sure I don't stain the white shirt of my uniform. I glance up and catch Reginald watching me, a thoughtful expression on his face.

"How did you know where to find me? Was it the blood bond?"

A frown crosses his face, but he doesn't look away or change the subject this time. "I could...*feel* you. It woke me up, actually. How hungry you were."

I stare at him, the ghost of that pull I'd felt still in my stomach. The images I'd seen had felt so real. But all I say is, "Why?"

"I know they taught you about the bond between

witches and vampires. The blood exchange helps those partnerships through that connection. But sharing blood with other vampires is…rare. It can form a much more *intense* bond. And it's more unpredictable."

That explains how he knew I needed help and where to find me, but then what had I been seeing? I stop breathing for a moment as it occurs to me maybe those images had been coming from him. Were those his…dreams?

"How is this different?" I ask. "I mean, you've been paired other times, so you know what it's supposed to feel like. I've read all of the textbook definitions, but reading it and feeling it for yourself are two totally different things. I don't know what I'm supposed to be feeling and what parts of this aren't normal."

He takes a long time before responding. "In the past, it's always been vague, I guess. You know how sometimes you have dreams that don't really make sense, or feelings you can't put into words? I think of it the way babies must think before they understand language—they have these abstract images and feelings that we can't understand. That's kind of what it felt like to be paired before. I could understand what my partner was trying to convey to me even if I couldn't put it into words. Even if I didn't know exactly what they were thinking, I could somehow feel what they wanted me to feel—like if they were in danger. I wouldn't be able to put into words where they were, but I could find them. If they were in distress, I could feel that distress."

He pauses, his eyes flitting over me again. "With you, it still is that way. Sometimes. Sometimes it's just a lot more. Sometimes I can hear exactly what you're thinking in perfect words as if you were speaking right next to me, or I can see what you see—like I saw you go into the bathroom. And the rest of it…whatever else is different…honestly, I'm not sure."

I nod, trying to process his words.

"Do you feel better now?" He gestures to the half-empty blood bag.

I nod again and wipe the back of my hand across my mouth.

"They don't usually lock this door. It's for visiting vampires. It's not much, but they keep the fridge stocked. So as long as you don't let anyone see you, you should be safe getting blood from here when you need it."

"You really think I can go on like nothing's changed?"

His expression doesn't change. "Yes."

My mouth falls open a little, but he's talking again before I can say anything.

"We should get you back to the headmistress about your tests. Just let me do the talking." He turns away, the conversation apparently over. I want to dig in my heels and refuse to leave until he answers all of my questions, but he's already halfway out the door. So I sigh, put the stopper back in the blood bag, stash it safely in my bag for later, and hurry after him.

———

WE'RE SUPPOSED to have the weekend off from initiation tasks as a break between final exams and the assembly on Monday announcing who is moving on to the second round of trials. I, however, get to spend my entire Saturday in the headmistress's office making up my tests. I suppose I should be grateful Reginald managed to convince her I'd had a devastating bout of food poisoning—whether she bought it or just wants to appease him, I'm not sure.

It's still light outside when I pull myself out of bed around 4 p.m. and cram in some last-minute studying—still no response from Connor. Every time I check my phone and his name isn't there, the knot in my stomach twists itself a little tighter. Maybe I should take the hint and give him some space. He'll talk to me when he's ready, and I have plenty of other things to worry about right now.

I squint at my window, the light burning my eyes and causing an instant headache to pound in my temples. I hold my arm out, and my skin tingles, but it doesn't hurt, exactly. Even if I don't get burned like a full vampire, this sun sensitivity thing is not ideal. Maybe I can find a spell workaround for it later.

I suck down the rest of a blood bag and a protein bar for breakfast—not the best combination, but judging by the way my stomach growls even after I've fed on blood, the witch half of me still needs regular food. Figuring out what foods don't taste disgusting with blood is the least of my problems. I throw a second bag of blood in my bag, just in case, then open my door to head to Coderre's office.

I skitter to a stop in the doorway at the sight of Monroe and Kirby. They're standing in the hall in pajamas, arms crossed over their chests. Despite the stance, their expressions don't look...*angry*, exactly. Their eyes search my face then drop to my backpack.

"I'm going to Coderre's office to make up my tests," I explain.

They exhale and drop their arms.

"We thought maybe you'd been cut," admits Kirby.

"Then when we heard you moving around so early this morning…" Monroe trails off.

I raise my eyebrows. "You thought I'd clear out without saying goodbye?"

"No," Kirby says, then winces. "Yes. I don't know. You've been acting so weird lately."

"And you ran out yesterday and never came back," adds Monroe.

"Is this about the Vexillium?" Kirby lowers her voice. "Because I was looking into it, and I found a few spells we could try to figure out where it's coming from—"

"Oh." I grimace and rub the back of my neck with one hand, momentarily disoriented at the mention of the poison. It somehow already feels like a problem from another lifetime, and in a way, it is. Everything that happened before I woke up in the prince's bed feels more distant, murky. I'd always thought my life was so compli-cated, and now looking back, I can't decide if I want to laugh or cry.

"I actually figured out where it was," I finally say.

"What?" they demand. "Where?"

"It was in my perfume…Reginald smelled it out. Vampire senses and all that."

Kirby's lips press together, and she looks away, but I don't miss the hurt that flashes across her face. "Why didn't you say anything?"

The words she doesn't say are just as clear. *Why would you talk to him but not us?*

It hadn't been intentional. It definitely hadn't been a conscious choice. Everything since that night has been an absolute whirlwind, and I haven't been able to clearly think about anything other than blood. Even now, I can *smell them*. Their pulses thud evenly at their throats, and for a moment, I can't help but focus on the curve of their necks. I wonder if they would taste the same as Beth did—

I shake my head and blink.

I stare at their faces—a mixture of hurt, confusion, and suspicion looking back at me. I want to. I want to tell them everything. They can keep a secret—I know they can. But something stops me.

I promised to keep this a secret. And even if I don't agree with him, I trust Reginald, for some reason. Maybe it's the bond connecting us, or maybe it's something else. But if he says I shouldn't talk about this, I believe him.

I check my watch, and a small jolt goes through me. I'll have to hurry to make it to Coderre's in time, and I'm already on thin ice. Showing up late might be the last straw.

"I'm really sorry, but I have to go. I can't be late for these tests." I start to edge around them, but look back before heading out the door. "We'll talk later, okay?"

When neither of them responds, I double back and throw my arms around their shoulders, crushing them to me. They hesitate for a moment, but then hug me back. "I love you guys," I say before pulling away. "We'll talk soon."

Monroe sighs and gives me a little shove, a smile threatening on her lips. "Go take your tests, slacker. We're having a party here tonight for everyone moving on to week two, and you better be there, okay?"

I nod before hurrying out the door. "Yes, ma'am!"

CHAPTER FOURTEEN

CODERRE DOESN'T SAY MUCH when I show up, just hands me my first test and pointedly ignores my presence as I work across the desk from her. When I finish the alchemy and poisons exam, she gives me a five-minute break, then we move on to languages and spells, and finally, history and foreign affairs. By the time I finish the final exam, my brain feels like mush, and I'm not sure if I could do another.

The door to the dorm is vibrating with music when I walk by—I'd almost forgotten about the party. My head definitely can't take that right now, so I keep walking. I'm not sure where I'm going until I reach the cemetery at the edge of the property. The gate creaks as I nudge it open.

It's quiet as I wind my way through the plots and head for the rows in the back. The path is well-worn, beaten down by however many feet have walked through here.

I don't come often. Probably not as often as I should. I did at first, but I learned quickly that coming here wasn't going to bring me the kind of comfort others sought out in such places.

Calla is the only Darkmore name here I recognize. The other headstones are carved with names of witches long since passed whom I never met and didn't do anything significant enough for me to hear about.

I hesitate in front of Calla's grave, waiting to get that feeling that always comes during our annual ritual on her birthday. To feel some kind of essence of her. But I don't. She's not here. It's just a rock in the ground and cold, wet earth. I sit down and lean against the headstone across from her anyway and pull my bag into my lap.

I'd been a freshman at the academy when she was going through initiation. And even though that was only two years ago, I still can't remember much from that time. I guess I hadn't been paying that much attention. I'd seen her in the halls. Sometimes we'd have lunch together. But our lives had been so separate. Whatever she'd been going through, it had been invisible to me. Until one day, it wasn't.

Sometimes I can't help but wonder if I'd paid more attention, maybe things would have turned out differently. Mom and Adrienne had been back at the Carrington estate. I had been the only one here with her. If something was wrong, I should have seen it.

"I wish you were here," I whisper, a small smirk rising to my lips. "I'm sure you'd have a lot to say about everything that's been going on."

The wind rustles through the cemetery, but of course, no response comes.

I take a blood bag out of my pack and raise it toward her stone. "Cheers." I take a small sip through the straw, and the moment the blood hits the back of my throat, relief courses through me.

Since Reginald showed me the blood stash, the hunger hasn't been as desperate. But it has been constant. Even when it's quiet and small and just the barest whisper in the back of my mind, it's always there, slowly growing and growing until I can't ignore it anymore.

It's only been a day, and I've already gone through five bags.

"In other news," I say, licking the blood from my lips. "There was poison in the perfume Mom gave me. What do you think? A sick test or a bad coincidence?"

It wouldn't be the first time Mom took extreme measures in our *lessons*. Back when Calla was sixteen, I was fourteen and late to go through puberty, so my powers hadn't fully formed yet. I could heal, but it took a while. Mom saw that as a great opportunity to help with Calla's training—slice open my arms to see if Calla could heal me before I passed out.

One of the few scars on my body is right below my left elbow crease from a time she went too deep, which was more of a message than anything else. Calla may not have been powerful enough at the time to heal me, but my mother certainly had been. Leaving the scar had been a choice, not an inevitability.

I run the pad of my thumb over the small patch of raised skin. If this is one of her sick tests…I don't know what the point is. To what end? What could she possibly hope to accomplish, especially when she hasn't been here at the academy to see if it was working?

"I could really use you in my corner right now," I whisper, then shake my head at myself, forcing the thoughts away. It's not going to help me figure out who is behind the poisoning. It's not going to help me pass these tasks.

It's not going to bring Calla back.

And it's certainly not going to help with whatever the hell happened to me when I took Reginald's blood.

The bushes behind me rustle, and I quickly shove the blood back into my bag. A girl stumbles into the cemetery —not just any girl, the first year who lives across the hall from me. She hits the ground on her knees, her entire body shaking and tears streaming down her face. She looks around wildly, taking a few moments before finally noticing me.

"Help," she whispers, nearly choking on the word. She pushes herself back to her feet. "Help," she repeats, louder this time. "He's—and there's—the blood and—"

Being the only person here, she must be talking to me, so I get up and hurry after her. The moment I rise to my feet, she turns and stumbles back into the trees.

"Wait!" I call.

Her form disappears almost immediately, so I follow the sound of her crashing through the leaves. She lets out a choked cry somewhere up ahead, then I break through the branches.

The body is by the lake, a few feet off from the frosted surface. I don't recognize him. Not at first. Even though his face is one of the only parts still intact. I inch forward, covering my mouth and nose with my hand to block out the rotting smell. It's so strong it coats the back of my throat. He must have been here for a while. At least a few days.

What's left of him is laid together in a neat pile. Several

pieces are missing, mostly larger chunks, like a full leg, his arm. Distinct bite marks are scattered across his skin, and there's a gaping hole where his abdomen used to be. But the shredded remains seem otherwise untouched. Like no other animals were willing to go near him after the initial attack.

The forest is quiet as I reach his body and lean down. His expression is frozen in a look of shock, but not fear. Just…surprise.

Like he knew whoever—or whatever—did this.

And he didn't expect them to come for him.

"Ryan," I say quietly, even though I know he can't hear me. Nausea surges up from the pit of my stomach, but it's not from the smell or the gore. It's from the picture I have of him in my head—very much alive—standing in the library, unable to meet my eyes.

But this can't have anything to do with that. The conversation—if you could call it that—had lasted less than a minute. No one else had been around to see us talking.

This can't be because of me. It can't.

It's a similar scene to the bodies I cleaned up at the parking garage, but there's something inherently different here. That first pile of bodies looked like they were ripped apart for sport—no missing limbs or bite marks. There were puncture wounds from vampire fangs, sure, but Ryan looks like he was mauled by an animal.

The girl behind me sniffles, and I glance up at her, almost having forgotten she was here. She covers her mouth with her hand.

"We should go get Coderre," I say.

She hugs her arms to herself. "What could have done this?"

I wince. "Something that clearly wanted to eat him."

"You think it was a vampire?"

I shake my head. "They wouldn't have left all of this blood wasted—and they'd have no use for taking all of those body parts with them. At least, none of that I know of…"

I trail off, the image of Daniel slumped against a tree rising up in my brain. The crazed look in that vampire's eyes as he'd forced his way toward me. Is this what he would have done to Daniel if we hadn't found him in time?

Silence falls between us, and we met each other's eyes over the body.

"We should go get Coderre," I say again.

She nods.

———

CODERRE'S FACE doesn't change when she sees the body. Her expression stays carefully blank as she takes in the scene, then juts her chin, and the two security guards waiting behind her head toward the body. Her eyes find me and the first year next.

"You two should go back to campus," she says.

The first year doesn't need to be told twice. She nods quickly and starts up the hill, hesitating only when she realizes I'm not following her. My gaze is still trained on Coderre.

"What's going on?" I ask.

"We'll do a thorough investigation, I can assure you," she says.

"Do you *see* him?" I demand. "There's barely any of him left! First Daniel, now this—"

"Valerie." She takes a step closer to me, and a muscle in her neck jumps. "Go back to campus. This isn't your place. We'll take it from here."

I hold her gaze for a moment longer, then turn my attention to the men near Ryan's body.

"Valerie," she warns.

I turn away without another word, passing the first year and heading straight into the trees. I can tell by the rushing footsteps behind me she's trying to catch up, but that just makes me walk faster. I can't deal with her shrill voice or wide, innocent eyes right now.

I don't know why I'm so *angry* all of a sudden, but it feels like a wild animal trying to claw out of my chest. I clench my jaw against it, my gums burning and throbbing.

The party is still raging on when I reach the dorm, the hall flooded with people, Kirby and Monroe included. They're both holding red plastic cups—Kirby in a cowboy hat, Monroe in a bikini top—and they grin when they see me.

"How'd the tests go?" asks Kirby.

I shoulder past them without a word, heading for my room, and force even breaths through my nose. My chest heaves as I try to calm myself down. I can hear the pulse of every person in this hallway, smell the sweat on their skin, imagine the way their blood would feel as it hit the back of my throat…

"Hey, Val—" Monroe tries to grab my arm, but I shake

177

her off. My control is hanging on by a thread. Sweat beads in my hairline. The last thing I see is Kirby's and Monroe's stunned expressions as I close the door between us.

The moment I'm alone, I let out a shuddering breath. My emotions are so…*vivid* right now. I feel like I'm about to explode.

Coderre knows more than she's saying. It was like I could *smell* it on her. And she keeps dismissing me when I ask about it—as if two attacks *on campus* aren't worth worrying about. How can she think we're all better off in the dark?

My hands shake at my sides, the rage building in me like fire, but then there's a tug in my stomach.

I pace back and forth along the length of the room when Reginald pulls on the bond again, and this time, I feel a bit of my rage seep out with it.

"Oh *hell* no." Monroe yanks the door open and struts into the room, Kirby a pace behind her. "What was that?" she demands.

I pinch the bridge of my nose with two fingers and hold up a hand to stop them. The noise from the party pulses against the inside of my skull, and I grit my teeth. "Guys, please, not right now."

"Did you stop at Bitchiness Incorporated on your way home to pick up this attitude? I hope you kept the receipt to return it, because *I'd* like my best friend back," Monroe goes on.

"Sorry I'm not in the mood for a party right now," I snap. "I just found a dead body outside."

"Wait, what?" Kirby closes the door and takes a step forward.

"Please." I rub my eyes with my hands and shake my head. "It's been a really long day, and I just want to be alone. My head is killing me."

Monroe pulls in a breath, but Kirby speaks before she can. "Sure, Val, we'll go. But keep whatever the hell this is up, and one of these days, we might not come back."

"Kirby…" I look up, and my gums burn as the hunger roars inside of me. If I just told them…if I could just *tell them*…

Kirby looks me up and down as Monroe crosses her arms over her chest.

"There's something going on with me," I say quietly, and tears cloud my vision. "And I can't tell you about it. I *want* to, but I can't. I'm just…struggling."

A hint of the anger bleeds out of Monroe's face, and she drops her arms to her sides. Kirby frowns, eyes flickering over my face.

I shove aside the tears that escape onto my cheek with a shaking hand. "I get why you're mad," I continue. "But I hope you can believe me when I say if I could tell you what's been going on, I would."

"I believe you," says Kirby.

"Fuck." Monroe gently punches me in the shoulder. "I wanted to stay mad."

I let out a breathy laugh and nod toward the door. "You guys go have fun. I'm just really not up for it, okay?"

"Well, I don't want to party if you're not going to be there." Monroe throws her arms up and lets them slap against her thighs. "Wes is already so drunk off his ass I bet he'll pass out in the next few hours. Now who's gonna draw on his face with me?"

"I'll do it," says Kirby.

Monroe rolls her eyes, but throws her arm over Kirby's shoulder and pulls her to her side. "No you won't. You'll say you will, but then chicken out at the last minute because you *feel bad*."

Kirby scowls, but doesn't try to pull away.

Monroe snaps her fingers a few times. "I have an idea! So no party tonight, but how about we go into town tomorrow and do Sunday brunch like we used to?"

They both turn to me again, faces expectant. I let out a small laugh and rub my nose with the back of my hand. "Yeah, brunch sounds good."

Monroe points at me. "We're holding you to that."

I smile a little and nod.

"Don't make us kidnap you and drag you there," adds Kirby.

"I won't."

The two stare at me for a moment longer, then nod, satisfied with whatever they see on my face. The moment they open the door, the volume of the party outside doubles, filling my room. I cringe, but they don't notice as they head back into the hall.

I collapse against the door when they're gone, my head still pounding, but at least the majority of the anger that had been consuming me on my way in has ebbed away. I don't know where it came from, but it was like as soon as it started building in my chest, there was no stopping it.

Is that a vampire thing? They're all rageaholics? Reginald doesn't have that problem. Most of the time he's infuriatingly calm. Maybe he just seems that way.

I pause. What if that's *exactly* it, and that rage hadn't

been coming from me at all? What if that was *him*? It would explain why it came out of nowhere. Maybe I was feeling his anger through the bond, unable to differentiate it from my own feelings.

Just thinking about the possibility makes my head hurt more. I prick my finger and press it to my forehead, hoping to relieve some of the pressure there, then collapse into bed, which is where I stay for the rest of the night as the party rages on outside my door.

CHAPTER FIFTEEN

I MEET Kirby and Monroe at the café Blood and Buzz at 5:30 p.m. With the sun setting around six these days, it's best to squeeze into places before they get too busy with the vampire clientele. Main Street is within walking distance from the academy, so it only takes me about five minutes.

The town of York is of modest size and fairly spread out. Most people here have miles between them and their nearest neighbors, making Main Street and the town square the congregating grounds. It's the type of town with hand-painted signs and flowerpots in the shop windows, the land-scaping meticulous and unnaturally bright-green.

The southern part of town, where the majority of humans live, has maintained most of its original architec-ture, whereas the farther north you go, the more the vampires have modernized and smoothed out all the edges. It's not as lively as the city, but they've tried to keep up—a new coffee shop or bar or movie theater popping up every few months.

Blood and Buzz appeared right before our freshman year. It's a small café, but it has the best pastries. And the owner is a plump older woman who tends to throw in free banana bread if she likes you.

The place is already vibrating with activity when I show up, nearly every seat filled, including the bar stools. The three of us manage to snag the last open booth by the windows at the front of the shop. My eyes are still burning from the sun as I slip off my sunglasses and set them on the table.

Freshman year, this had been our routine. We didn't have many classes together, so we would reconvene on Sundays to debrief and tell each other how things were going at the academy. I don't know when we stopped doing it. Maybe because as years go on and the academy narrows down who gets to stay, the classes get smaller, so we started seeing each other more throughout the week. Or maybe it was because of how busy and stressful all of our schedules got.

Sitting with them now, I feel eighteen again. Still more excited than anything to be at the academy. Not yet stressed. Not yet mourning the loss of Calla. And definitely not yet dealing with all of the things I have going on today.

Once we order our coffees and our waitress disappears into the back, Kirby and Monroe turn to me with expectant faces.

So. We're going to jump straight into it then.

"Did you guys hear about the human?" I ask. I know that's not really what they want to talk about, but I still don't know what I'm going to say about the rest of it yet, so maybe this will distract them long enough for me to figure it out.

They stare at me a minute, and the clanging of silverware and surrounding conversations fills my ears. I try to force my focus back on the table in front of me, blocking out the rest of the noise. If I'm not careful, I'm learning, it's all too easy to get swept up in my surroundings. The larger the crowd, the harder it is to focus. I smell the burning pieces of bacon on the grill in the back, the chocolate melting in the pastries in the oven, the blood they keep in the fridge for vampire drinks, though the scent is somehow…*flatter* when it's cold.

"I've heard rumors," Kirby says, drawing me back to the table. "I heard they found him down by a lake, and he was torn apart."

"I think he worked in the library here," I say. "I ran into him before."

A chill breaks out over my skin at the memory of him standing in the stacks, very much alive. I'd half expected Coderre to call me to her office for a statement or something this morning—*some* hint of an ongoing investigation—but I still haven't heard anything.

Monroe shivers and hunches her shoulders beneath her leather jacket. "That's awful. Did it look like another vampire attack, like with Daniel?"

I shake my head, the image of his body rising back up in my mind. The blood in the snow, the missing pieces of flesh. The bitter smell of his fear still lingering behind even though he was long gone. "Maybe, I don't know. It seemed a lot more brutal than that, like an animal."

"Has anyone been to see Daniel?" Kirby asks. "Does anyone know how he's doing?"

Monroe and I both shake our heads.

"Not since the blood moon," I say, suddenly feeling bad. It hadn't even occurred to me to go check on him again with everything else that's been going on.

"I heard he's still staying in the hospital," says Monroe.

"What about his initiation? Is he out?" asks Kirby.

"I guess we'll find out at the assembly tomorrow, but they have to make an exception for him, right?" I say. "I mean, it happened on academy grounds, *during a class.* The school has to be liable for that."

"I heard he *still* hasn't healed," says Monroe.

Kirby shakes her head. "That's insane. Have you ever heard of anything like that?" Four eyes dart to me for a second. I know she's thinking about the poison.

Apparently my attempts to distract them have already failed.

"I'm sorry I didn't tell you guys about the poison sooner. I honestly just forgot. There's been...other things going on."

"*Other things?*" echoes Monroe.

I grimace, but then the waitress reappears with our drinks and sets them on the table in front of us, saving me. Her scent washes over me as she leans across the table. Human. They smell different than witches, I'm noticing. Less sweet. She pops back up and pulls out a notepad, all rosy red cheeks and curly black hair.

"Are y'all ready to order?"

Monroe and Kirby get pancakes, and I go for the breakfast sandwich with extra hash browns on the side. The moment our waitress walks away, they turn back to me.

"I don't know who did it. It was in some perfume my mom got me. But the timeline doesn't really add up. Like, I didn't start feeling bad until I already had the bottle for a few weeks, so honestly, it could have been anyone who slipped it in after the fact, right?"

Kirby chews on her lip.

"Do you have any suspicions?" asks Monroe.

I shake my head again. "You don't know a spell for that, do you?"

Kirby's mouth quirks. "I don't know if there *is* a spell for that."

Monroe, on the other hand, does not look nearly as amused. Her gaze is as intense as before. "If it wasn't the poison, what happened with the exams?"

I run my tongue over my incisors, remembering how *loud* everyone's blood had been in that room, then startle a bit as I realize my teeth don't feel as sharp right now. I never asked Reginald how that worked, if he would even know. For regular vampires, their fangs can retract when they're not using them. Mine don't seem to do that, but they also definitely aren't as sharp as a full vampire's would be. They're in some weird in-between state.

My gaze shifts between my two best friends. I don't think I've ever successfully kept a secret from them before, so what makes me think I can get away with it now? And more importantly, I don't *want* to. If Reginald hadn't warned me away from telling anyone, they would've been the first people to know.

And how bad would it *really* be if I told them?

I sigh and clamp my hands together on the table in front of me. "The other night, something happened. And I got...sick. And then when I was taking the exams, it hit me again. And I had to get out of there."

"You really should get an award for the most vague answers ever," mutters Monroe.

Maybe Reginald is rubbing off on me.

"What do you mean by *sick*?" Kirby asks.

I glance around, but no one is paying attention to us. The room is so loud people with normal senses are probably having trouble hearing their own conversations.

I let out a low laugh and shake my head. "I don't even think you'd believe me."

"Val." Kirby nudges me under the table with her shoe. "What is it?"

I blow the air out of my cheeks and push the hair away from my face. My heart thuds a little harder against my ribs. "When we did the blood exchange, something happened to me."

Monroe's eyebrows furrow, and Kirby folds her arms on the table to lean closer.

"And I—" My eyes flick to the side again. I open my mouth and tap on one of my canines, then lean back in my seat.

Monroe and Kirby continue to stare at me, and it's like I can see their brains working behind their eyes. Monroe's the first to realize. She sits up straight and covers her mouth with her hand.

Kirby opens her mouth to say something, but my phone cuts her off as it buzzes on the table. I scan the messages on the screen and sigh. Reginald insisting I come back to the

estate tonight. No one is supposed to have tasks this weekend, but I have a feeling this has more to do with *recent devel-
opments* than initiation. Considering he seems to know a lot
more about what's going on than I do, passing him up
would probably be a pretty stupid idea.

The waitress reappears with our food, smiling as she
sets each plate in front of us. Monroe presses her lips
together and looks around, frustration seeping into her
expression as she realizes she can't speak freely. The
moment the waitress is gone, she points a finger at me.

"We are not done talking about this."

I stab my fork into my hash browns and raise my
eyebrows. "Oh trust me, I know."

Reginald sends another half dozen texts by the time I
leave the café, and as if that hadn't been enough, I can *feel*
his impatience radiating in my chest.

I have half the mind to take the train back just to annoy
him, but with the poison out of my system and all of this
blood inside me making me feel three times as strong as
usual, I don't have an excuse.

I barely feel the teleportation spell this time, and the
gash in my arm heals before my feet touch the grounds of
the estate. There's an empty plot of grass between the
outdoor pool and the garden—this is where I'm supposed
to meet the prince.

He's standing with his back to me, a woman I've never
seen before in front of him. She's dressed in the same white
uniform as the rest of the servants here, so she must work

for the estate. I wouldn't have given her a second thought, if not for the way she laid her hand on his arm while she talked—the kind of familiar touch that only comes with knowing someone for a long time.

Before either of them notices my approach, she squeezes his arm and turns to head back toward the estate, exposing the long braid of red hair down her back, tinged with gray, just at the roots. He leans against one of the stone pillars and watches as she goes, his face turned so I can't see his expression. Once the estate doors close behind her, he tilts his head back to look at the stars overhead and lets out a slow breath.

The grounds suddenly feel eerily empty in her absence.

I brace myself as I approach, wondering if he somehow heard what I talked about with Monroe and Kirby earlier through the bond despite my attempts to keep it from him. I don't know exactly how much I can control what translates over, but hell if I'm not going to try to build some kind of block there.

"How'd the tests go?" he asks without looking at me.

"Better than the first one."

How long has he known I was here? I set my bag on the grass, trying to gauge his mood, but he doesn't seem upset. I can feel him vaguely through the bond, not even a feeling, just that he's there. Surely, if he were furious, I'd feel *that*.

"You know," I say. "You're kind of failing at this whole initiation thing."

He rolls up his shirtsleeves and glances down at me. He's in a suit—he must have been somewhere important before this. "How so?"

"I've seen other witches get kidnapped and dragged

away from the school...I heard some guy had a bunch of vampires ambush him in the bathroom...and you just text me."

He presses his lips together like he's trying not to laugh. "Are you asking me to kidnap you?"

"No." I shift my weight. "I guess I'm just hoping you're not taking it easy on me because of everything going on. I'm just as capable—"

"I can assure you, Darkmore, I'm not taking it easy on you. I'm just not that theatrical. *Although*, if you're really feeling left out with your classmates, I'm sure I can come up with something."

"That's not what I was saying—"

He grins.

I sigh, immediately regretting bringing it up, but I have a feeling the more I try to discourage him, the more he'll want to do it now. "Why are we out here?"

"I thought it might be wise for you and I to get a handle on this bond—or at least figure out exactly what we're dealing with."

I wave a finger between us. "Is there any way to...turn it down?"

He raises an eyebrow. "Turn it down?"

"Yeah." I wave my hand vaguely toward myself. "Sometimes you're just so *loud*. Like I can feel you more than I can feel me." I hesitate, wondering if I should ask him about the anger I'd felt yesterday, if that really had been coming from him.

"Oh, trust me," he says before I have the chance, "I have the worse end of that deal with your baby vampire hunger. It's quite unpleasant."

"Yeah, well, that hasn't been very pleasant for me either," I mumble.

He ignores me and pushes off the pillar. "I do think we can build up walls, so to speak, to keep things from transferring over. We can work on that. But how about we start with seeing what you can send over intentionally? A thought, a feeling. Concentrate on something specific." As he says it, an image rises up in my mind. It slides in seamlessly, like it's my own thought, but there's something about it that's inherently foreign. Something about the colors, the perspective.

It's me, standing in the middle of the gardens. I know I'm looking through Reginald's eyes, but still, a small jolt goes through my chest as the sight of *me* looking back at me. I stare into that version of me's eyes—and for the first time in a long time, she doesn't look nearly as tired as the versions of myself I've seen in the mirror. Her skin is full of color again, her eyes bright and focused. She looks...pretty. She turns away from me and starts walking into the trees.

The moment she's out of my sight, the image disappears, and I'm looking at Reginald in front of me again. He stands with his arms crossed over his chest, watching me.

"I thought pairs could only exchange vague things—feelings, general locations, that kind of thing."

He nods. "What did you get then?"

"I saw it perfectly. Like, every detail."

He waves his hand for me to try. I clench my jaw, trying to focus on that place I occasionally feel the bond tug, just behind my navel. It warms as I rest my attention on it.

"Good," Reginald says softly.

I try to craft an image in my head, but it feels like

molding something out of dry clay. The pieces keep crumbling between my fingers. I picture him standing here in the garden, the way he's standing now. Once the image feels solid, I have him turn toward the pool and start walking. As the background shifts behind him, it gets more and more difficult to hold on to. Just before I feel the image slip away, I have him walk to the edge of the pool, then keep going until his body crashes down into the water.

I jolt out of my trance as the water splashes and find the real Reginald scowling at me.

"Of all the things you could have thought of, *that* was the first thing that popped into your head?"

"But you saw it too?"

"Yes," he sighs. "I saw it. Well done, I suppose."

I grin, but my amusement is short-lived. The water makes me think of the lake, and the lake makes me think of Ryan.

Reginald frowns. "What is it?"

I consider evading the question, then it occurs to me he probably *felt* my shift in mood instead of seeing it on my face. "Are you still looking into James Westcott?"

His eyes quickly flicker around us, ensuring we're alone, then he lets out a breath and shakes his head. "Truth be told, I wasn't finding much, and with plenty of other things to worry about for the time being, I've put it aside."

"Don't."

He raises his eyebrows. "Don't?"

"I mean, I don't think you should stop looking into it."

He closes the rest of the distance between us until we're barely inches apart. "What do you know, Darkmore?" he asks quietly.

"There was a human in the academy's library the other day. I asked him about James—" I hold up a hand to stop him as his expression shifts. "And he reacted really weirdly. Like he was scared or something. And then a few days later, he showed up dead on the academy grounds."

Reginald studies my face for a second, then crosses his arms over his chest and nods. "How?"

A small shiver runs through me. "I don't know what could have done it. He was completely torn up—pieces of him missing, bite marks. It was brutal."

His frown deepens.

"I don't know if it's actually connected," I add. "I just thought you should know."

He presses his lips together. "Can you show me?"

"Show you?"

He meets my eyes again, a bit of the tension easing from his features. "Can you *show* me what you saw?"

I guess it shouldn't be too hard since the image is permanently seared into my head now. I focus on the bond first, then try to picture the scene again. His body by the water. The bloodless, pale skin. The first year hopelessly sobbing beside him.

The image shifts, playing back the memory like a movie. Coderre walks onto the scene, looking at the body, and then at me, her expression blank. As she starts to talk, the image breaks, and I blink back to Reginald in front of me.

His expression is even more troubled than before, a harsh line now between his eyebrows. "His body had been there for a while. You can tell."

I nod, agreeing. I'd had the same thought.

"The academy does sweeps of the grounds daily," he continues. "They wouldn't have missed that. So why was he still there?"

My stomach drops to my feet. Because he's right. We do have patrols that sweep the campus every single day, leaving no inch unturned. So unless some of the guards are really bad at their jobs and about to get fired, why would they have allowed his body to lie there for so long?

Maybe that's why Coderre didn't look surprised to see him.

"You still think it's not worth looking into James Westcott anymore?" I ask.

"We should…" He trails off as he notices something behind my head. I start to turn, and he appears beside me, his hand circling my wrist. "You should go inside."

"What? I just got here—"

He silences me with a look. Every line of his face is hard, his jaw clenched tight enough it looks like the bone might break through skin.

I bend down to retrieve my bag as footsteps draw closer.

"How you doing there, Reginald?" says a low voice behind me, the words buried beneath a Russian accent.

I turn to see two men approaching us, both also wearing three-piece suits. The one with darker hair looks me up and down and grins. "Who is this?"

Reginald takes another step forward, angling his body so he's blocking me slightly from view. "Valerie Darkmore. Her mother is the queen's right hand."

"Darkmore," he muses. "The blood witches?"

"Can I help you gentlemen with something?" Reginald says, his voice full of sharp edges. "Are you lost, Viktor?"

"Just exploring," says the other one. "Seeing all that your great region has to offer."

Reginald is so tense I can feel it, even without the bond. *Go. Inside.* His voice practically growls inside my head.

I glance at him, but his attention is locked on the two men in front of us, so I shoulder my bag and do as he says, heading back toward the estate without a word.

"It was nice to meet you, Valerie!" one calls after me, and something about his voice sends a shiver down my spine.

I PUSH open Connor's door to reveal an empty room. The bed is neatly made, as always, the surrounding surfaces clear of his usual belongings. I could wait for him to come back, but if he's in the middle of a shift, it could be hours.

I haven't spoken to him in days now—the longest we've gone without talking in a while. At first I'd thought he was just busy…but maybe it's more than that. Maybe me being half-vampire is something he can't get over. But if he was struggling with it, why wouldn't he talk to me? This silent treatment isn't like him. Should I be…worried?

I slump against the wall.

I haven't been able to shake this chill since running into those Russian guys outside. Somehow it didn't click until I was back inside that they were likely the vampires responsible for the bodies I helped Reginald clean up. Goosebumps rise on my arms at the thought, at the way their eyes had looked me up and down like maybe I was something they'd like to eat too. What was most troubling was Reginald's reaction. As the prince, he's arguably one of the most powerful vampires at the estate. What does he have to be afraid of?

"He's not here."

I jump at the voice behind me. Adrienne stands at the end of the hall, one foot propped on the stairs. There's a pile of books in her arms—she probably just finished her classes for the night with the estate's tutor.

She nods at Connor's door. "He probably won't be back for a while. Honestly, he hasn't been around much lately."

I nod and close the door again.

Adrienne doesn't move. "What are you doing here?" she asks.

I wave my hand vaguely in the direction of the garden. "I had a thing with the prince earlier."

She nods, and an awkward silence falls between us. After a moment, she shrugs, lifts the books in her arms, and turns back to continue down the stairs. "See you."

"Adrienne?"

She pauses and regards me over her shoulder.

I don't really have anything else to say to her, but I feel like I *should*. She and I have never been close, but we've also never felt this distant before. And with each new day that Calla's still gone, the wall between us grows thicker and thicker.

And now this thing with the poison in the perfume...I don't know if I actually believe our mother would be capable of that, but if she *were*, would Adrienne have known about it? Would she have stood by and let that happen? I wish I could immediately dismiss the thought, but I honestly don't know.

If I went into her den, I'd probably find Vexillium in there, but that wouldn't mean much. She has hundreds of herbs and poisons in there, always has. I study Adrienne's face for a moment, as if the answer might be written there, but of course, it gives nothing away.

"It's good to see you," I finally say.

Her brow furrows, but she nods, then heads downstairs. More footsteps thud as human servants scurry back and forth. I push off the wall and turn to leave as a woman appears around the corner.

My blood runs cold at the sight of her, but she doesn't even spare me a glance. Her dark hair bounces around her shoulders as she struts past me and straight to Connor's door. When she opens it and finds he's not inside, she lets out a low hiss.

My heart races in my chest, images from that night rising up in my mind no matter how much I try to push them back. When she turns and catches me staring at her, she flashes her fangs. If she recognizes me from the last time I found her in his room, she doesn't show it.

"Leave Connor alone," I say lowly.

Her eyebrows lift, and she prowls toward me. "Connor? Is that its name?"

My entire body tenses at the word *it*, but I don't back down, not even when she's barely a pace away from me. She's much taller than I am, even more so in the high heels, and she looks at me over her nose.

She reaches down and takes my chin between two fingers, her long nails digging into my skin, and tilts my head back and forth. She sighs and releases me. "A Dark-more, is it?"

"Just leave Connor alone," I repeat.

"Why? Are you trying to claim him? Didn't anyone ever teach you to share your toys?" She takes another step toward me, and I back up despite myself. Her grin returns, and she keeps advancing until my back is pressed against the wall. "How is it that you intend to stop me, Darkmore?" she whispers, and her breath washes over my cheek.

I force myself to stand up straighter. "He's from a family that's been loyal to the Carringtons for decades. If they found out you were—"

"They would do nothing because he's a *human*."

Anger builds in me like boiling water, and my hands shake at my sides, but as much as she's not allowed to harm me here, I'm also sworn not to hurt her. Somehow the only person without that protection is the one who needs it most.

"Don't you have anything better to do? Or is your life so boring that the only way you can get off is to take someone against their will—"

She grabs me by the throat and slams me against the wall, knocking all of the oxygen from my lungs. She presses down, and I let out a small choked sound as she leans in close. Her lips brush my ear.

"Don't test me. I don't care what your last name is…"

Frowning, she pulls back, then loosens her grip just enough for me to gasp in a breath. But she doesn't release me. I stare at her, eyes wide, as she leans her face down to the crook of my neck. My heart races, but instead of sinking her fangs into my skin, she inhales deeply.

"You smell like…" She looks at me again, *really* looks at me.

My heart pounds against my ribs even harder. There's no way she could tell from my smell…could she?

"Oh." She squints at my face, finally letting her hand drop from my throat. "*Now* you've got me interested."

I turn to leave, but she grabs my arm, her nails digging in above my elbow.

"I'd be careful if I were you, little Darkmore," she hisses.

"Candace."

She releases me at the sound of Reginald's voice. He stands at the mouth of the hallway, eyes flickering from me to her. Candace bows her head marginally as he approaches, but the satisfied smile never leaves her face.

Reginald's eyes linger on my neck for a moment before turning back to Candace. My skin burns as my body fights to heal whatever bruises she caused. "What business do you have on the human floor?"

"Why don't you ask the halfling?"

Reginald goes very, very still.

Candace tilts her head to the side. "So you *did* know. Interesting. I wonder what Queen C—"

The bond tightens in my stomach, then Reginald turns into a flurry of movement. One moment, he's standing beside me, the next, he's beside Candace, his teeth tearing into her throat. Her blood splatters across the wall, then her body slumps to the ground between us.

I stare, immobile, as Reginald rips a handkerchief from his pocket and wipes the blood from his mouth.

"Well don't just stand there," he says. "Help me clean her up."

I stand motionless for another second, then my entire

body starts to tremble as Candace's blood drips down my face. Blood still oozes out of her torn-open throat into the carpet.

Reginald sighs and hands me the handkerchief. I take it with shaking hands and quickly scrub my skin.

"It had to be done."

"Did it?" I ask, my voice high and on the verge of breaking.

He steps up in front of me, forcing me to look at him. "It did," he says lowly. "Now let's clean this up before any of the humans see."

When I glance down, Candace's open eyes lock on mine, and I quickly look away. My hand shakes as I switch out my blade to perform the same spell I did in the parking garage. Reginald lays his hand over mine as I struggle to line the blade up with my arm.

"Are you all right?" he asks quietly. "Did she hurt you?"

"I'm fine." I rub the back of my hand along my mouth.

"What happened before I got up here? What was she doing on this floor—what are *you* doing here?"

"I could ask you the same question," I say, but my voice comes out weak.

"I felt your fear all the way outside."

My focus drifts back to Connor's door. Unable to say it aloud, I hope it transfers through the bond. Reginald doesn't say anything for several moments.

"Do you know how many other vampires have been involved in this?" he finally asks.

I shake my head, gaze still trained on the door.

"I'll take care of it. They won't be bothering him anymore." I turn to look at him, but his face gives nothing away. When I still don't move, his expression softens. "You have my word."

"And her?" I gesture to Candace's unmoving body. A missing vampire at the estate won't go unnoticed.

"I'll take care of it," he says again.

I meet his eyes, but his expression invites no further conversation. I swallow hard and bring the blade to my skin again. "Let's just get this over with."

CHAPTER SIXTEEN

THREE SHOWERS later and there's still blood under my fingernails. I tuck my hands into my sleeves so I don't have to see it as I shoulder my way into the empty lobby of the annex building. The assembly must be in one of the basement halls. I take the wide, spiral staircase down, following the sounds of voices until I come to the right room. It's one of the smaller lecture halls, and the majority of the seats are already filled when I slip in the back door. There was a little over a hundred students in our year in the running for the Marionettes, but by the looks of it, at least half of us have already been eliminated.

I grab the first empty seat I see and sweep the room, searching for Monroe or Kirby.

"Hey, Darkmore." Wes slides into the seat beside me and pushes the hair out of his eyes.

I quirk an eyebrow at him, but bite back the snarky comment on my tongue about him sitting with me. With

Daniel still in the hospital, he probably doesn't have anyone else to sit with.

"You nervous?" I ask instead.

He leans back in his chair and props his feet out. "Nah. They'd be crazy to cut me. *You* on the other hand…" He glances at me sideways and winks.

I elbow him. "I'm not the one whose group members hated him so much they tried to poison him."

He blows the air out of his cheeks and shakes his head, but he's smiling. "Low blow." He runs his hands up and down his thighs. "Daniel said you went to see him. He'll never tell you this—and *I'll* personally push you off the clock tower if you tell him I said anything—but I think it meant a lot to him. No one else—well, it was just cool of you."

The seriousness of his expression is so out of place, it leaves me momentarily speechless.

I clear my throat. "He doing any better?"

Wes presses his lips together and nods once. "Think they're gonna let him sleep in his own bed tonight. So that's something."

Not knowing what else to say, I reach over and give his arm a brief squeeze. Any other time, he'd probably shove me off. But today, he just takes a deep breath and lays his hand over mine, his gaze trained forward and the line of his jaw hard. I don't think I've ever seen him with facial hair before, but it looks like he hasn't shaved in days, the stubble coming in thick and dark.

"I'm still gonna kick your ass in the second week of trials," he murmurs, releasing me.

"You can try."

A hush falls over the crowd as the door at the front of the room bangs open and Coderre steps up to the podium. She shuffles the papers and folds her hands in front of her.

"Today I'll be announcing which of you will not be continuing on with the second week of initiation, which also means your time at this academy has come to an end. I think I speak for all of the faculty here at York Academy when I say your efforts this past week have done us proud. But unfortunately, not everyone has what it takes to be a Marionette. Let's get started, shall we?"

As she starts listing off names, one by one, the people who have been cut rise from their seats and hurry from the room. My shoulders tense a little more each time. The anxiety in the room is palpable, and it's like I can *feel* everyone else's as much as my own. Dozens of different thundering pulses pound in my ears, building on each other and layering until I can't focus on anything else.

My throat isn't aching nearly as much now that I've had some blood, so at least I'm not fighting the urge to rip out the throat of the girl next to me. But I can smell the sweat beading on her forehead as she leans forward, hanging on to the headmistress's every word. I can smell her fear like a perfume, smell the despair of the guy currently heading up the steps, his head hung low.

Their anxiety builds on my skin like static electricity, and I can't tell which feelings are *mine* anymore. I hang my head forward and look at my hands, but then I notice the dark lines of dried blood under my nails again.

The images come rushing back—the look on Candace's face, the way her eyes had seemed to follow me as Reginald and I cleaned up the hall. He didn't say a word after that.

No explanation. Which was worse than anything he could have said.

He'd said he didn't want me telling anyone, that he didn't want anyone to know…but I didn't realize that meant anyone who *did* find out had to die. If keeping it a secret is more important than their sacred laws against killing other vampires in the region…

"Valerie?" Wes says next to me, but his voice sounds far away.

A second, sharper spike of anxiety fills the air as the headmistress narrows down to the last few names, drawing me back to the room. The voices get so loud that my head pulses, and I lean forward, holding my forehead with both hands, trying to block it all out and force myself to focus on my breath. Even with my eyes closed, I can hear the wooden stairs groan under the footsteps of each person as they leave, the hushed voices across the room.

"What does she have to worry about?" whispers a girl behind me. "Of course they're not going to cut a Darkmore."

My head pops up, and I blink hard, trying to clear the voices from my head.

"*And* I hear someone caught her in the prince's room back at the estate."

When my vision refocuses, I realize half the room has already left. Through the empty seats, I catch sight of the back of Kirby's and Monroe's heads in the front row.

The blanket of anxiety in the air eases, and now Coderre is moving back toward the door.

Kirby and Monroe look back and catch my eye. Kirby offers a hesitant wave, her eyebrows drawn together. My ears fill with the buzzing again as I push to my feet and head for the exit. Wes says something, but I don't hear it. The sounds of everyone else leaving are so loud in my head that it's almost unbearable.

I slam into the door and break into the cool night air, sucking as much into my lungs as I can. I need to get away from all these people.

"Valerie," someone says behind me, or maybe I just think they're behind me. Maybe they're all the way back in the lecture hall talking about me, and I can still *hear them.*

A tug in the center of my stomach makes me stop and let my back fall against the cold bricks of the building. It's a faint feeling, the barest tug of the string connecting us. He tugs again, lighter this time, but it's enough to pull me out of my head and back into my surroundings. It's not enough to quiet all of the noise, but it's a start.

I walk back toward the dorms. The more distance I put between me and the crowd, the less my head pounds. It can't always be like this. There must be a way to turn it all off.

When I make it home, I collapse into bed. I didn't get cut before the second round, so at least that's one fewer thing to worry about today. On top of all the new worries my last visit to the estate prompted, I don't think I could handle any more.

WHEN I OPEN my eyes again, the entire world is upside down. My back is pressed against a ceiling, held up by some invisible force. I try to stretch my arms out to my sides, but my body won't move.

A moan pulls my attention to the bed below me—not mine, but one I recognize. One with thick, red curtains and intricately carved wooden posts.

A girl is on her knees on the bed, her skin shiny with sweat, her dark hair splayed out around her as she buries her face in the silk pillows. A man is kneeling behind her, the muscles of his back rippling as he grips her hips and pounds himself into her again and again. She cries out each time, her hands fisting in the sheets.

"Fuck," the man grunts and leans over the girl, grabbing her hair in one fist.

My entire body goes cold at his voice. I try to look away, but my head won't move.

I must be dreaming. I squeeze my eyes closed, trying to wake up, but the pounding and the moaning and the creaking of the bed all continue on.

Reginald grabs the girl and flips her onto her back. She lets out a breathy laugh and leans back on the pillows, revealing a black silk blindfold over her eyes. Then her feet are on Reginald's shoulders, and they're going again. She cries out as he slams into her, harder each time, as he utters something in a voice too low for me to hear.

"Fuck yes," she breathes.

She's human, I realize with a start. He spreads her legs wide around him, revealing a bite mark on her inner thigh, and a small trail of blood runs down her skin. He pulls away from her for a moment, and she whimpers. A light chuckle shakes his shoulders, and he leans down until his lips are right next to her ear.

"You haven't had enough yet?" he murmurs.

She bites her lip and shakes her head, then hooks her legs around his waist and flips him onto the bed so she can climb on top. He grins up at her, his hands finding her hips as she braces her hands on his chest and repositions herself. Just as she guides herself back onto him, Reginald's eyes flicker up to the ceiling.

And then widen, locking directly onto mine.

I gasp and lurch up in my bed. Whipping my head back and forth, I take in the familiar surroundings of my dorm room and let out a shaky breath. When I bring my hand to my chest, my heart races against my palm.

"Fuck." I push the sweaty hair out of my face. "It was just a dream," I whisper as my heart finally starts to slow. But as I lie back down, the shock lingers in my body, right behind my navel.

And it doesn't feel like it's coming from me.

CHAPTER SEVENTEEN

I DON'T HEAR from Reginald for the rest of the weekend—
not a text, not even a feeling through the bond. I can't stop
thinking about Candace and whatever the hell that dream
was. But I can't tell if this silence is normal and he's just
busy—maybe getting ready to surprise me with a task after
that conversation at the estate—or if I should be…worried.

After class on Monday, Kirby and I head into town to
work on our paper. Blood and Buzz is quiet this time of day
in the brief period between the early evening rush and
lunch. A man carting in a shipment of blood for the
vampire drinks holds the door open for us, and every
muscle in my body tenses, though the smell is faint through
the wooden boxes. At least I'd had the foresight to down a
blood bag in my room before coming here. I hold my
breath as we pass, and Kirby and I head for one of the
booths in the back corner. A neon sign hangs directly above
us—bright red lips with fangs—and it casts a pink tint over

our table. A few other girls from school are sitting on the bar stools, but other than that, the shop is empty.

"Latte?" Kirby asks, then pauses, her eyes flickering from me to the menu. "Or do you want...*you know?*"

I smirk. "Latte is fine."

She smiles, seeming relieved, and sets her things down before heading to the counter to order. I pull up all of the materials we have about wendigos and a notebook, pausing again at the illustration on the first page. What's probably so unnerving about them is how they manage to look so human and yet not human at all. They're somehow emaciated and gluttonous at the same time. They often appear skeletal, but no matter how much they consume, it never satisfies.

Kirby reappears with the drinks and slides one of the coffees toward me. She twists her own cup in her hands over and over again, her teeth deep in her lower lip. "How are you doing?" she asks.

"I'm okay." I sip the coffee, relieved to find the taste isn't much different for me now, just stronger. I should probably cut back how many pumps of syrup I have them put in though. It nearly coats my tongue. I wince and set the cup back down. "Adjusting. How has your initiation been going?"

"Clearly not as exciting as yours has, but I like Alice. She's been a good partner."

"Tell me about her! I want to know everything. I'm sorry I've been kind of...AWOL."

She sits up straighter and tosses her hair over her shoulders. "Well, it certainly makes a lot more sense now. And as far as excuses go, it's a pretty good one." A small smile crosses her face. "Alice is around the prince's age, I think. And she's never been paired, so I'm her first. She's actually, like, really funny. She and Monroe would probably get along. She's from the estate in Norway, but was transferred here when she turned eighteen. She still has an accent—it's cute."

I try to fold my smile between my lips, but it comes out just the same. "Kirby…do you have a *crush* on her?"

Kirby's eyes widen, and she reaches across the table to smack my arm, but a hint of a blush creeps up her cheeks. "Shut up."

I hold up my palms. "Okay, okay. We only have a few days to get this project done though, so we should get to work." I point to one of the passages and push the book toward her. "You think we should focus the paper on Wendigo Psychosis?"

Kirby sips her drink. "Wendigo what now?"

"Psychosis." I pull a highlighter out of my bag. "Didn't you read *anything* about them before picking them for our subject?"

She shrugs. "Nope. We should've just done something easy like werewolves. What's Monroe's group doing?"

I flip the page. "I don't know, maybe a harpy?"

I nudge the book toward her again, and she finally glances down. "So if they don't eat you, they possess you, or they make you want to eat people," she concludes.

"Not necessarily eat people." I pull up another article and highlight the final paragraph. "It says it can cause *extreme greed, gluttony, and excess*—which, yes, often shows up as cannibalism—but there have also been cases with other symptoms, depending on how the wendigo was created in the first place."

Kirby blows on her drink and narrows her eyes at me over the cup. "Why do you seem, like, weirdly into this?"

"You're not going to help me at all with this paper, are you?"

"I am helping!" She wags a finger between us. "This is me helping!"

Sighing, I pull the article back up and scan the rest of the page. "The first recorded legends believed wendigos were once humans who were forced to consume human flesh to survive—it made them stronger, but they also couldn't stop. The more flesh they consumed, the less human they became themselves, until eventually they were completely driven by their never-ending hunger. We know now, that's not necessarily true." I flip back to the textbook. "In order for someone to become a wendigo, they either had to have some kind of magic in them to begin with, or the help of a witch to purposefully transform them."

"Who would do that on purpose?" Kirby mutters.

The bells above the front door ding as someone steps inside. I'm already scanning the next page when Kirby reaches across the table and nudges me.

I turn and see Daniel walking toward the counter. The girls on the bar stools are staring, too, as the woman behind the register turns away to get his order. I half expect to see Wes standing behind him, but he's alone.

My stomach sinks the same way it had at brunch yesterday—has anyone else been to see him since I did?

Based on what Wes said at the assembly yesterday, it doesn't sound like it. Everyone else has probably been too swept up in initiation. I can't imagine what it would be like to lie in that hospital bed all this time and have no one even come to see me. We might not like each other half the time, but being brought up in this kind of environment creates a weird camaraderie. He looks around him as he waits for his order, like he's trying to find a place to sit.

I'm sliding out from my seat before I realize it, and I step up beside him. "Hey, Daniel."

He glances down at me, and there's a slight sheen over his eyes. He looks a lot better than he did that day in the hospital, but his skin is still pale, the circles beneath his eyes dark. A weak smile appears. "Hey, Darkmore."

"I didn't know you were out yet—it's good to see you."

"Here's your order." The woman sets his cup on the counter, and he nods a quick thanks. His hand shakes as he picks up the cup.

"How are you feeling?" I ask.

"Not a hundred percent, but they let me go back to staying at my own place today, so at least that's something."

"They still don't know why…" I trail off.

He smirks. "I look like I should be on my deathbed? No."

"Well, I wasn't going to say it like *that*."

"Oh, don't go soft on me now, Darkmore. You're the only one who tells it like it is."

I smile, relieved he's still in the mood to joke around at least. He glances around the shop at the other empty tables again.

"Do you"—I nod back toward our table—"want to come sit with us?"

He doesn't say anything, but follows me over and takes the seat next to Kirby. No one says anything, and we all sip our drinks. A heavy silence settles over the table, and I can't help but think about how Daniel was always the one to lighten the room, always the first to start a conversation, the first to laugh, even when his comments were annoying half the time. He appraises the books strewn across the table and tugs out the paper sticking out of my notebook.

"Samantha Hawthorne?" he asks. "What's this for?"

"Nothing." I grab the obituary back from him, and he raises his eyebrows. "I—uh—was looking into some other blood witches the other day. Just curiosity and whatnot."

Daniel frowns. "She looks…sick."

We meet each other's eyes, and I can't help but compare Samantha's picture to Daniel's face. The lines under his eyes are in the same places, so are the hollow curves of his cheeks. I wish I could check her neck for bite marks, but it's covered by her hair.

He nods at the paper. "How'd she die?"

"It doesn't say."

Daniel's frown deepens, and Kirby's head swivels between the two of us. "Why do I feel like you two are having a conversation that I don't understand right now?"

Daniel's gaze doesn't leave my hands. "Can I see that?"

I hand the obituary back over, then fish around in my bag for the other article I printed about her and slide it across the table.

"She was a blood witch, right?" he asks.

"You said her last name was Hawthorne?" Kirby asks.

I nod.

"They're all down in the cemetery behind the school—the Hawthornes, I mean. I think most of the old blood witch families are back there."

I stare at her, my mind working, and she shifts her weight. "What?"

Daniel meets my eyes again. "These might not be able to tell us what happened to her." He sets the papers back on the table. "But we could ask her."

<hr />

"I CANNOT BELIEVE you guys talked me into this," says Kirby as she jogs after us down the hill, her high-heeled boots barely finding purchase in the frozen earth.

"No one forced you to come," I remind her over my shoulder.

She huffs. "I cannot *believe* you're trying to get rid of me."

The campus is quiet as we head toward the cemetery. Daniel is silent beside me as Kirby trails behind, cursing as she goes. My bag slaps against my side with each step as we follow the old, rocky path, and I hunch my shoulders against the cold. It had been so warm earlier, but the temperature dropped out of nowhere.

The campus's light fixtures stop about halfway there, and we hike the rest of the way in near-darkness. With my newly heightened sight, I can still tell it's dark, but my eyes can see every detail of my surroundings as if it were the middle of the day. Kirby and Daniel, however, spend the first few minutes stumbling after me before one of them finally pulls out a light.

The iron gate creaks as I push it aside, and we continue past the small plots at the front. All of the major family mausoleums are toward the back. A lump rises in my throat as we pass the Darkmore section, but I keep my gaze averted from Calla's grave.

The Hawthorne mausoleum is on the smaller side, carved from white stone with two pillars at the front. It takes a few shoves with my shoulder before I get the door open. Dust puffs up around me as I step inside, and I cough.

Kirby shines her flashlight around the space. There's a single window on the far wall that lets in the barest trace of moonlight. Dead flowers line the floor, though with the entire family gone now, I'm not sure who would still be coming in here.

Daniel lingers by the door as Kirby and I pace inside. We'd stopped at the dorm after the coffee shop to grab some supplies, and I'd picked a few of the flowers that grew along the paths at the last minute. Maybe it was silly, but it felt right. Showing some respect, especially if we want to get on her good graces, can't hurt.

I pull the small bouquet of white flowers from my bag and set them against the marble wall as I scan the rows for one name in particular. At the very bottom corner, I see it.

Samantha Hawthorne.

Whether she's actually buried in here, or it's just her name with an empty drawer behind it, I'm not sure. Hopefully it won't matter.

One by one, I pull the supplies from my bag and lay them out on the floor. Samantha's obituary is last, and I lay it beside her name, hoping it'll be the next best thing to having something that belonged to her. I wouldn't have the faintest idea of how to get something like that, seeing as she's been dead for a century and she's not even from my bloodline.

Once the summoning candles are perfectly positioned, I light them going clockwise around the triangle, and Kirby sprinkles some herbs into the flames. They immediately fill the mausoleum with their earthy, floral scents. As I reach the final candle, Daniel appears beside me and sinks onto his knees. I meet his eyes, and he nods.

"Please work," I mutter under my breath as I bring my blade across my palm, letting the blood spill onto the obituary and surrounding herbs.

We don't officially cover summoning spells until our final year at the academy, but how hard can it be?

Daniel offers his hand, and I do the same. Kirby cuts her own with a small knife, and we layer our palms on top of each other.

"Samantha Hawthorne, we summon you."

The wind picks up outside, and tree branches crash against the roof overhead. I squeeze my hand into a fist, forcing more blood to drip onto the concrete as the candles flicker.

"Samantha Hawthorne," I repeat, my voice wavering this time. "We need you."

The candles all snuff out at once, sending winding trails of smoke into the air.

Thunder rolls outside, and a flash of lightning cuts

through the room. A figure illuminates in the corner, and I gasp and shove myself back.

She's in a long, white nightdress, though her skin is even paler, and her long hair is braided down her back. She flickers, like she's barely holding her foot in this realm. I might not have much time.

I stand, and her wide, black eyes lock on to me.

"Samantha Hawthorne?" I whisper.

She looks me up and down. Tree branches knock against the roof, and she flinches, head whipping back and forth to take in her surroundings.

Daniel and Kirby rise to their feet, looking around wildly. Their heads snap from me to the space Samantha Hawthorne is hovering, but their eyes don't focus.

"Is she here?" Daniel whispers.

Samantha glances at him, then back to me. "Why have you called on me?"

"I—" I pull out the stack of papers I'd printed about her—everything I could find, which wasn't much. "We need to know what happened to you."

Her eyes narrow and then fall to the mess of blood on the floor.

"Please," I say.

"You're not safe here," she says, and her body flickers again, this time taking longer to reappear. "None of us are."

"What do you mean? At the academy?" I nod to Daniel and Kirby. "Why can't they see you?"

She turns her head as if to look at something, though all that's there is a blank wall. "Only blood can call to blood."

"You mean blood witches?"

She turns to me again, a sad look on her face now. She takes in the sheen of sweat on Daniel's forehead, the paleness of his skin. "It's already started again, hasn't it?"

"Again? What's happening? Please—"

"Be careful where you go alone, Valerie Darkmore."

Another strike of lightning illuminates the room, and I jump at the crack of thunder. Once the light disappears, she's gone with it.

CHAPTER EIGHTEEN

I LET my first cigarette fall to the ground, snuff it out with the heel of my boot, and immediately pull out a second. The moon is high and bright above me as I lean against a headstone, tilt my head back, and blow a cloud of smoke into the air. I glance at Calla's grave and can practically *feel* her judgment radiating from wherever she is.

I can picture the face she'd make perfectly—pursed lips, arched eyebrows. And if you asked her *What?* she'd sniff, look away, and say something along the lines of *Oh, nothing.* She invented passive aggressive. But then she'd smile, never staying annoyed with us for more than a few seconds.

My fingers shake as I bring the cigarette back to my mouth.

Thoroughly creeped out and frustrated from the lack of actual answers, Daniel and Kirby trudged back to school shortly after Samantha Hawthorne disappeared, but I still haven't been able to bring myself to head back.

A cold breeze tickles the back of my neck, sending a

shiver down my spine. I could try to summon her again, try to get some real answers, but something tells me she wouldn't come back. Even as a ghost—someone already dead and untouchable—she seemed scared to be here. However Samantha Hawthorne died, she died afraid.

Footsteps crunch on the ground behind me, but somehow, I know exactly who it is without turning. He comes up and leans against the headstone on my right. Neither of us says anything for a while, and I blow out another cloud of smoke.

"You trying to avoid our next task?" he asks. "Is that why you're hiding out here?"

"You can find me anywhere, so what kind of stupid plan would that be?"

"Congrats on making it to the second round, by the way."

I roll my eyes. We both know nothing I did caused that to happen. "What can I help you with, *Your Highness*?"

"Well, we could start with why you were in my bedroom the other night."

My heart stops in my chest, and the cigarette falls from my fingers. I turn to him, eyes wide. He stares back, expressionless.

"I thought I was dreaming," I murmur.

"Do you typically dream about me that way?" he muses. "*I* don't mind, but my partners may have thoughts about it."

My face flames. "I didn't—I was going to bed," I sputter. "And when I woke up, I was *there*. And I couldn't leave."

He frowns thoughtfully and looks straight ahead again. "Interesting."

A long beat of silence stretches between us, and images of that night materialize back into my head unbidden. The flashes of skin and sweat and hands fisted in sheets. The sound of their bodies coming together, and Reginald's low voice as he murmured in her ear—

I force the memories away and cross my arms over my chest.

"Well," he says finally. "See anything you like?"

I pick up a stick and throw it at him. "What the hell is happening? What *is* this bond between us?"

He bends over to retrieve the stick and spins it between his hands. "I'm not sure. I've bonded with two other witches before—my previous partners—but it was never like this. It's...peculiar."

"Peculiar? It's fucking weird. How do we make it stop?"

He turns to me, the barest whisper of a smile on his lips, and shrugs. "I don't think we can."

The wind picks up again, and I wrap my arms around myself.

"What are you doing out here anyway?" he asks.

"I thought you knew *everything* about me now."

He chuckles. "I can feel when you're so hungry you're about to rip someone's throat out. I can't read your mind."

I glance at the Hawthorne mausoleum and think back to Samantha's ominous, but not at all helpful, warning. It could've meant anything. *You're not safe here.*

The second part, however, there was no mixing that up.

Be careful where you go alone.

Reginald follows my gaze, and his frown deepens.

"Who were those guys at the estate the other night?" I blurt out, hoping to distract him enough to drop it.

If he looked unhappy before, it's nothing compared to the shadow that falls over his face now. "Some of the vampires from the Vasiliev estate in Russia are visiting my mother. I...have a history with some of them. They're not particularly good company to keep."

I lift an eyebrow. "A history?"

"If you come by the estate again before they leave, avoid them, if you can, okay?"

I frown, but nod.

He claps his hands together. "Anyway. You may have made it past the first round, but we *do* still have something to do tonight."

I sigh. "You're not going to make me go all the way back to the estate again, are you?"

He shakes his head as he rises to his feet and waves for me to join him. "Just into town this time. Promise."

———

THE CHURCH IS on the corner of the human side of town—a part I definitely do not frequent. I think in the three years I've been at the academy I may have come this far down Main Street once.

This appears to be where Reginald is taking me today. We head toward the front entrance, and humans bow their heads and quickly step out of our path when they see Reginald, murmuring something I don't catch under their breath. He continues on like he doesn't see them, but a muscle in his jaw jumps.

We head straight for the priest's office in the back, passing a dozen empty lines of pews. A man wanders through the rows with cleaning equipment, sanitizing the donation centers placed at the front of each seat—a small wooden box with an opening for the human to slide their hand inside. The box has a sensor and automatically drains the required amount of blood from their wrist, then bandages it. They must have just had a service.

The priest rises from behind his desk, head bowed. When he looks back up, his eyes are glistening with something that looks like awe. "Your Highness."

Reginald nods his head toward me. "My partner is here to check your logs for this week."

"Of course. Of course." The priest rustles through one of his desk drawers and pulls out a clipboard. He bows to Reginald again as he comes around the side of the desk and hands the papers to me. "If you'll excuse me, I have an appointment…?"

The priest lingers in the doorway, gaze drifting back to Reginald as if waiting for permission.

"Yes, of course," mutters Reginald.

The priest bows yet again before finally slipping from the room. I raise my eyebrows, but say nothing. It's been a while since I've been around humans—at least, humans who don't work directly for vampires. I almost forgot how *annoying* their worship can be. How thoroughly they believe the vampire propaganda that highlights them all as gods.

I busy myself with scanning the page—on the left side is a printed list of names. There's a slot beside the names for each week of the month, where the person is required to sign off after they've given their weekly blood donation. Nearly every box is filled on the sheet, except one name is crossed out altogether—deceased—and one name at the bottom has an empty box for this week and no signature from the priest for an excusable absence.

"Derek Brown." I hand the clipboard to Reginald. "He missed this week."

Reginald sighs heavily and sets the clipboard back on the priest's desk. "I'll take you back to the academy now," he says without looking at me.

"You don't want me to come with you?" I ask. "Isn't it normally the Marionettes' job to find the person and collect their skipped donation?"

Reginald meets my eyes, suddenly looking exhausted. "This is his fourth time."

I inhale sharply but steel myself. "I should still come."

He doesn't say anything at first. He just turns away and starts heading for the door, leaving me to jog to catch up with him. Once I'm at his side again, he looks at me out of the corner of his eyes, his expression unreadable. "If you insist."

———————

DEREK BROWN LIVES in the opposite direction of the academy in the apartment on top of the apothecary on Main Street. Our car idles out front, and Reginald looks over at me, hesitating before opening his door and climbing out. I try to brace myself as we head up the stairs to the second floor, my heart fluttering in my chest. Despite my efforts to hide my nerves from my expression, I know Reginald can feel it, because I can feel *his* dread like a steady drum in my stomach.

Reginald knocks on the door and waits. My hearing

picks up on a cacophony of noises—the TV next door, the dishwasher downstairs, a woman laughing at the end of the hall—but I try to focus on the room in front of us. Then, slowly, a racing heartbeat comes to the forefront of my attention.

Oh, Derek Brown is inside, all right. And he knows we're here.

"He's trying to climb out the back window," I mutter.

Reginald sighs, already turning for the stairs. "I know."

He picks up the pace, his long strides eating up the distance seemingly with no effort. Just as we reach the back of the building, Derek Brown tumbles from his window and lands in the bushes below.

"Derek Brown," Reginald says calmly.

Derek's bushy red hair pops up from the weeds, his bulging eyes taking in our approach. He pivots like he's going to run, but I've already pricked my finger and let the drop of blood fall onto the earth. I imagine the blood running through his veins turning to ice, hardening his muscles into stone. Derek freezes midstride, unable to move.

Reginald considers me over his shoulder with a raised eyebrow.

I shrug.

"I was hoping you'd taken our conversation from a few weeks ago to heart, Derek," says Reginald as he paces closer, coming to a stop inches from the human. His voice comes out cold, hard. "This was your fourth strike."

"Please," whispers Derek, his entire body trembling now.

Reginald moves so fast my eyes can hardly detect it. His fangs tear through Derek's throat, splattering his blood across the grass. I gasp and jump back a step as his limp body collapses into the bushes. When Reginald turns back around, his fangs are still extended, dripping with Derek's blood, his eyes glowing in the moonlight.

The scent of blood crashes into me like a wave a moment later, and my mouth waters. I suck in a sharp breath and take another step back, as if putting more distance between us will lessen the pulsing in my gums.

Reginald whips the handkerchief from his pocket and cleans his face. He glances at me, practically vibrating with need where I stand. "Fuck," he mutters, already walking past me and back toward the car.

"I—" I look from Derek's crumpled body to Reginald's retreating form.

"Come on. Alexander will get it," he calls without looking back.

Sure enough, his driver—Alexander, evidently—comes around the corner with a large tarp in his hands. He doesn't meet my eyes as he passes me, and I silently follow Reginald back to the car. He's already in his seat and looking out the window when I climb in, and I can't help but wonder how many times he's done this. If it fazes him anymore—the death, the blood, the bodies. He didn't even hesitate.

Candace's unseeing eyes flash into my mind, and I shake my head, trying to clear it. He hadn't hesitated then either. We'd cleaned up the body, but surely the estate won't overlook one of their vampires disappearing. What happens then?

The bond is eerily quiet like he's purposefully blocking me from whatever he's feeling. If he hadn't killed Derek Brown, someone else would have—I know that. The law is the law. And if his sentence was an execution, then he must have had a lot more on his record, otherwise he would've been dragged to the closest blood farm.

But if he doesn't want me to dispose of the body, what are they going to do with it?

The car dips as Alexander deposits the body in the trunk, then silently climbs back into the driver's seat.

"Are you taking me back to the academy?"

A muscle in Reginald's jaw jumps. "No."

I don't ask any more questions, and no one else offers any more information. People amble along the sidewalk as we head back down Main Street, coming to the park at the center. There's a crumbling statue above the fountain—a human on a horse who must have been significant at one point, but I don't recognize him—surrounded by benches and stretches of grass. This is where Alexander parks, and when Reginald climbs out of the car, he doesn't look at me.

People stop and stare as Reginald and Alexander pop the trunk and pull out the tarp. Derek hits the ground hard, and he rolls out, his blood smearing across the pavement. I linger by the car, hugging my arms to myself as a crowd accumulates on the sidewalk. We all watch silently as they pull Derek's body toward the statue. Alexander returns to the car and grabs rope out of the trunk, then they get to stringing him up.

When they're done, he hangs with his arms spread wide, blood dripping from his shoes and staining the fountain below him red. I can't look away. His head lolls against his chest, hair still stirring in the breeze. I don't notice Reginald has come back to the car until he's right behind me, fingers brushing my elbow.

"Let's go," he says, voice low.

I climb back in and stare out the window as we pull away from the curb. Crowds of humans linger on the sidewalk.

"It's to send some kind of message, right?" I ask, my voice thick.

Reginald doesn't answer.

"How many times have you done that? How many people?"

He doesn't answer that either.

It's not until Alexander is pulling up to the academy's gates that he finally speaks again. "We only have one task left together before your final trial in front of the court. I haven't scheduled it yet, so I'll have to let you know."

I stare at him, but when it's clear that's all he's going to say, I nod and climb out into the cold night. They drive away before I have a chance to start walking, and I stand there staring at the smear of blood along their taillights until they disappear into the darkness.

CHAPTER NINETEEN

My dreams are full of blood that night. We're in the city, Reginald and I, and there's a list of names in my pocket. I point out people on the streets as we pass, and Reginald grabs them by the throat, holding them still so I can sink my teeth into their necks and drink until they stop struggling. It's intoxicating, the blood. It runs down my lips, over my chin. It's so warm when it hits the back of my throat. We go through human after human, faceless body after faceless body. But it's not enough. Never enough. When we're done, the street is full of their lifeless corpses piled on top of each other, and blood covers my face, my chest, and my hands. Reginald grins at me under the streetlights, his fangs protruding over his lips.

I wake with a start, gasping for air and covered in sweat. It takes a minute for my vision to focus on the room around me. I lift my hands in front of my face, still warm from the dream. There's no blood on them despite the feeling of it being under my nails, so I drop them back to my sides and stare at the ceiling. I feel nothing through the bond this time, so this dream must have been all mine.

The clock beside my bed informs me I have less than twenty minutes to pull myself together and get down to the field for today's practical test, but instead of the usual urgency this would evoke, I lie there for another minute, still waiting for my heart to slow.

Once I've slipped on my uniform and pulled my hair into a high ponytail, I instinctively reach for the perfume bottle on my desk and stare at my empty hand when it catches air. I haven't had any more fainting spells or issues with my powers since Reginald took it, and yet, that doesn't bring me much comfort. Especially not after my encounter with Samantha Hawthorne's ghost yesterday.

"You look like shit," says Monroe as I take my spot beside her in line. The sky is full of clouds, casting a gray tint over the campus. The rest of the class is already here, but as I look around the field, Zouche is noticeably absent.

My mind is still caught somewhere between the memory of last night with Derek Brown and that dream. I can't shake either of them. I bite my lip, double-checking no one is within hearing range, before I whisper, "Have you had to check the blood logs yet?"

Monroe's eyes widen, and a smile quickly spreads across her face. Far too excited about me breaking the rules, as usual. "That was my first task, actually."

"And did you have any skips?"

She nods. "A college student. It was her first offense though, so she just got a warning."

I blow the air out of my cheeks, Derek's body hanging

from the statue burned into my memory. His blood dripping from Reginald's face…

Is his body still there? How long will they leave him like that before someone cuts him down? Until he starts to rot or animals find him?

I shiver and shake my head, trying to clear it. "We had an execution last night."

Monroe gasps and looks around again before leaning toward me. "Did you have to do it?" she whispers.

I shake my head. "Reginald did."

Her eyebrows shoot up, and a small, satisfied smile finds her face. "*Reginald*, huh? Sounds like you two are getting *awfully close*."

I shove her in the shoulder. "Shut up."

"On a real note though, how is everything with Connor? Have you two patched things up?"

"I…" I trail off, my stomach sinking. I don't really know how to answer that question. I haven't heard from him in days. Not since the night of the blood exchange. And as more time goes on that he hasn't called, I can't help but think his girlfriend suddenly being half vampire…*changes* things for him. I've left him two voice mails over the past few days, but I haven't seen so much as a text in response. Even if this turned out to be some kind of deal breaker, I can't believe he wouldn't want to talk about it first. We've been together for six years, but we've been friends for more than twenty. That has to mean more than this.

I have to mean more to him than this.

"All right everyone!" Zouche calls as she jogs onto the field in an all-black tracksuit, her pixie cut standing up in sharp spikes. "Welcome to your final practical of initiation.

Congrats on making it this far. Today, you'll be tested in groups!"

Monroe and I exchange a sidelong glance as Zouche starts spouting off names and pointing to different spots around the field.

"Today is all about teamwork," she says. "When you join the Marionettes, you never know what other witches you'll be working with and from which disciplines. Valerie." She steps in front of me. "You'll be with Daniel, Beth, and Andie today." She waves the four of us over toward the forest-facing side of the clearing and moves on to the next group.

Andie practically skips over to us, a grin stretched from one end of her face to the other. I wonder if she realizes how cartoonish she looks. I guess she can't help that she's pocket-sized. Daniel has to crane his head down just to see her. I can't bring myself to look Beth in the eyes, despite her trying to catch my attention. The innocent gap-toothed smile is too much. Honestly, I'd feel better if she hated me. I keep hearing her muffled screams and how hot her blood had felt on my skin. How had I looked to Reginald—eyes crazed, blood dripping down my face?

Probably a lot like what I'd seen in that dream.

I step up beside Daniel, and he gives me a pained smile, though he looks better than he did yesterday. There's a little more color in his cheeks, a little less haze in his eyes. We all settle into an awkward circle, arms crossed over our chests, no one making eye contact.

Once the rest of the groups are assembled, Zouche returns to the center of the field and claps her hands to get everyone's attention. "Today's task is simple. I want you all to join energies so you can get to know and appreciate one another's powers. Channel each other. Once you've formed a secure connection, we'll go from there."

Andie bounces on her heels. I can *feel* her energy, and we haven't even started yet. Daniel takes Andie's hand first, his skin strikingly pale in comparison to hers, then reaches for me. I try not to cringe as I join hands with Beth on the other side.

The moment Beth's skin brushes mine, a ripple runs through our circle, like a jolt of electricity coursing between us. Daniel's hand tightens around mine as we all close our eyes and sync our breath together.

At first, the energy is an indiscernible, tangled web. Slowly, the different threads start to break apart, and I can see them as different colors in my mind's eye—red for my blood magic, green for Andie's elemental magic, silver for Beth's lunar magic, and orange for Daniel's skinwalking. The threads slowly spiral together in the space between us, and my skin warms.

But then something shifts. The darkness behind my eyes fades as an image swims into view—the heart of the forest behind us. I whip my head around, confused. The trees appear like smoke, slowly sinking into their places, the darkness itself like fog clinging to the ground.

I can still feel the others like sunlight against my skin, but when I look around, I'm alone. A light breeze rustles through the trees, scattering dead leaves at my feet. The temperature drops, the coldness pressing in from all sides. My breath puffs up in a cloud in front of me, and something moves to my right.

I spin around, and my entire body goes still. There are

three figures, possibly more, considering the fog is too thick to see beyond them. Their eyes glow in the darkness, and their long, black cloaks blend in with the shadows. Antlers sprout from each of their heads, though the one in the middle's are noticeably larger. They're deathly still, but I know they see me.

They're watching me.

I swallow hard and take a step back. A stick cracks beneath my foot and echoes in the silence. Slowly, the figure in the middle rises into the air like it's floating.

My breath catches in my throat as it continues up until it's levitating several feet in the air, the end of its frayed cloak just reaching the antlers of its companions. Slowly, it spreads its arms to the side, revealing long, slender fingers that end in claws.

My heart pounds in my chest, and the one on the right tilts its head as if sniffing the air. As if it can smell my fear. The hood falls back to reveal its gaunt face—a face I've seen in all of the books for my project with Kirby.

No.

I clench my hands into fists at my sides and try to look around without moving my head. The forest stretches endlessly in every direction.

This isn't real, I remind myself. I'm in the field with Andie, Daniel, and Beth. Whatever this is, it's some kind of projection.

A hallucination. A dream. A test.

This must be the real task today. Maybe Madame Darlington shared my project's subject with Zouche. That's what this is.

It must be.

All I need to do is break the connection.

I try squeezing my eyes shut and opening them, pinching myself—but the figures don't disappear.

The one in the center creeps toward me, its cloak trailing behind and swaying in the breeze. Maybe I'm supposed to use what I know to kill them, but I don't have any fire, and I don't have any silver. I hold my ground, lifting my chin. At the very least, I can control whether I give them any fear to feed off of.

But as it approaches and lowers onto the ground a pace away from me, a flicker of doubt flames in my chest. It towers over me by several feet and casts me into shadow. It makes no noise as it moves—it doesn't even appear to breathe. The hood of its cloak covers the top half of its face, the bottom half covered by an animal's skull.

Behind it, the others lift slowly into the air, and I realize there are more of them—many more. Their dark silhouettes lift into the fog, one after the other after the other, until I can't differentiate their forms from the trees.

They can't expect me to fight all of them. I don't stand a chance.

I have to wake up.

Wake up. Wake *up*. *Wake up.*

I can no longer feel the heat of the others on my skin. It's just me here in the cold, with this creature looming above me, silent and still.

"You're not real," I whisper, trying to convince myself.

The sleeve of its cloak falls back, revealing its long, jagged claws. Before I have a chance to react, it thrusts its claws forward and digs them into my chest.

My entire body ignites with a different kind of heat, and I scream.

———

ONCE I'VE STARTED SCREAMING, I can't stop. They come out one after the other, barely taking a pause for breath. My throat aches as blood wells on my chest, and the pain spreads like flames consuming my skin. Darkness surrounds me, and I squeeze my eyes shut.

"Valerie."

"Oh my God."

"*Valerie.*"

Something presses against my chest, and the pain sears into me like a hot brand tearing through skin. My eyes fly open to see the dark sky and stars above me. A blurry face hovers to my right, and slowly, Daniel's face swims into view.

"Can you hear me?" he asks.

I gasp, and my hands fly to my chest. They come away slick with blood.

"What happened?" barks Zouche. She stomps over and appears on my left side, her face creased in worry despite the annoyed tone of her voice.

Andie starts stuttering out a nonsensical answer as Zouche bends to inspect my chest. I try to look down, but all I see is the shreds of fabric soaked in blood.

Like claws tore through my chest.

And the way fresh blood keeps seeping out—it doesn't look like it's healing.

"What the hell happened?" Zouche demands as she

wedges her hands under my shoulders. "Help me get her up. We need to take her to the healer. Class is dismissed! Valerie?" She leans toward me and lowers her voice as several pairs of hands hoist me into the air. "What was it? What did this?"

What was I supposed to see? I try to ask, but I only manage to cough up blood all over myself.

"Mrs. Zouche," says Andie, her voice wavering.

"We need to hurry," she says. The hands around me tighten, and then we're moving.

CHAPTER TWENTY

"Oh my God, *back up*. You're breathing on her."

"Well *sorry* for being concerned."

"Girls, you really need to leave."

A fuzzy version of the vaulted ceiling swims in overhead as I blink. Sunlight is streaming through the glass panels along the peaks of the building, filling the room with light. My vision slants like it's drunkenly trying to pick itself back up, but eventually clears.

"Getting kicked out of the hospital," I murmur. "That's a first, even for you two."

"Oh my God, Val." Monroe's hair falls onto my shoulder as she leans over me and plants a hand on either side of my head. Whatever she sees in my face eases the concern in her own, which is quickly replaced with a smirk. "It's about time your lazy ass joined us. You've been asleep for like a day."

Kirby's head appears beside hers. "Honestly, very dramatic."

"You know me. I live for the drama."

My eyes involuntarily flicker to Monroe's neck hovering above me, and my throat burns. I swallow hard. Whatever healing my body just had to do accelerated my hunger, and my gums ache with it.

The healer on call, Madame Fiona, throws her hands up, apparently giving up on insisting on my rest, and disappears into the back office. Monroe watches until the curtain flutters shut behind her, then leans close to whisper, "What happened out there?"

I shake my head, still trying to make sense of it myself. Had I been the only one to see them?

Monroe and Kirby exchange a glance, but before either can say anything else, the entrance to the hospital opens. My breath catches in my throat at the sight of my mother strutting her way toward us. Adrienne follows quickly behind, with Headmistress Coderre bringing up the rear.

My mother examines me on the bed, her expression blank. As she notices my friends, her face transforms into an outright glare.

"Right." Kirby coughs. "We'll come back and see you later."

Monroe squeezes my shoulder. "We're glad you're okay."

Adrienne grimaces and meets my eyes over Mom's head as they hurry from the room.

"Valerie," says the headmistress. "How are you feeling?"

Another flash of irritation shows on my mother's face as she comes around to the other side of the bed. I flick my eyes between her and Coderre.

"Okay," I say, my fingers subconsciously coming up to brush my chest, and I glance down, startled when I feel a bandage there. I'm still in my uniform, but judging by the oversize shirt now hanging from my shoulders, mine was too destroyed to salvage. "It hasn't healed yet?"

My mother bristles again, and I realize she's not annoyed with *me* for once—she's glaring at Coderre.

"Wounds from wendigos can be slower to heal. Even for blood witches," Coderre says softly. "But it *will* heal."

"You know about the wendigos?" I ask.

Her brow furrows. "You told us about it on your way in. You don't remember?"

Everything after we started the practical is a blur—well, except for what I saw. That is still perfectly intact. But everything after their claws connected with my chest is fuzzy.

"You're lucky she's not dead," my mother snaps before I can respond. "You've had no fewer than *three* undocumented vampires spotted in town, one who attacked one of your students on these very grounds, a dead human, and now a *wendigo*? And what have you done?"

The headmistress stares at my mother, her expression still perfectly composed. "I understand your frustrations, Rosemarie, and your concern for your daughter's well-being—"

"I don't think you understand much."

"Mom," I start.

She silences me with a look.

"As I was saying," continues Coderre, still undisturbed by my mother's outbursts. That's probably what's riling Mom up so much in the first place. "We understand your concerns. The entire faculty has been looking into these matters, and we're putting the academy on a temporary lockdown as we sweep the area and come up with a plan."

I clear my throat. "Can I say something?"

My mother rolls her eyes and paces away, but Coderre looks down with a sad smile and nods.

"I'm not sure if sweeping the grounds is enough. That *thing* wasn't out in the fields. Not really, at least. It was like they got into my head."

Adrienne shivers and wraps her arms around herself.

"I don't want you to worry about this," Coderre says. "We're going to handle it."

"You know if she got away, it's just because the wendigo wanted her to," Adrienne murmurs.

The headmistress's jaw jumps—the first crack in her demeanor.

"I don't think you should stay here anymore." Mom reappears at my side, her hard gaze firmly set on Coderre. "I think you should come home with me and your sister, at least until the end of your initiation, and wait for the fools around here to clean up this mess."

"*Mom.*"

"These *fools* have been handpicked by me. Watch your mouth, Rosemarie, or I'll give your job back to Coderre. Just because you're my favorite doesn't mean I won't add one of your canines to my crown."

The queen sweeps through the open doorway. Her two guards hesitate by the entrance as she comes to stand at the foot of my bed. Coderre visibly straightens at the sight of her and bows her head respectfully. I keep my eyes on the door for a moment too long, half expecting Reginald to come in next, but there's no one else, and the bond in my core is quiet.

The queen is strikingly out of place with her gold crown and floor-length red dress, surrounded by gurneys and tables of healing supplies. She gives Mom a hard look before turning to me, and her features soften.

My eyes flicker between her and Coderre. *Give your job back…?* Coderre was the queen's right hand before Mom? How did I not know this? Coderre catches me looking and frowns.

"Valerie, how are you doing?" asks the queen.

I fidget, my fingers running over the bandage on my chest. "Good as can be expected, I guess."

The queen nods. "I have a meeting in town and thought I'd stop by and see how you were. All things considered, you've been excused from your last task with Prince Reginald, so we'll just see you for the final task at court."

I force a smile. "I look forward to it."

"As do we." The queen nods at her guards and starts to turn away, but then juts her chin at my mother. "Rosemarie."

Mom follows after her without another word.

Adrienne lingers at the foot of my bed as the headmistress walks over to Madame Fiona, and the two start talking in hushed voices. I look up to see Adrienne staring at me, her teeth sunk deep into her bottom lip.

"You don't have to look so worried." My voice comes out raspy, and I clear my throat. "I'm fine."

Her lips move, and it takes my brain a moment too long to process her words. *For now.* She shifts her weight and looks back at the door.

"Have you heard from Connor?" I ask.

"No. I haven't seen him around in a while though."

I try not to let how much her words affect me show on my face, but my stomach roils like I might be sick. If he wouldn't show up for something like this—even just to see if I was okay and then leave—then maybe I am holding on to something that's already gone. Could I really mean so little to him so quickly? To not even warrant a conversation?

"Adrienne!" my mother calls from the hall.

She looks from me to the door again. "I'm glad you're okay," she says, then turns and follows our mother without looking back.

"Valerie, honey," says Madame Fiona. "How are you feeling? Can I get you anything?" She and the headmistress watch me closely, like they're waiting for something.

I try to swallow the lump in my throat again. "Some water?"

"Of course. Of course." Madame Fiona jumps up and brings over a glass while the headmistress continues studying me from across the room.

I eagerly drink down the contents of the cup, the cold water relieving the itch in the back of my throat. I know it won't tide me over for long, but I can't very well ask for what my body is actually craving, even if it probably would speed up the healing process.

I freeze with the glass a few inches from my face, the pieces finally clicking together in my brain. That's it. That's why they're looking at me like that. Why they've *all* been looking at me like that.

Wendigo Psychosis. They're worried I'm about to go off the rails and start ripping people apart.

"I feel normal," I insist. "No murderous urges, if that's what you're worried about."

They exchange a look.

"We'd like to keep you overnight for observation anyway," says Madame Fiona. "Just to play it safe."

I sigh, pull the scratchy sheets up over the bandage on my chest, and meet Coderre's gaze. "Does this mean I failed the last practical?"

She blinks, surprised. "I think given the circumstances you can be excused, Valerie."

"I was the only one who saw them, right?"

"Them?" says Madame Fiona.

The headmistress gets up from her chair and comes closer. "How many did you see?"

I shiver, remembering the endless rows of bodies rising into the fog. "Too many to count."

Madame Fiona lays a hand on my leg. "You're safe now."

"We've locked down the academy, and I have everyone I can looking into the matter," adds the headmistress. "This won't be brushed under the rug. I can promise you that."

Madame Fiona pats my leg. "Why don't you get some rest, and we can reevaluate your condition tomorrow?"

I nod, fingers picking at the edges of my bandage, and they rise and disappear behind the curtain in the back.

SLEEP DOESN'T FIND me easily. I toss and turn in the narrow hospital bed, the wound in my chest twinging at the slightest pressure. When I'd peeled back the bandage to check on it a few hours ago, it seemed mostly healed. The thick scars are still visible though—four jagged lines from my collarbone to my sternum.

The UV-blocking curtains are drawn down over the windows, though the faintest trace of sun peeks through. It must still be the middle of the day.

I roll over again and blindly reach for the glass of water on the table beside me—instead, I touch something warm. Something that feels an awful lot like skin.

I jerk back, surprised, and open my eyes expecting to see someone watching over me for the night—maybe the healer. But my gaze locks on an unfamiliar man standing beside my bed, so large I can't take in his entire form at once. I know in my gut he's not supposed to be here. Adrenaline shoots through my system, and I start to scream.

The man clamps a hand over my mouth, and a second pair of hands grabs my shoulders from behind. A needle bites into my neck, and I gasp. My vision blurs rapidly, blotting out the face of the dark figure, and he releases his hold on my mouth as my body goes limp against the bed. One of them grabs my arms, and a second pair of hands grabs my legs.

"Hurry," a deep voice barks, and they hoist me into the air.

I try to wrestle myself away, but my body won't move, paralyzed by whatever they injected. Soon, the darkness crashes into me, and then I can't feel anything at all.

CHAPTER TWENTY-ONE

I WAKE to another sharp pain in my neck in an unfamiliar room with plain walls and a concrete floor. A single, naked bulb buzzes over my head. A man moves into my peripheral vision, a needle in his hand. I flinch away, but he's already backing up, the syringe empty. Whatever it was, my entire body feels heavy and numb, a dull sort of heat coursing through my blood, and a weird taste sits in the back of my mouth.

I inhale sharply and whip my head to look around the room, but it's just me and the man. He didn't bother to cover his face, which I suppose should be more cause for concern than anything else. Or maybe I should be more concerned that I've seen him before. Once. On the estate grounds that day with Reginald—he's one of the Russian visitors. I search my memory for his name, but come up blank.

The amusement he'd had in his expression that day is gone. He crosses his bulging arms over his chest as he leans against the wall and studies me, his dark hair covering his eyes.

I try to move, but rope is bound around my wrists, securing me to a metal chair. I yank against the restraints until my skin burns. The pain remains even when I stop struggling.

I inhale through my nose—and there it is. Just the faintest trace, but a scent I'm starting to become far more familiar with than I'd like.

Vexillium.

"Why are you doing this?" I ask through my teeth. "What do you want?"

The man says nothing. He watches me for a moment more, then turns and slips out the door, closing it behind him. I hear the lock latch, and then, silence.

I suck in a sharp breath and look around the room again. There has to be a way out of here. No windows, no other exits besides that door. I glance down, and my stomach tightens. There's a drain in the floor beneath my chair.

Am I in a blood farm?

I stop breathing for a second.

Calm. I just have to stay calm. I've been trained for this. Panicking will not help me. Options. What are my options?

I pull against the ropes on my wrists until blood trickles down my fingers, but I can't feel even a whisper of my magic inside of me.

They've been using Vexillium, but the poison isn't uncommon. Does this mean they've been the ones poisoning me all along, or is it a coincidence? How would they have had access to my things? And the timeline doesn't add up—as far as I know, they hadn't gotten to the estate yet when I'd first started to notice the effects.

But the attacks…were those them? The witches in the parking garage, Daniel, Ryan…me. My mind spins, desperately trying to form connections, but there are too many missing pieces. Too many variables. Too many attacks. Too much blood. Too much death—

Calm. I have to stay calm. *I have to stay calm.* Plan. I just need a plan.

I pull against the ropes around my wrists again but only dig them deeper into my raw skin. A small whimper escapes me despite myself.

Then something occurs to me. I stop struggling and sit up straighter. They managed to subdue my magic, but they don't know about the bond. Even if I can't convey anything specific to Reginald like he'd been trying to teach me, all I need is for him to *feel* me. Ideally, feel where I am.

I search for that familiar thread in my gut, but it's like I'm grasping around blindly in the dark, and every time I get close, it slips through my fingers like smoke.

I swallow the lump in my throat.

Whatever was in that syringe must have cut me off from him too. Wherever I am, I'm alone. And no one is coming to find me.

I DON'T KNOW how much time passes before the man comes back. Despite my efforts, I fall asleep in the chair, the exhaustion taking over. He doesn't say anything when he returns, but he leaves the door open. I try to look behind him, but it's too dark to see whatever is outside of this room.

"What do you want with me?" I ask.

He doesn't answer, of course. He walks straight to my chair, and I try to shrink away, but he grabs me by the shoulder and plunges another needle into the side of my neck. I gasp at the spark of pain and brace myself for what-ever comes next, but he walks to the other side of the room and leans against the wall again, watching me. I stare back, unblinking, until a second figure strides through the door, this one closing it behind him. He's just as large as the other man, but with shorter hair and darker skin—he was at the estate too.

The two mutter something to each other in Russian—the language I'm the worst at, of course. But I manage to pick out a few words—*start, time, soon.* They exchange a knowing look, their lips curled.

Whatever they've brought me here for, I have a sinking feeling I'm about to find out. And they're…looking forward to it.

Sweat breaks out at the back of my neck, and my chest rises and falls as my breathing quickens. The newer arrival slips back out the door while the other comes closer. He scans me from head to toe then pulls a knife out of his pocket. It looks sharp.

I flatten my back against the chair, my heart pounding against my ribs as my eyes dart from the blade to his face, imagining all of the creative things he could do with it. If he wanted to kill me and be done with it, he probably would've brought something bigger. This one is small, easy to hold.

Easy to use for extended periods of time.

"Is this about James Westcott?" I blurt. I have no idea what I'm hoping to accomplish with this other than stalling, but everyone else I've asked has reacted pretty strongly to the name.

"Кто?" he grunts.

Who?

I have no reason to believe they'd tell me anything, but there isn't even a flicker of recognition in his expression. He leans toward me.

I try to pull away again, but I have nowhere to go. "Just ask me what you want to know—"

The man ignores me and grabs my shirt by the collar. He yanks the knife through the thin material, a straight line all the way down, and tears it away from my body, leaving me in my bra and uniform skirt.

I close my eyes, waiting for the blade to sink into my skin, but it doesn't come. Letting out a shaky breath, I open my eyes again as the second man returns. He's carrying a small brown bag that clangs as he moves, like it's full of glass.

I swallow hard, pulling against the ropes again. They must have pumped me with a much stronger dose of Vexillium than what had been in my perfume for my powers to desert me altogether. Even my half-vampire side is useless if I don't have fangs or anything I can summon. I feel completely…human.

Which, right now, makes me helpless.

They tied my ankles to the legs of the chair while I was asleep, and the chair is bolted to the floor, so I couldn't tip it over if I tried. Not that it would break—it's solid metal.

The second man hands a glass vial to his companion, full of Vexillium in its herb form. He grunts something in Russian that I can't make out, then the man with the longer hair prowls toward me, the herbs in one hand, a knife in the other.

My entire body pulses with my heartbeat as he kneels in front of my chair, but I don't let the fear show on my face. I refuse to give him that. I stare him down as he dusts the herb along the blade—whatever he's about to do, he doesn't want it to heal. The second man comes up behind me and pins my shoulders down.

"Why are you doing this?" I bite out through clenched teeth.

The man doesn't look at me. He reaches forward and starts to dig the knife into my stomach. I gasp at the sudden fire spreading across my skin. The man's hands tighten around my shoulders, holding me back as the knife carves lines down my abdomen.

My entire body fills with heat, and I break out in a sweat as I tighten my fists against the arms of the chair until my veins pop. A choked sound squeezes out of my throat. When he's finished, he takes more of the herb and shoves it in the open wound.

I lock my teeth together to keep from crying out as he starts again, this time in a different direction. With each cut he makes, he shoves the herbs into my skin. My body trembles with the pain, but I lock it inside, biting down on the inside of my cheek until blood fills my mouth. I won't let them see me afraid. I won't.

I *won't.*

Every time I think he's done, he pauses, considers the

space he has left, then starts again. *They're letters*, I realize. One by one, he builds a message—for whom, I'm not sure. My vision is too blurry with unshed tears to make out what it says.

By the second word, my resolve fades, and I start to scream.

I PASS out somewhere between letters six and seven and wake up alone. My skin is covered in sweat, and suddenly the room is unbearably hot. It's more likely that I'm feverish. My head lulls against my chest, my vision black around the corners and too blurry to see whatever they wrote, though the throbbing emanating from every inch of my stomach tells me whatever they did is still there.

The pain is dull though. Distant. They shoved another needle in my neck about halfway through, something that made my entire body go numb for a while, which was more confusing than anything else. Why would they try to help with the pain they'd just caused? Or was the numbing drug for something else?

And yet, I'm no longer afraid. Not as much, at least. Because if they're going through all of this trouble to send some kind of message, I'm not staying here. They'll have to deliver me at some point. Until then, it's a matter of waiting.

I suppose it's wishful thinking they'll want to deliver the message with me still alive.

I try to think of all the people they could be targeting —why they'd choose *me*. Or maybe it didn't matter.

Maybe it was random. But I can't help but feel this is personal.

Since they're with the Russian estate who have been negotiating with the queen, it must be someone in the court, right?

The queen? It's unlikely. There are many people closer to her they could've used instead of me.

My mother? Possibly. But something about it doesn't feel right.

The door creaks open, and my entire body stiffens as not just the two men step into the room, but this time, they have a woman with them. She's carrying a large black bag, and it jerks to the side, as if something is moving in there.

I watch under half-closed lids as the three talk among themselves in Russian. The two men stand up much straighter with her in the room now, their heads slightly bowed as if in respect. I try to blow the sweaty strands of hair out of my eyes and lift my head, but I can't muster the energy.

Maybe this is it. Maybe we're leaving.

The woman turns to look at me. Her eyes are cold and completely devoid of emotion as she looks me up and down then turns back to her companions.

I swallow hard as ice-cold fear slithers down my spine.

She's a witch. I can smell it on her.

This time, when she speaks, I understand her perfectly.

"Откройте её рот."

Open her mouth.

CHAPTER TWENTY-TWO

WHATEVER NUMBING drugs they'd been injecting are long gone now. The pain is so great, my entire body is shaking with it, but I can't scream. I can't do anything more than let out low, desperate groans between pockets of consciousness as my body slips in and out of the dark.

I come to in familiar surroundings and blink, confused.

Someone shoves me onto my knees from behind, and I hit the bright red carpet of the hallway hard. I look up at the wooden door in front of me, tears leaking out of the corners of my eyes. Someone holds on to my hair from behind, and it's the only thing keeping me up. My feet are free, but my wrists are still bound behind my back. My shoulders ache from being in the position for so long.

But that is nothing compared to everything else.

A large hand reaches over me and pounds on the door. Footsteps sound on the other side, then the air behind me whistles, and the hand disappears from my hair.

I slump to the side, and pain lances up my shoulder as I desperately suck in air through my nose.

The door swings open, and feet appear in front of me, but my vision is too hazy to see anything else.

"Valerie? *Valerie?*"

Hands brush against my skin, but I can already feel myself slipping back into the dark.

"Go get a healer. *Now.*"

"I'll get her mother—"

"No." There's a pause, and then: "Get someone else. Anyone else."

Something rips the restraints from my wrists, but the relief is short-lived. Arms wrap around me and hoist me off the floor. My head dangles against an arm, and I blink up at Reginald as he carries me into the room.

"Who did this?" he demands as he gently lays me out on his bed. His jaw flexes, and for a moment, the bond runs hot between us.

I shake my head and groan, trying to motion to my mouth, but my hand feels heavy and like it doesn't belong on my body.

He stares at me, and it takes a moment for realization to dawn. "You can't talk."

I shake my head again, tears dripping down the sides of my face. He glances down at my abdomen, the message fully on display now, and his entire body goes still.

The door bursts open, and two people hurry inside. He runs a hand through his hair and lets out a harsh breath, his gaze still on my stomach.

"We should clean out the wounds first," one of the women says.

Reginald looks from them to me, his chest rising and falling rapidly. "Her mouth too—they, they sealed it."

An older woman frowns as she looks me over, pausing only a moment on the wounds. A younger woman with the same brown eyes appears on the other side of the bed and hands a bowl to her.

My chest aches as I wrestle for air, but it never reaches my lungs. Black spots appear in my vision.

"I think she's hyperventilating," says the younger woman.

Reginald kneels beside my head and takes my hand in his, his grip so tight it almost hurts. "Valerie," he says, his voice raw and low.

Something jolts inside my stomach, and I arch against the bed, my scream getting trapped behind my sealed lips.

Everyone lurches back.

"What was that?" Reginald demands.

It comes again, and this time when I look down, I *see* the movement in my stomach straining against my skin.

"Do something!" Reginald shouts.

"What on earth is it?" the younger girl asks.

I thrash against the bed as it twists inside of me, coiling and stretching like it's trying to rip my insides apart.

"Here."

A hand smears something cold and gritty across my lips, and I gasp as my mouth finally unseals.

"Get it—out," I pant, choking around something deep in my throat. "Get—out—" My throat burns around the words like it's tearing open.

"You're going to have to hold her down."

Reginald climbs up beside me and pushes my shoulders into the bed with trembling hands.

It surges up so hard against my stomach it feels like it's ripping through my skin, and I scream and kick my legs against the pain. My body tries to roll to the side and coil in on itself.

"Hurry," Reginald says through his teeth.

"Hold her still," snaps the woman.

"Fuck." Reginald climbs all the way on top of me, pinning my legs with his legs and my arms with his hands. The thing moves inside of me again, and my back arches involuntarily. *"Hurry."*

The women join hands over my head and chant rapidly under their breath. It moves inside of me, inching up higher and higher until it lodges itself in my throat and presses down so hard on my windpipes it completely cuts off my air. I gasp and grab on to Reginald's wrist. Black starts to creep in at the edges of my vision, then someone splashes a handful of cold water onto my face.

"Tilt her head to the side," the old woman orders.

The younger one pushes my head to face the older woman, and then I feel it. Whatever is in there is not coming out willingly. It pulls and latches on to every last inch as the old woman slowly forces it up. I gag, tears running down the sides of my face, and Reginald's hold on me tightens.

The tail comes out first. I dig my fingers into Reginald's arm until I draw blood, as inch by inch, they extract the snake. Once there's enough of the tail to grab on to, the older woman seizes it and starts to pull as the younger woman's chants intensify. With every yank of the snake, my body clenches. Until, finally, she pulls it the rest of the way out.

For a moment, its red eyes meet mine as she pulls it away.

"What the hell kind of magic is this?" cries the younger girl.

I retch, covering the bed beside me in blood and the contents of my stomach, heaving and gasping and sobbing.

"Ivy," barks the older woman.

"I'm on it."

"Reid," I whimper.

"Valerie." He pushes the sweaty hair out of my face and leans down. "Valerie, look at me."

I turn my head, just an inch, and he stares down at me, eyes as wide as I'm sure mine are. "You're okay," he murmurs. "You're okay."

I turn my head again and cough, splattering the sheets with more blood.

"Here," says the older woman. "She needs to drink this. Then we'll get started on her stomach."

Reid tries to lift my head, but the thought of swallowing anything—of putting anything in my body right now—

"Try."

Eyes closed, I let him pull my head up to tilt the cup to my lips. The moment the liquid—thick and cold—hits my tongue, I gag and shudder.

"The whole thing," says the woman.

"Just one more sip," whispers Reid. "You just have one more sip."

I squint an eye open at the nearly full cup. Liar.

He smirks, but it doesn't reach his eyes.

He lifts the cup again and tips the contents back. I try to swallow as much at once as I can. As soon as it hits the back of my throat, it takes the edge off the pain, and it's enough to keep me drinking. Reid watches me, then sets the cup aside when I'm finished.

"We need to clean out whatever they put in those wounds," says the woman.

"Here, honey, take this." Ivy, the younger of two, kneels down and offers me a spoon full of a clear syrup. Reid stands behind her, arms crossed tightly over his chest. I close my eyes as I swallow, and almost immediately, sleep pulls me under.

———

Reid is asleep in the chair next to the bed, his head tilted back, legs splayed out in front of him. He snores lightly, and his eyelashes flutter against his cheeks. I squint at the windows, trying to figure out how much time has passed, but the UV-blocking tint makes every time of day look the same.

The rest of the room is empty—no sign of the healers. I glance down at myself. The sheets are soaked in sweat and blood, and they're tangled around my legs. I'm in one of Reid's shirts now. I slide my hand under the hem and run it across my stomach. The skin is smooth—the wounds completely healed now.

"You're awake." Reid straightens in his chair and rubs his eyes.

Still too weak to sit up, I roll my head to the side to look at him.

"How are you feeling?" he asks.

Like every part of my body weighs three times as much as usual. Even the idea of talking is exhausting. I try to clear my throat and wince.

He gets up and brings over a glass of water. I eye it, still not moving, and he braces a hand behind my shoulders to prop me up before bringing the glass to my lips. It's cold against my throat, but doesn't bring much relief. I shake my head when he tries to tilt it again, and he returns to his seat beside the bed.

The moment I meet his eyes, he looks away, dropping his gaze to his hands in his lap.

"Adrienne came by to see you while you were asleep. We contacted the academy and everyone to let them know you're all right."

I glance around the empty room. "And my mother?" My voice comes out raspy and low.

A muscle in his jaw jumps. "We told her you were here. She's probably just busy with the final trials."

I look back up at the ceiling. *Of course.* I'd laugh if it didn't hurt so much.

"I'm going to request you get reassigned," he adds quietly. "To a different partner after your initiation. This was—this was me. They were after me. And if you're my partner, that means they'll always be after you too."

"Reid—" I start.

"Both of my previous partners died," he continues, still not looking at me. "Both of them. Because of me. I won't let it happen a third time. I'm not going to watch—I can't—I won't allow it to happen to you too."

I stare at him, waiting for him to look at me, but he

doesn't. I open my mouth to speak, but my voice comes out hoarse and in broken pieces. "You can't—really think—that's the solution here."

He doesn't respond.

I clear my throat and wince, but my voice comes out stronger now. "But if it's not me, it would just be someone else."

He presses his lips together in a hard line.

I look back at the ceiling, every inch of my body aching. And yet, the worst of the pain is focused in the center of my abdomen, far deeper than the cuts had been. It takes me a moment to realize it's not mine. His pain is heavy and thick, and it seeps out of the bond like hot tar.

I wet my lips as I turn my head to look at him. "Let me ask you something."

He hesitates, then slowly raises his eyes to meet mine.

"If I had been paired with someone else, do you think I still would have turned when I did the blood exchange?"

"I believe so, yes," he whispers.

"And do you think if I had been paired with anyone else that they would have helped me? What do you think they would have done when they found out?"

He doesn't say anything, and that's more than enough of an answer.

"I know you feel like being paired with you put me in harm's way, but the way I see it, if I'd been paired with anyone else, I'm pretty sure I'd be dead right now."

He looks down at his hands again. When it's clear he's not going to say anything, I ask, "What did it say?"

He shakes his head.

"If I had to be the messenger, I think at the very least I deserve to know what it said."

He gets up, paces to the end of the room, and leaves his back to me. "It said, *We remember.*"

My eyebrows pull together. "Who are they, Reid? What do they want? And *don't* avoid the question this time. You can't keep me in the dark if I'm just going to get pulled in the middle of it anyway."

He sighs and rubs the heels of his hands into his eyes. "You asked me before where I went when I left here. I didn't *leave*, exactly. My mother sent me to go stay at the other estates. I spent the last ten years bouncing around between them, but I was with the Russians for about a year. And those guys, we have some...history."

He stops for a long enough time that I think he's not going to continue. But as I open my mouth to say something, he pulls in a deep breath and stands up a little straighter. "They're brothers, those two. There used to be three of them. And they were all friends with Prince Alexei at the Vasiliev estate. We never got along, but for months, we just avoided each other. Things work...differently at Vasiliev. Different rules. Different procedures. And those three, they were getting away with murder. Literally. They made their own little blood farm for fun in this shack a few miles outside of the estate. Sometimes they'd forget to go check on the humans for weeks at a time, then they'd show up, and they'd all died of thirst or starvation, so they'd go back into the city and collect some more, whether they'd broken the law or not. And no one was doing anything about it. No one—" He breaks off, and his shoulders heave as his breathing quickens.

"I followed them there the week before I came back here," he continues, his voice barely above a whisper. "I don't know why I did it. It's not like I thought it would stop them from bringing in more humans. But there were a lot of kids in this batch, and I..." He turns back to face me, but he's looking somewhere over my head. "I let them go. The humans. One of the brothers, Sacha, came back to the farm alone—I guess he'd forgotten something. The brothers had confiscated anything on the humans when they'd arrived, but then just left all of their things sitting outside the cages. A few of the humans had been carrying guns with wooden bullets and..."

He shakes his head again. "I knew Viktor and Mikhail wouldn't just let it go. But I didn't expect them to come here. And I didn't expect—they killed three of the academy's guards to get you, and the healer on call. They left the bodies there, like they wanted people to know what they'd done."

Slowly, he meets my eyes again. "They blame me for their brother's death. But that's all I know. I don't know what this was. I don't know if they want revenge, if this was just for fun...if this was just the start."

We stare at each other for a while, and his guilt presses into me through the bond like a weight sitting on my chest.

"Are they still staying here?" I whisper. "At the estate?"

"No one has seen them since they dropped you here. I think they took off."

For now is what neither of us needs to say. He searches my face for a moment, and the bond weighs heavier inside of me, sinking like a weight in the water.

The door creaks open, and one of the maids pokes her head in.

"Excuse me, sir, but I was sent up to remind you Miss Darkmore is needed in the throne room for her final task in half an hour."

"She's not going," says Reid.

"What?" I shove myself up in the bed and immediately have to lean back against the headboard to steady myself. "Of course I'm going."

"Valerie." He turns to me and lowers his voice. "You can't even stand."

He can't possibly be suggesting I miss the final task. "Well I can't just not show up."

The maid shifts her weight awkwardly in the doorway until Reid turns back to her, mutters a quick thank-you, and dismisses her. He rubs his hand along his jaw. "Valerie, I don't think it's a good idea."

"You know I can't pass initiation without this final task." My legs threaten to buckle as I roll myself out of bed, but I manage to stay upright.

He stares at me, and I can see there's something he's not saying.

"Why don't you want me to go?"

He opens his mouth like he wants to say something, but something stops him—something *else*. He presses his lips together and exhales through his nose.

I know that look. He *can't* tell me. Whatever it is, he's been spelled to secrecy.

He knows whatever my final task is.

And it's bad enough that he doesn't want me to go.

"I have to."

265

He turns his back to me and nods a few times, seemingly to himself. "I can give you my blood," he finally says. "It will make you feel stronger. Strong enough to get through the task, at least." He doesn't look at me as he rolls up his shirtsleeve and comes over to the side of the bed.

I want to yell at him. To grab his chin between my fingers and force him to *look at me*. To explain what the hell is going on. But he can't, and I won't, and I'm running out of time. And as much as I don't want to admit it, he's right. I'm not strong enough for whatever the queen is about to have me do, not without his blood.

I make the cut along the inside of his wrist and hesitantly bring his skin to my lips. My mouth waters at the smell of his blood, and my eyes close involuntarily as the sweet taste hits my tongue.

"I'll have one of the maids bring you up something to wear," he says as I finish. His eyebrows are drawn tightly together like he's thinking hard about something. I wipe my mouth with the back of my hand, then he quickly turns his back to me and strides from the room.

"Reid—"

He closes the door behind him.

CHAPTER TWENTY-THREE

THE FINAL TRIALS are the estate's best kept secret. They're different for everyone, perfectly designed to test each initiate's weaknesses, and afterward, everyone in the room is bound to secrecy with a spell. Over the years, I couldn't help but wonder what Calla's task had been. If whatever had happened in this room was what pushed her over the edge.

When I enter, the queen is smiling down at me from her throne, fresh blood shining on the front teeth of her crown. My mother is at her side, her expression impassive as I approach. Reid stands near the dais with a few of the queen's guards. His hands are clasped in front of him. Even as I reach my place in the center of the glass circle, he doesn't look at me.

The queen rises from her throne. "Valerie Darkmore. Welcome to your final task. Yours is a bit of a special one, I must admit. Here at the court, we have no doubts about your abilities. No doubts about your knowledge. What we've chosen to test you on today is your loyalty."

I stop breathing, a cold sweat immediately breaking out on my skin. When I look to my mother, no emotion shows on her face. Reid's jaw flexes.

"There are many traits we look for in prospective Marionettes. Power. Intelligence. Tenacity. The ability to do whatever is necessary for the good of all. For your first priority to be with us." She nods at a guard, and he disappears into one of the back doors.

I stare after him, waiting for him to reappear, my anxiety like boiling water rising up inside of me.

And then: the faintest of tugs on the bond draws my attention.

I glance over at Reid, but he's still looking at the floor, his eyebrows drawn together. The bond tugs again, harder, and this time, he lifts his head and meets my eyes. The blood I drank from him earlier seems to have strengthened the bond, and two words appear in my mind, loud and clear, in his voice:

Trust me.

I face forward again as the door reopens and the guard steps through with another person in tow.

My heart skitters to a complete stop in my chest.

He's bound tightly—ropes around his wrists, a gag in his mouth. They put him on his knees a few feet in front of me. He shakes the hair out of his eyes, and then Connor looks up.

I stare back at him, my horror probably evident on my face, and yet, somehow, Connor's face is the perfect picture of calm. Stubble lines his jaw, like he hasn't shaved in days, and his clothes are covered in dirt and sweat. Dark circles ring his eyes.

"Your task is simple," says the queen. "We'll let you decide how to do it. All you have to do is kill him."

Tears cloud my vision as I look up at my mother again. She stares back at me, unflinching. How long has this been planned? How long has she known? How could she sit there and listen to me beg her to protect him when she knew it was going to come to this?

"We'll give you five minutes to decide," adds the queen.

"Killing humans is against the law," I say quietly.

The queen's face hardens. "I *am* the law."

Reid tugs on the bond again, but I can't even look at him. He knew about this. How long has he known?

All of these days I've been worried Connor wasn't calling me back, that he wouldn't want to be with me anymore, but really, he was—

Where have they been keeping him? In some kind of jail cell?

My breath hitches, and a tear trails down my cheek as Connor holds my gaze and nods. His face is so open, so trusting. No trace of anger or sadness. Just…resignation.

I've worked my entire life to get here, but as I look at his face, all I can think about is all of the nights he snuck into my room and held me while I cried. The way he'd chase me through the gardens when we were younger and I needed to get away from my mother's incessant lessons. His hand holding mine as we watched my sister get lowered into the ground. Our first kiss by the pool after my mother used me as a cutting board to test Calla for the first time and he'd found me crying.

Joining the Marionettes is all I've ever wanted…but I don't know if I can do it without him.

I don't know if I can do anything without him.

"Valerie," my mother says. "He's one human boy. This is your legacy as a Darkmore. This will pass. Don't forget who you are."

The coldness in her voice hits harder than any slap she's given me. She watched Connor grow up. He was as much her child as I was, and now, she won't even look at him. Won't even say his name.

I shake my head. I can't. *I can't.*

The bond pulls so hard I physically take a step forward. Reid's gaze is piercing, demanding. For some reason, looking at him causes a sense of calm to wash over me, settling on like a second skin. I blink, and the tangled web of emotions tightening my chest loosens. A comforting warmth spreads through my veins.

You can.

His voice fills my head like smoke, and I find myself taking another step toward Connor, who nods at me again.

You can.

There are so many ways to kill people—different options for different species. Humans are the easiest—so many ways to end a life. We had an entire class on it at the academy sophomore year. Though one factor that was never discussed was the pain. Only the efficiency.

You can.

I suppose the most humane way would simply be to stop his heart. I could do it quickly.

You can.

He wouldn't feel much pain. There wouldn't be any blood spilt to add to the queen's collection below us.

You can.

I reach down and tear the gag from his mouth. He swallows hard, his eyes never leaving mine, and whispers, "It's okay."

The sound of his voice sends an electric current through me, and I pause. This is Connor. *Connor.* I don't know what life looks like without him, and I don't want to find out.

The fog crashes into me again, flooding my senses.

You can. You can. You can.

I love you, he mouths and lets out a shuddering breath.

"Your time is running out, and I'm getting impatient," says the queen.

Connor nods and closes his eyes.

The rest of the room fades around us until it's just me and him. Me and him and this one thing left for me to do.

I twist the blade out of my ring and draw a small line along my palm. Tears drip from my chin and mingle with the blood as I close my hand into a fist, and Connor's body drops to the floor.

CHAPTER TWENTY-FOUR

No one comes to get him. His body lies in front of me as the queen stands, smiling. Blood roars in my ears as the fog clears from my mind, and everything around me is muffled. I think she's saying something about when I'll get my results, but I can't hear her. I can't hear anything but the pounding of my heart as I stare at Connor on the floor.

Something shifts inside of me at the sight of him like that. Something breaks. His legs are folded to one side, and his wrists are still bound, leaving them nowhere to go but his chest, which is so very, very still.

My body trembles as I look up at Reid. A stricken expression weighs down his features, and it takes everything in me not to scream.

He glamoured me.

He *glamoured* me, and now Connor is *dead*.

Blood drips from my fingers, and it sinks beneath the glass under my feet. I pull in a shaky breath as the queen flicks her wrist toward Connor's body.

"Someone clean that up. Make sure it's dead first."

Reid paces across the floor and leans over him.

"Don't touch him," I growl.

"Valerie," he says lowly as he straightens again, a warning in his voice. I know if they find out what just happened all of this will have been for nothing, but my anger is thrashing inside of me like a wave in a storm, out of control and overflowing. He grabs my wrist to pull me from the room, but I resist, trying to get around him, desperate for another glimpse of Connor. This can't be the last time I see him. Not here. Not like this. It can't—

I pause, cocking my head at the smear of blood on his lips.

Then his eyes fly open.

I gasp, and he is a blur of motion. Something crashes into me so hard it knocks the breath from my lungs. Suddenly I'm on the ground on my back, and the last thing I see is Connor's glowing red eyes before he throws my head to the side and sinks his teeth into my neck.

I scream.

SEE WHAT HAPPENS NEXT

Thank you so much for reading *The Marionettes!* If you enjoyed it, **it would mean so much if you left a review!**

Continue with Valerie's story in the second book in the series, *Wicked Souls,* available now.

Good news! I also have a bonus scene **from Reid's point of view**, available through my newsletter. Find out why Valerie and Reid were *really* paired together.

Want even **more** bonus material? **The hardcover** copies of this series all contain exclusive content like bonus scenes from the love interest's point of view, character art, annotated chapters, letters from the author, and more!

ABOUT THE AUTHOR

Katie Wismer writes books with a little blood and a little spice (sometimes contemporary, sometimes paranormal...and sometimes even poetry.)

Be the first to know about upcoming projects, exclusive content, and more by signing up for her newsletter at katiewismer.com.

Signed books are also available on her website, and she posts monthly bonus content on her Patreon (including a Patreon-exclusive book!)

When she's not reading, writing, or wrangling her two perfect cats, you can find her on her YouTube, Instagram, or TikTok.

patreon.com/katiewismer

tiktok.com/@authorkatiewismer

instagram.com/katesbookdate

youtube.com/katesbookdate

goodreads.com/katesbookdate

amazon.com/author/katiewismer

bookbub.com/authors/katie-wismer

Printed in Great Britain
by Amazon

47039843R00169